HUNG JURY

By the same author

The Right to Silence
Abuse of Process

HUNG JURY

Rankin Davis

Hodder & Stoughton

First published in Great Britain in 1997 by Hodder and Stoughton
A division of Hodder Headline PLC

A CIP catalogue record for this title
is available from the British Library

ISBN 0 340 69572 2

Typeset by Palimpsest Book Production Limited,
Polmont, Stirlingshire
Printed and bound in Great Britain by
Mackays of Chatham PLC, Chatham, Kent

Hodder and Stoughton
A division of Hodder Headline PLC
338 Euston Road
London NW1 3BH

To the 'Liquidators'
600,000 'volunteers' now dead or dying, who cleaned up the avoidable mess the world knows as Chernobyl.

ACKNOWLEDGEMENTS

Pesticides are real. The Circle of Poison is real. Cancer is all too real. So are the people who assisted in the writing of this book. David Weir and Mark Shapiro, two remarkable American researchers who gave the circle its deadly name.

To the many eco-warriors who cannot be named for obvious reasons who gave an insight to the commitment required to save the planet from its allegedly most intelligent inhabitants. Cheers especially to Salamander Bill, Black Frank and the Hobbit for the digging experience.

To the 144 jurors who shared their experiences of the law and lawyers over too many drinks and laughs. If you can see your face on this jury then an apology is due.

To Mr F. T. Wilson, the finest police officer I have ever had the privilege of knowing, who passed on his wisdom and expertise and who was too modest to allow me to mention his honours.

To Kate Lyall Grant, like a good claret getting better with each vintage.

And finally to Keith and Tony without whose continued support and belief this book would never have been written.

Warmest thanks.

R.D. County Durham. 1997.

'I durst not laugh for fear of opening my lips and receiving the bad air'
'Casca' in Shakespeare's *Julius Caesar*, Act 1, Scene 2

PROLOGUE

Sunday, July 20th, Mayfair, London

Geoffrey Haversham reached for the 1972 volume of the *All England Law Reports* from the bulging bookshelf. Wearily, he slumped back into the green leather chair and opened the heavy manual. He quickly located the case he wanted: Regina v. Fitzpatrick. It was the sixteenth he'd read that evening concerning extradition treaties. Haversham was tired; it had been a long but ultimately satisfying weekend. The next day the government should accept his advice, and a long-sought-after drug baron sheltering in Guatemala would be on the receiving end of a nasty package for a change.

He rapidly read through the judgement, making notes on a yellow legal pad in his tiny, neat handwriting. Another fifteen minutes were lost in concentration before a soft mournful whimpering from the corner of the study interrupted him. He checked the eighteenth-century carriage clock and was surprised to see that it was a little after eight.

'Two ticks, old boy,' he whispered over his shoulder, but he knew that Frazer, his chocolate-brown Labrador, wasn't renowned for his patience come walk time. It was a well-rehearsed routine: first the whimpering, then the rattling of his silver lead and, if that didn't precipitate a response, an irritating low groan usually did the trick.

Reluctantly, Haversham replaced the top on his treasured gold Mont Blanc, a gift from his younger brother, and placed his files in the red leather briefcase embossed with the gold crest of high office. Just as he was rising from the desk he heard Frazer dragging his lead across the beech-wood flooring heading for the door.

'All right, all right, I'm coming.' Haversham paused for a moment and eyed the black leather medical kit perched on the window ledge warily, reached towards it, then retracted his hand, he wouldn't be long; no need. Ten minutes later the duo were taking their favourite route alongside the lake. Haversham lit a cigar and watched Frazer scamper around the edge of the Serpentine. The summer sun was low in the sky but the Hyde Park flowerbed displays were alive with colour: deep red begonias and snow-white alyssum contrasting with cool blue lobelia. A few people were still scattered around the grassy areas, picnic hampers packed and children finishing their games. He heard the soulful whine of a harmonica player blowing his blues from a nearby bench. They could have been playing for Dr Jenny Fox, the defendant in the case he had been prosecuting for the last month. Haversham had little doubt what the jury's verdict would be and where the eco-terrorist would spend the rest of her life. But, as the old legal chestnut said, 'If you can't do the time, don't do the crime.'

As they rounded the corner of the Serpentine gallery heading for the bridle path, Frazer's ears suddenly pointed to the sky. Haversham looked ahead and noticed one of those confounded kids rollerblading towards him. A ludicrous flash of technicoloured Lycra hurtled fast and low out of the setting sun, about a hundred metres away: head down, swaggering from side to side, one arm locked behind its back, the other swinging in front, knuckles almost scraping the floor in a pendulous motion. Haversham made a quick, churlish, mental note to get on their case: he would ban the activity altogether if he could. Such a tiresome nuisance; as if the footpaths of this great space were made for anything other than walking. Surely there was an ancient by-law he could invoke. At that speed Haversham couldn't tell if the rollerblader was male or female, and he couldn't see the figure reaching into the pouch strapped around a slim waist. He took a firm hold on Frazer's collar and reluctantly moved to the side of the walkway.

Twenty yards and closing, still he didn't register the gun – the sound of wheels sizzling across the tarmac were louder than the spit of the barrel – and a nanosecond later the Attorney General of England and Wales crumpled to the ground clutching frantically at the dart embedded in his neck.

Frazer barked furiously but Haversham couldn't hear him nor did he register the wet tongue licking his face: he couldn't move or speak. His head lolled indolently to one side, cheek flat against the ground as paralysis set in. Seconds later he saw the moulded plastic skates circling his head before halting inches from his face. His hand offered no resistance as it was pulled away from his neck and the dart ripped from his flesh. From the corner of his eye he could see the face of a woman bearing down upon him; she checked the vein in his neck for a pulse. Tight features, slight sweat across her brow, olive skin and dark brown curls framing an angular jaw with pencil-thin lips. Haversham tried, couldn't see her eyes behind the mirrored wraparounds, could only see his own pathetic reflection as she dispassionately rolled him on to his back.

From nowhere two more faces appeared, kinder faces carrying the frown of genuine concern. Haversham tried but failed to tell them anything with his eyes as his kidnapper assumed control. Suddenly he registered the blue strobe light flashing somewhere to his left, but knew that its response was too fast to be an authentic London ambulance. He made one last attempt to open his mouth but it was useless; his throat was desert dry and his jaw wheel-clamp locked. Ironically, he couldn't even prevent the friendly passers-by unwittingly assisting in his abduction. He was manoeuvred onto the stretcher by a less than careful and clearly bogus paramedic.

As soon as the doors to the ambulance closed he felt a mask being strapped to his face and wondered for the first time whether he would ever see the light of day again.

Monday, July 21st

Alex Parrish was bone-weary of murder. This was the twentieth time. There were three of them: two burly men brandishing assault rifles, and a svelte woman, all in tight black ski-suits and masks. The victim wore a once-white lab coat, now crimson, which flapped behind him as he crawled away from their ferocious attack, squealing like a scalded toddler. Alex watched in morbid fascination as the victim's face leaked blood on to the research centre's sterilised flooring, which his scrambling elbows smeared like a sidewinder in the Sahara; and still he squeaked and whimpered.

The three followed, faces hidden by their woollen masks, the men lashing out with heavy black combat boots at the victim's face. The woman – self-possessed, calm personified – followed behind, tenderly cradling a powerful handgun.

When Dr Charles Easterman, the corpse in waiting, reached the end of the corridor, he inched his back up against its aluminium wall and covered his battered face with his hands. Alex exhaled deeply; it would be the killing time soon.

The woman gestured languidly with a roll of her left wrist: her compatriots each took an arm and flipped Easterman on to his stomach. Alex felt his bile rise. The woman sat down astride the slender spread of his back, legs tucked under his shoulders, her groin hard against the back of his neck.

'Jesus,' Alex muttered under his breath, though he should have been well used to it by now.

Her companions watched her actions intently, hungrily. The dull nose of her weapon was placed delicately against the base of his skull. There was no struggle from Easterman; he seemed to freeze, as if he knew true futility.

5

The first high-velocity bullet entered his brain and ended his life. The following pair, one to either side of his shattered cranium, were vicious over-kill, but Easterman wasn't complaining.

Then she stood and rolled her hand again; her accomplices complied once more. The bullets had peeled the front of his skull away: a once-brilliant man reduced to mashed pomegranate. She reached down with her hand to his lips, which she took with her thumb and forefinger and pushed into a grisly grin.

The men laughed, but a stern turn of her head silenced them immediately. She walked briskly away from the execution; the men followed behind. Dr Charles Easterman smiled stupidly for the video camera.

A click later and the screen of the monitor transformed to white noise and video blurring. A court usher solemnly turned off the apparatus. Alex and the other eleven members of the jury returned their attention to the trial judge.

'The prosecution claim that the woman in the video was the defendant, Dr Jennifer Fox, and I have reminded you at some length in this summing up of the evidence, some might say compelling evidence, that drives you to that conclusion.'

11.50 a.m., Court Two, The Old Bailey, London

'Did Dr Jennifer Fox murder Dr Charles Easterman on the night of October the thirteenth last?'

The ermine-robed High Court judge let the words hang in the air, glancing momentarily from face to face of the twelve of them. He had made his own views startlingly clear during the trial and summing up, then informed the jury that they were free to disregard his opinion if they disagreed with it; as if.

Alex Parrish leaned back against the padded leather buffer of the jury box, in Old Bailey court number two, and could almost feel the presence of ten thousand other backs that had performed an identical action down the long history of English crime. The courtroom was high ceilinged with intricate plasterwork. The highly polished dark wood, finest English oak, looked as old as the Common Law. As an architect with a burgeoning practice, Alex could appreciate its design and purpose: it said 'take me seriously or suffer the consequences'. The other eleven sat rapt or slumped, indifferent or keen, in the two rows of the oak-built box; Alex just wanted to see the end of the trial.

Murder was such an ugly, graceless word, or was it the word's meaning that made him uneasy? Mur-der. Two syllables, six letters, a simple word that could mean so much to the world yet so little to the murderer. For four long, gruelling weeks, they had listened to the case against Dr Jenny Fox, whilst the world's press had force-fed the facts down the hungry public's gullet. He flicked his attention to the crammed press box and eager public gallery: didn't these people have lives?

Alex was surprised that Geoffrey Haversham – the Attorney General, who had prosecuted the case so tenaciously – was absent; obviously fulfilling other public duties. Then again, jury service was the last public service Alex needed. When the letter arrived from the Lord Chancellor's Department, it had almost cost him the contract to design a leisure centre in Essex; it could still do so. It had only been secured by sharp work and slightly sharp practice.

The weary judge concluded his summing up, reading carefully from the great ledger that held his thoughts and the evidence of the preceding weeks.

'Those, members of the jury, are the issues you must resolve. You will find it convenient to elect one of your number to act as spokesperson and chairman of your discussions.'

Alex saw his fellow jurors' eyes flash along the line to 'Uncle Bob', who sat in the seat in front of him. Alex couldn't remember when the nickname had first been coined for the avuncular retired watch-repairer, but since its inception they had all used it; all but Alex that was.

The judge's domed head nodded dully to the black-robed clerk of the court as two middle-aged ushers scuttled forward, between them clutching a single King James Bible in their right hands. The pale, rotund clerk clambered to his feet and monotonously intoned the ushers' oath.

'Do you swear by almighty God, that you will take this jury to some private and convenient place and that you will suffer no person to speak to them, neither will you speak to them yourselves unless it be to ask them if they are agreed upon their verdicts, so help you God?'

The ushers muttered their agreement with the Almighty: more lip service, Alex thought. He looked across the room to the ashen face of the defendant, Dr Jenny Fox: eco-terrorist or freedom fighter? Whatever the label, a man was dead, shot three times through the back of the skull: years of education and learning smeared on the floor of a government-funded research centre in the dead of night.

She looked tiny in the dock, flanked by two burly female prison warders. Her Nordic blue eyes, twin vortexes at the centre of whirlpools of dark rings, stared unflinchingly ahead. Her fine features were more Jane Austen than Myra Hindley. Finely arched eyebrows, long dark lashes, milk-white teeth inside firm lips that were more intellectual than sensual. Still, all in all, a postgraduate pin-up for the maximum-security wing. She had shown little or no emotion during the last month. The Attorney General, Geoffrey Haversham, had laboured that point during his closing address.

"Has she shown any remorse, members of the jury? Has she shown one iota of regret for the summary execution of a rival academic? You have the evidence of your own eyes as an answer to that question.'

He had a point, a point that might well find favour with the other jury members, but Alex preferred the hard facts, not the gut instinct of a thousand would-be diviners of human behaviour.

The ushers separated; one to open the small latched door from the jury box, the other the door to the private exit from the court to the jury retiring room. Alex picked up his heavily notated bundle of jury documents that had amassed during the trial. He glanced up at the simple white-faced courtroom clock. It was one minute to midday, almost high noon for Dr Jenny Fox. He followed the ushers and the other jury members from the throbbing court into the relative quiet of the corridor leading to the sanctity of their room.

He passed through the portal and the door closed behind him with a gentle click.

The room smelled like a new car, pristine and virgin. It was the air-conditioning. A quick glance to the large barred windows and the recently thumbed putty confirmed Alex's suspicion that it had been newly decorated, probably in their honour.

A large round melamine table and matching chairs dominated its centre. To the side more comfortable low-slung, padded, plastic seats squatted against the wall as if in shame. Alex removed his black leather coat and dropped it unceremoniously on to one of them. He could hear Uncle Bob talking quietly in the background.

'No, like everything else, this has to be done by vote, democratic like. It's the proper way, Dave.'

He was talking to the big, balding figure of Dave Conran, a baby-boomer with a booming voice and thick black moustache, which probably made him appear more sinister than he was, though Alex was dubious about that. Alex called him 'Stalin' after the Communist dictator, though only in his thoughts.

'You're clearly the man for the job, Bob,' Dave's East End accent elasticating the word 'clearly' to impossible length. 'Stands to reason: horses for courses, senior man and all that.'

Alex folded his arms and waited for the others to remove their coats and place overnightbags and briefcases on the floor. Uncle Bob waited patiently for them to settle but as yet no one had taken a seat. Alex watched the compact man carefully. He wore a serge suit that had seen more birthdays than Alex, yet it was still smart: more lived in than tired out. A startling white shirt, a little frayed around the collar but Alex knew it would be crisply laundered, was finished with a proudly worn regimental tie. Bob's face was as small and compact as his body and as neat as his mind. His dark little eyes looked as wet as a mouse's, but Alex had seen them sharpen to those of the rodent's larger, more ferocious cousin twice during the course of the last few weeks. The transformation had been fleeting but uneasily illuminating. Now they were in their naturally benign state as he thoughtfully scratched his right cheek. Alex saw the wedding ring catch the light, but knew from snippets of talk that Bob was a long-term widower.

One by one they fell silent, until all that could be heard was the hum of the air conditioning and a repetitive clicking sound. Alex flicked his eyes to the left and there, unperturbed and smiling, sat Elsie Brimstone, pensioner and demon knitter with the growing sleeve of a baby's cardigan dangling over her own.

'Don't mind me, you youngsters. I'll have to finish this soon or little Demi will be too big for it.' Her activity never faltered as she spoke. Alex had grown accustomed to the noise. In the canteen, in the jury waiting room, probably in the toilet, the constant soft clicking counted out the adjournments, like a plastic metronome. Alex half-expected to see her at it during the trial. Her kindly, rounded face, like a Dickensian favourite aunt, was a warm copper colour from winters in the Spanish sun, courtesy of her six doting sons, tempered with steel. Alex called her 'Pearl'.

Uncle Bob coughed in light disapproval at her reference to him as a 'youngster'. What was it about the elderly? Alex thought. They all want to be considered as young for their age, yet would fight to the grim death to be the most senior citizen, if only by a day.

'Well I think we should make a start,' Bob said quietly. 'We all heard what the judge said about electing a foreman.'

'Does that term include the female as well as the male gender?'

Alex and the others turned their attention to 'Princess Grace'. Helena, Alex reminded himself, but the cool blonde's resemblance to the fifties movie star was unmistakable. Tall and willowy, like Grace in *High Society*, but more barbed, brittle ice, too used to her own way. Bob smiled evenly.

'The judge didn't strike me as a sexist, Helena,' Stalin said. 'Obviously thought the good Doc was up to a spot of brutal execution; chairing a jury should be a piece of pi—'

'Ladies present,' Bob interrupted.

'Should be a breeze,' he countered, whilst failing to appear remotely embarrassed. 'Doesn't mean it's what we want though, does it, dear?'

Alex watched Grace flush slightly, as her arms folded across her flat stomach.

'I am not your dear and shudder to think at the poor specimen of womanhood who is.'

It was Stalin's turn to colour up. He glared at her.

'What you need is a . . .'

'Some respect,' Pearl chipped in. She continued to knit. 'Just like my grandchildren, squabbling over nonsense, when what we all need is to settle down to our homework. That girl, Jenny, she's the important one here, that's why we are here; at least I thought so.'

Alex smiled broadly, it was impossible to take offence at Pearl but she hammered her message home like a regimental sergeant major.

'Let's all calm down and sit down,' Bob suggested, his right arm sweeping towards the table. Slowly the others began to take their places. Alex waited until they were all seated before moving. He noticed the two young men in the jury: 'Pitbull', a savage looking man-dog with a shaven head, and 'Danno', a Eurasian, like Steve Magarrat's sidekick in *Hawaii 50*; each moved towards the seat at Uncle Bob's right, but a simple nod from the forceful pensioner guided them to other seats. They sat next to each other. Bob raised his head and stared straight at Alex, who shrugged and sat down next to him; it was the only seat left.

'Now,' Bob began, 'do we have any proposals for fore-' – he smiled warmly at Grace – 'person?'

Stalin raised his hand quickly.

'You, Bob, are best man, I mean person of either gender, for the job.' He grinned smugly around the gathering.

'I second that,' a deep male middle-class voice added.

'Why, thank you, Alex,' said Bob, a hint of surprise in his tone, without turning. Alex didn't want the bickering, he wanted to get this over and pick up the rest of his life, but he had surprised himself and, quite obviously, Bob too.

'Any other nominations?' Bob continued, all eyes and faces turned to Grace, whose own gaze focused unblinkingly on the man to her right. A handsome half-caste with the bone structure of a Calvin Klein model, Frank Stroyan, or 'Denzel', as in 'Washington', as Alex knew him in the roll-call of his head, stared straight ahead, a polite smile on his fine features. Grace sucked in and blew out some of the rapidly supercharging air. Alex suspected there might be something going on between the two, but this was the first public showing of the possibility. Grace dropped her eyes and shook her head quickly, savagely. Stalin snorted his amusement. Uncle Bob took up the reins.

'We need to keep these things nice and democratic: let's have a vote.' All but Pearl raised their hands in the air in Bob's favour, she continued to click away, unfazed.

'Now,' Bob continued, 'we all have our own views about this case, and that means we are all entitled to our say.'

He looked around to agreeing nods.

'What I propose is this: as some of you may know, before I retired I spent a lifetime, man and boy, working with clocks and watches. All kinds, any make from any country, could patch 'em up a treat, even made a few from scratch.'

Alex watched, impressed. Any other pensioner who talked like this would have been yawned away from his dotage reminiscence, but there was something powerful about Bob's delivery that demanded attention; even Alex's.

'Clocks work, you see, if they're put together right, tick-tock, right around the dial, like clockwork, that's the expression. This table is the clock face and each of you one of the twelve one-hour markers.'

Alex watched each of the others fixing the idea in their minds.

'Where's twelve o'clock?' he asked their newly elected foreman, who swivelled his head to look deeply into Alex's eyes.

'Why, right here,' he whispered. 'Only right that the foreman goes last and doesn't hog all the limelight. Besides, I'm sure that all you lot have better minds than a retired watch-mender from the East End of London.'

Alex sincerely doubted that proposition.

'What we'll do is this: each of us in turn asks a question or makes a point about the case, then we'll discuss that until we are all happy about it, then move on,' Bob continued. Another voice cut in: Stalin.

'Let's just have a vote, find the murdering bitch guilty, then go home.'

'Not quite as simple as that,' Bob answered.

'You heard the evidence,' Stalin continued, 'bleeding overwhelming.'

'These are the most serious charges you can face,' Bob answered. 'Life imprisonment if she's convicted.'

'Should be the rope,' Stalin pushed. Bob raised a hand to quiet him.

'We aren't here to argue about the death penalty, just her guilt.'

'Or innocence,' Alex interjected.

'Exactly,' Bob continued, 'as I was about to say.' But the mouse eyes had momentarily flickered from prey to predator. Alex wondered if he was the only one to notice the stark transformation.

'Back to the clock face,' the foreman suggested. 'If I am at twelve,' he turned to Stalin, 'then that puts you at one o'clock.'

'Lovely stuff,' number one replied, 'over in a jiffy. Let's not waste any more time.'

Alex waited patiently as Stalin grinned confidently at the other eleven. Bob smiled back as if his right-hand man was sat for once just to his left.

12.19 p.m., Prime Minister's Study, 10 Downing Street

For the fiftieth time that morning, Edward Haversham replaced the handset into its cradle and pushed his lean, tanned fingers into the thick, dark, wavy hair that had become his trademark. The unruly boyish locks which had endeared him to the party faithful when he first appeared on the political merry-go-round had now reluctantly given way to a media-friendly grooming. Today, however, it would take more than a hairdresser and make-up girl to make him acceptable to the critical public eye. He looked and felt terrible, a gastro-bubbling fear had gripped the pit of his stomach since the news had first come through. Where the hell was his brother?

He had been woken at 3 a.m. by a call from the Cabinet Office Briefing Room at the Home Office. The Samaritans had contacted Scotland Yard shortly after two o'clock with a faxed message requiring urgent advice upon what they suspected was another crank call, but procedure demanded immediate attention for even the most ludicrous calls. The message revealed that a caller using a computer-generated voice-box had informed the duty counsellor that he was holding the Attorney General Geoffrey Haversham as a hostage. There would be no further communications until 1.15 p.m., at which time they expected to speak with the Prime

15

Minister himself: if not, then the Attorney General would be killed. To underline the sincerity of the threat, an interweb site number was given with precise instructions for the necessary hardware and installed software, including a video driver, high-resolution screen and industrial-performance modem so the act could be witnessed on-line.

TO25, the Central Communications branch at Scotland Yard, wasted little time in making the decision to dispatch officers to the Attorney General's townhouse in Grosvenor Crescent Mews in Mayfair. On arrival, all that could be found was a whimpering chocolate-brown Labrador stretched across the entrance porch of the stucco-fronted building. At 2.47 a.m. the matter became an official crisis situation with a codename, level 1 security tag and the full attention of Paul Goodswen – Deputy Assistant Commissioner, head of SO12, Flying Squad, B Division – who had the unpleasant task of first contacting the Home Secretary and then waking the Prime Minister.

Edward Haversham rose from the leather-topped desk and walked the length of the room to the large Georgian window overlooking the rear gardens of his new home. He'd occupied it for less than three months now and its full extent was still a mystery. As he gazed on to the neatly manicured grass square below, the clouds parted briefly, allowing the midday sun to burst into the room. He turned sharply away from the light and his eye was drawn to the collection of silver-framed family photographs perched on the walnut bureau next to the window.

Picking up the small double-frame compact at the front he looked at the image of the two of them, his own six-year-old toothless grin and Geoffrey's self-conscious nine-year-old frown. It was one of his favourites, insisted upon by their mother. January 1956, just like yesterday, he remembered it vividly. It had been their first visit to London from the North. Their mother had taken them on an open-topped double-decker tour of the city. The excitement of the big gleaming red bus, the huge buildings and the people – so many people – was overwhelming, but there was one moment that was burnt into his memory just as clearly as the film in his mother's Kodak Instamatic.

As they had crossed the Westminster Bridge and stood on the

western side of the shimmering Thames below the enormous stone clock tower, the great chimes of Big Ben had struck the eleventh hour. Momentarily he was frozen to the spot, paralysed by the noise, vibrations shaking his tiny frame, and Geoffrey's arm tight around his shoulder. They craned their necks up to the face of the world's most famous timepiece when their mother shouted, 'Say cheese.' He turned to the lens and somehow realised then that one day he would come to know every nuance, every pitch and every different note of that bell.

It was strange fate that on that same day, moments after the booming had stopped in his ears, another sight steered his destiny, subliminally altering his life for ever. As the three of them wandered along St Margaret Street, hugging the great gothic façade of the Houses of Parliament and past New Palace Yard heading towards Westminster Abbey, crowds had gathered, blocking their progress. The brothers had frantically burrowed their way to the front, much to the annoyance of their mother.

A sombre procession was taking place of men wearing long grey wigs and others following dressed in morning suits. As the line filed past them, his mother pointed out the Prime Minister. He had immediately asked her loudly who the Prime Minister was, and she replied that he was 'the most important man in the country'. Confusion abounded in the young Haversham, for up until that point he had always regarded his father as the holder of that honour. He expressed that very view to the laughter of those around them. It wasn't so much a disappointment as a reality rush when a nearby policeman confirmed that his mother was telling the truth. A lesser boy may have left the matter there, but not him. Without a second's hesitation, the young Edward Haversham declared that some day he would also be Prime Minister. None of the smiling faces around him could ever have realised just how serious he was.

A sharp rap on the door interrupted his thoughts and brought him crashing back to the present. He hastily replaced the photograph as Donald Taylor, his Personal Secretary, entered the room.

'Everyone is present, Prime Minister. The press office are screaming for a comment but I thought you'd want to take the security briefing immediately. They're assembled in the anteroom. All this afternoon's engagements have been cancelled. The deputy PM has been apprised of the situation and will chair the cabinet at two thirty,' said the efficient Yorkshireman.

'Thanks. Show them in.'

Haversham returned to his desk, glancing at the portrait of Winston Churchill that hung above the fireplace with his firmly set jaw and familiar brown Cuban torpedo. He composed himself as best he could but it was going to take more than a couple of deep breaths and a long-dead predecessor to quell the dual action of helplessness and anger. Within moments, his secretary had returned, followed by a group of four people. Elizabeth Arlington, M15 liaison officer to SO12, was the first to hold out her hand. Haversham had met her before on two or three occasions since the election at security briefings from the protection squad. Despite his newly elevated status as leader of Her Majesty's Government, there was a side to this woman which clearly wasn't to be influenced by men in power. When he thought about it he guessed that she wasn't likely to be influenced by men, full stop. The two of them hadn't exactly hit it off in the chemistry stakes when Haversham had questioned the high level of personnel required for even the most routine of public engagements.

He had made no secret of his distaste for the seemingly endless ambition of the security services to acquire a more than significant role in mainstream policing without relinquishing what he saw as their paranoid grasp on unaccountability. To make matters worse he had also seen a confidential memorandum signed by Arlington warning the head of M15 that the security arrangements of the two Haversham brothers were being hampered by the Attorney General's flat refusal to entertain twenty-four hour personal protection.

She was a tall, raven-haired woman, a similar age to himself, with a full mouth and sleepy brown eyes that gave nothing away, set into a highly sculptured face that lent itself perfectly to caricature. Haversham greeted her as warmly as he could under the circumstances, before she introduced the rest of the group. Superintendent Ray Prince from the Counter Terrorism Contingency Planning Branch of SO13, with his tight blond crew-cut and preppy tortoiseshells, looked too young for his title but suitably studious for an analyst.

In direct contrast was the next in line, Detective Chief Inspector

Brian Chance, lead hostage negotiator from SO10. Haversham remembered seeing Chance interviewed on television following the successful release of fifty-eight passengers from a US-bound Jumbo some time last year during yet another Libyan-driven anti-imperialist attack. He guessed that Chance was somewhere in his mid-fifties and looked as if he had always been that age. Sporting a shabby tweed jacket and old school tie, Chance had slicked-back, grey, thinning hair and a sharp nose that looked too elegant for his big, friendly face.

Finally Paul Goodswen stepped forward: he was acting head of the operation and would give the technical details during the briefing. Haversham shook hands with the police officer; so this was the man with overall control, the man who held the steering wheel of his brother's fate. Goodswen was relatively short for a police officer but his frame filled the blue linen suit he was wearing to capacity. Strangely, the fact that clearly he hadn't had the time or deference to shave for the occasion gave Haversham some real comfort. These were action people, just like himself, and a vague sense of hope began urging itself back on to the playing field after a nine-hour absence. The two men locked eyes momentarily and Haversham found himself repeatedly muttering a sincere thank you.

Arlington's rhythmical Morningside brogue, with its clipped consonants and inherent precision bred from generations of Edinburgh old money, helped him focus on the reality of the situation as they sat around the conference table.

'Prime Minister,' she opened softly, 'I know that a man such as yourself expects candour at all times. I do not, therefore, apologise for my bluntness now. We are all deeply concerned that you will find it extremely difficult to sustain objectivity despite your undoubted qualities. This is not only a matter of national security but also a time of great emotional strain for your family.'

'I'm not sure whether to feel insulted or complimented,' he replied quickly without altering his expression. Then after a moment's pause he leant forward, forearms on the table-top and palms spread wide. 'Rest assured that if the time comes when I feel compromised in my duty to the citizens of this country, control will be relinquished. So far my objectivity, as you so delicately put it, is intact.' He delivered the line in his best electioneering voice, direct and sincere. In all the years that he had campaigned and debated, he'd learned that even the most hopeless of points if practised enough could be made to sound as if it had emanated from the heart. This time he could hear the hollowness of doubt in his words. He could only hope that the panel of scrutineers sitting opposite him didn't pick up the resonance of a man trying to convince himself of the truth.

He stared almost indignantly into those inscrutable brown eyes but saw nothing; he had to hold on, for there was one thing Edward Haversham was sure about. As he saw it, the best chance that his brother had of making it through this alive was if he was calling the shots.

'Nevertheless, Prime Minister,' she pressed, gazing back at him, 'this situation is unique: the temptation to ignore policy will be immense.'

'Ms Arlington, we still don't have a demand. It may be a politically motivated action or it may be for financial gain; either way, my previous comments still apply.'

'With the greatest respect, sir, we believe it highly unlikely that there could be any motive other than terrorist action.'

'One thing politics has taught me is that the best mind is an open mind. I would have thought it important in your line of work too,' he said a little too tersely and regretted it immediately. Point-scoring still. He kicked himself mentally.

'Of course,' she replied, 'but would we be doing our jobs properly if we didn't ventilate all matters?'

'I understand your concerns, Ms Arlington, although I confess to finding it insulting that you will not accept my word. Let me crystallise the issues for you. Firstly, this government would never have sanctioned the appointment of my brother as Attorney General had he not shown the qualities to meet the position both personally and professionally. He is a strong individual of high principle. Secondly, the fact that he is my brother has no bearing upon the manner in which you will deal with the situation. Do I make myself clear?' He managed to sound convincing enough as Paul Goodswen gave a slightly uncomfortable cough designed to temper Arlington's crusade. Thankfully she took the hint and retreated.

'Understood, Prime Minister.' She almost tripped over the words. 'All yours, Paul.' Goodswen took up the briefing.

'I have been appointed Incident Commander and I will be

reporting directly to the Commissioner, the Home Secretary and, of course, yourself. The command structure is a pyramid with the incident room at the apex. I am assisted by the technical support team and have at my disposal the firearms units and hostage negotiators headed by DCI Chance. Superintendent Prince will be shadowing every moment of the operation from a remote location with officers from "A" squad. They work on what we call "slow-time" decision-making and co-ordinate and constantly update contingency plans: he's there to make an unhurried assessment away from the crisis management of the front line, which is my team. The Cabinet Office briefing room is on stand-by for military intervention should our methods prove inadequate.

'All in all, we have every conceivable safeguard in place to ensure that your brother comes out alive.'

Haversham exhaled slowly; these were the words he longed to hear.

'The kidnappers have requested contact with you and our decision at this stage is that you clearly must comply. We don't know who we're dealing with yet, but there's every reason to believe that they want to negotiate. This is an expertly planned operation. It's unlikely to be the Irish, given the lack of recognised Provo or UDR codewords used.'

'Unless it's a splinter group,' Prince reminded him.

'Even so, we believe in two possibilities. Firstly, we know that the Attorney General was working on extradition treaties for the Puma drugs cartel; they have the money and resources to carry out this sort of job. Secondly, any number of Middle-Eastern groups could be responsible and the security services are currently pooling all intelligence together in the hope of discovering a lead. The high-spec technology needed for the computer link-up shows the level of professionalism here. Our IT department has attempted to contact the Internet number provided, but so far we've been jammed. We'll be using mobile communications for the modem which will be linked back to the incident room at the Yard: we don't want them hacking into the databases held on Downing Street's computers.'

'Is there any possibility of tracking the source once we get through?' asked Haversham. 'I mean, I'm assuming that if we keep them on the line long enough then some sort of trace is available.'

'Extremely unlikely that they'll give us the time, wouldn't you say, Brian?' The Commander looked to DCI Chance, who was studying the Prime Minister's reactions closely.

After a few moments' slightly uncomfortable silence he unfolded his arms, leant forward resting his elbows on his knees, and looked up into Haversham's eyes.

'To be honest, sir, I haven't got the faintest idea what sort of timescale we're dealing with here. I could give you some guesswork, but I can tell that you're not interested in that, are you, Prime Minister?'

'I prefer specifics. Fire away, Chief Inspector.'

'There are no hard lines around the edges in a hostage situation. Kidnappers fall into three categories: the mad, the bad, and those who have a cause. The mad ones are genuinely unbalanced; potential suicides. I've yet to come across a case with this level of planning and patience orchestrated by a madman, but there's always the first. The bad ones are common criminals and you can safely say some of them are slightly deranged; normally after money. But then' – his face seemed to darken as he turned to the third category – 'you have the offenders for a cause: more committed than unequivocally criminal. The difference lies in what they demand.

'The bad rarely take hostages if they can help it: there's nothing to be gained in taking a hostage and so most sieges occur by accident when a crime goes wrong. You know the scenario: bank job, not quick enough, and boom' – Chance slapped his hands together for effect – 'suddenly the place is swarming with cops and then you're left with a sobbing woman in the crick of your arm and a gun to her head. That's giving us the best chance. We can offer them another way out, talk to them, plead with them, ask 'em why they want to add on four years for unlawful imprisonment to the sentence: they can't get away, so why bother?

'But here, you see, things are quite different. There's no doubt in my mind we're dealing with terrorists and we have no understanding of what their agenda is; but they know ours all right. We don't give in.'

The finality of the last statement bored through Haversham's psyche like a power drill piercing a lump of softwood. The DCI was right. Policy demanded that the authorities never give in to terrorists and right now he was that authority. He sat silently with his palms pressed together and wished he had a God to pray to.

12.37 p.m., The Jury Room

'Let's get this thing over with, I've got my own business to run,' Stalin said. He wasn't one to mess around. This trial had robbed him of a month of empire building his mobile phone business. Things could be going better. Another writ had arrived that morning from yet another whingeing punter; didn't they bother to read the contract? 'And I mean business,' he warned.

Alex could believe it. There was something pugnaciously pushy about the man that smacked of avarice. His clothes were expensive but ill-fitting. A blue sports jacket with cream slacks and garish tie had been his chosen uniform during the past weeks. Alex marvelled at Stalin's ability to produce increasingly objectionable neckwear on a daily basis and he had saved the worst till last: purple paisley with lemon stripes. Stalin slackened off the thick knot and unbuttoned his collar.

'I have to say, I think this is a waste of time. She's not only guilty, she's very guilty.'

Uncle Bob narrowed his eyes slightly and Alex saw that the small gesture was enough to halt the fearsome juror's complaint. Stalin shrugged.

'Go ahead,' Alex whispered, but it was to the foreman that Stalin looked for permission to continue – it was granted with a wave of his pipe. Stalin laced his fingers together and began.

'Like I said, I have my own business, cellular phones. Got in at the beginning, before the cowboys rode into town.'

Alex smiled wryly.

'But it wasn't easy, a lot of competition. Some say that's healthy, I never thought so myself. Anyway, there was this one bloke undercutting like crazy and it wasn't competition, it was suicide. So he had to be sorted out, given the word.'

'Threatened, you mean.'

It was Princess Grace, smiling like she had witnessed the event, but Stalin was not for backing down.

'Best-learned lessons are hard ones.'

'What's your point?' Alex muttered, and was aware of a sidelong glance from Uncle Bob.

'The point is how can we possibly ignore her motive for blowing him away? I mean, look at what we heard during the trial about her and Easterman.'

The Old Bailey, Day Four

Alex's back was stiff with inertia and there was still half an hour of evidence before the luncheon adjournment. Before him sat a thick bundle of photocopied documents provided by the prosecution: a catalogue of the articles and researches written both by the defendant and the deceased, which chronicled a bitter public disagreement between them. In the witness box the editor of the *Lancet* outlined the history of the debate. Half-rimmed glasses balanced theatrically on a long thin nose that was pushed slightly into the air.

'Professor Keeley, it was your decision to publish these articles?'

'Indeed, and I had no hesitation in doing so. It was a matter of public importance.'

'Could you briefly précis the matter of debate?'

'Certainly: leukaemia clusters, that is groups of significantly higher than expected rates of the disease, in localised areas, particularly in the young. Most research has centred on nuclear sites such as Sellafield and Dounreay in Scotland, but Dr Fox and the deceased were concerned with pesticide plants.'

Alex glanced across to Jenny Fox. She was waiting to pounce, if she were misrepresented, with alert and watchful eyes. As yet she appeared satisfied with the description.

'And were they in disagreement?'

The Professor nodded gravely

'They were poles apart; worlds apart, one might say.'

The Attorney General paused for effect, swept his eyes towards the jury then spoke.

'Please explain.'

The witness gestured towards his own bundle of documents.

'It is all in there, but basically Dr Fox is something of a maverick in her field and Easterman exposed the political nature of her findings.'

'What is – I'm sorry, was – Mr Easterman's standing in this field of research?'

The witness removed his glasses and held them by one of their arms.

'Without doubt, the leading light of his and every other generation, a quite brilliant man.'

'And Dr Fox's reputation?'

Alex heard a commotion from further along counsel's benches as the defence QC, Milton, climbed quickly to his feet.

'My lord, I object. The defendant is to be tried on the evidence, not on the opinion of this witness.'

The judge listened to the objection then pursed his lips before speaking.

'Expert evidence is always based on an opinion, Mr Milton. I will allow the witness to answer the question.'

Keeley smiled thinly.

'Her objectivity was in question. One's researches often throw up results that one would have preferred them not to. Science is based on hard fact, not wish fulfilment.'

'And how,' the prosecutor continued, 'did the deceased view her findings?'

'With the utmost suspicion. Indeed he went on the attack and began dismantling her reputation – and I might add he was very successful in that regard.'

You're not doing a bad job yourself, Alex had thought.

It was several days later that a police interview with the defendant was read to the court by the interviewing police officer:

'But you hated him.'

'Yes, I did,' she had replied, 'but not enough to want to kill him.'

'He had destroyed your reputation.'

'Not to those who knew the truth, the ones who counted.'

'What truth?'

'That the only results that were falsified were Easterman's own, not mine. He's employed by the government: do you think for one moment they would allow him to publish the truth?'

'So this is a huge conspiracy, is it?'

'Yes,' she had replied, 'that is precisely what it is. It's what I've been telling you all along: this is a set-up, you may even be part of it, I don't know. I don't know anything any more. All I do know is that when I arrived at the research centre he was already dead.'

'Is that really the best you can come up with?'

'Look, he telephoned me, said he'd had a change of heart and that he wanted to share the results with me, but wouldn't say any more on the phone. He thought it might be bugged and he was right. Whoever killed him knew me and my friends were coming and murdered them too.'

The interview had been terminated as Jenny Fox was too upset to continue.

'That's bull,' Stalin shouted across the table in the jury room towards Princess Grace, 'she had every reason to kill him. Never cross a woman, I know what frigging women are like.'

'Steady,' Uncle Bob warned.

'I can fight my own battles,' Grace replied. 'It's not the word frigging I find distasteful, it's not even that smug, self-satisfied smirk on your face, it's your ignorance. In the last month I have endured your bigotry, your racism, your hypocrisy, so it does not surprise me in the slightest that you have now added women to your list of prejudices.'

'See what I mean?' responded Stalin, appealing to the others, arms outstretched, palms facing upward.

'She's right.'

The voice came from Alex's right. In the four weeks of the

trial Kalsi Abadom had barely spoken a word to any of the other members of the jury. Now she was attacking a belligerent fascist. A tall white girl in her mid-twenties, clad in a yashmak, who had chosen to swear her juror's oath on the Koran she now stared unflinchingly into Stalin's eyes.

'Whether she committed this murder or not, it has nothing to do with her gender.'

'Of course she did it. Christ, am I the only one here with any sense?'

'No, you're not.' Alex could hear the anger in his own voice.

'Let's all just calm down,' Uncle Bob demanded.

'Look I'm at one o'clock,' Stalin blustered. 'That means it's my turn in the spotlight. When the hand sweeps past then fair enough, but I know my rights and I want my say.'

'Your time's up,' Uncle Bob warned.

'What?'

Stalin looked like a puppy that had been smacked. Alex glanced sideways at the foreman whose face was set in rigid determination. So, he thought, you still have all your own teeth, and they're sharp too.

'What we do know,' Uncle Bob continued, 'is that Jenny Fox had every reason to want to kill Easterman.'

'Does that mean she did?' Alex asked, thinking out loud.

'That's not what I said, but it does suggest that she had a reason to kill him.'

'Murder him,' said the Prof, at number four, proud of his grasp of the English language.

'Murder him, then,' Uncle Bob responded through lightly clenched teeth. 'But do we really believe that after all this' – he waved the copy of the rivals' vitriolic correspondence in the air – 'Easterman would really invite her around for a chat and an apology?'

Alex looked around the table at the unimpressed faces of the jury members. The Mouse at number two, dropped her gaze to the table-top and Stalin was grinning. The Prof shook his head slowly and Kaftan at three had her eyebrows raised. Princess Grace and Denzel looked briefly at each other then a little too quickly away. The two young jury members, Danno and Pitbull, at five and six on Uncle Bob's human timepiece both shrugged almost

27

apologetically, whilst Kalsi shook her head slowly from side to side. Alex swivelled his eyes to Uncle Bob and could just detect a flicker in the foreman's right cheek. Alex attempted to interpret what it was, then in an instant he knew. Uncle Bob was desperately trying to stop himself smiling.

12.51 p.m., Victoria Embankment, London

T o anyone strolling along the northern bank of the River Thames on this gloriously sunny afternoon it looked just like any other ambulance passing by. That's the way Pavel had planned it. Not so much guesswork as sheer intuitive genius. At least that's what they had always said of him. From his earliest memories of calculating the number of loaves his mother could bake from the wheat rations the Party gave her, to the relative luxury of the Military Academy where he did very different kinds of sums, they'd always said he was a genius. He had never been one to dwell upon his own abilities even as a child: stolen from his parents, and thrust among other carefully selected prodigies, he had been too busy exploiting those talents to concern himself with how others regarded him. Special boy. Special man.

He watched calmly out of the blackened windows as the vehicle drew to a halt. Double yellow lines and threatening fluorescent orange clamp-zone signs marked the area as a no-go for others but not for the emergency services; just the way he planned it. People were passing by but none gave the van a second look. Two young lovers draped over each other on a bench by the river were the only stationary objects within a hundred metres. Pavel ran a mental observation check through habit, not serious conviction: he knew that ninety per cent of genius is thoroughness.

Clothing: loose, bright sportswear, probably imported design. Male: perhaps twenty-two, thin face, no physical threat. Two points of concern: Walkman and sunglasses. The former could be cover for a communication link and the latter could house a miniature camera unit, but the youth was looking over at the South Bank and his lips didn't move. Female: a little younger, Mediterranean complexion, eyes closed, enjoying the sun. The pink seersucker jacket gave it away, though: on the lapel he spotted a plastic badge bearing the legend Victoria English Language School. Pavel allowed himself a brief smile of satisfaction as he matched the lettering on the namebadge to a large wooden sign across the carriageway outside an imposing spire-clad gothic building.

'Students.' He gestured towards the couple with a nod. The young woman sitting beside him looked up impassively from one of the two monitors she was studying. She'd changed now from the technicoloured lycra jumpsuit she'd worn in the park the previous night into a more appropriate white and blue nurse's uniform. Pavel turned his attention to the hatch separating the driver's cab from the hold and gave the signal to Serge to cut the engine. Only the gentle humming of the computers and the dull sound of passing traffic could be heard as Serge followed his order. Pavel took one long, deep intake of breath and positioned himself on the swivel chair in front of the makeshift steel bench. On top sat a mesmerising array of technology blinking and flashing in an unashamedly unchoreographed demonstration of silicon power.

'Time check, Lydia,' he demanded.

'Twelve fifty-five and fourteen seconds. Switching to satellite tracking program and transferring to your monitor now,' the woman said in a flat, Eastern European accent. Her smooth olive brow had just the suggestion of dampness and her pupils were dilated from the adrenaline rush.

'OK, got it,' Pavel replied, grabbing the headset next to the keyboard and manipulating the flexicord microphone over his mouth. 'Stand by, commence countdown now.'

'Twenty . . .' The first number, slightly croaky, fought its way out; it wasn't every day you got to hack into the US military global satellite system. She swallowed hard and continued, following the chronometer syncronised to GMT. 'Nineteen, eighteen . . .'

'Opening commport three, initialising modem link at 56Kbps.'

'Fifteen, fourteen, thirteen . . .' They'd been through this a hundred times in preparation but never with the juice turned on. Her confidence grew as she watched the modems light up.

'Dialling GPSS.'

'Ten, nine, eight . . .' Lydia continued as Pavel's fingers flashed over the characterless keyboard with the deftness of a concert pianist.

'Connected. We're hooked into GPSS online and still counting. Switching back to monitor two now. Downloading access code to telecommunications/GPSS/satcode directory in your C drive.'

'Three, two, one. Exploding dump files now,' she said, her mouth drying rapidly as she watched the monitor burst into furious activity. They had only another thirty seconds before the trace program would be automatically locked on to their position from 500 miles up in space. The graphics display box showed the file copying at breakneck speed. Within fifteen seconds it was done.

'File transfer complete,' she said, relaxing a little. 'Global Navigation Satellite System accessible. US satellite Senator Two will enter into range in two minutes. Estimated exposure time nine minutes. Time now twelve fifty-seven and three seconds. Awaiting instructions.'

'OK. They should be operational now. Open web site at WWW.Gov/Att.Gen./htlm, but hold the encryption program.'

'Affirmative. Web site open; scrambler still active.'

'Perfect, Lydia. And now we wait. De-encrypt scrambler code at one fifteen and fifty-five seconds. We'll find out then if they are taking us seriously.' Pavel removed the headset, reached for the brown bottle of pills on the bench, hurriedly swallowed two, then closed his eyes and swivelled away from Lydia's concerned expression. After five years of watching this man ply his cause across the planet she had no room for doubt. And if ever she or anyone else needed confirmation of his convictions they only need witness the pathetic sight of Geoffrey Haversham lying strapped to the stretcher bed at the other side of the van. Pavel had to be taken seriously. Very seriously.

12.58 p.m., 10 Downing Street

Edward Haversham headed the group making its way along the narrow, red-carpeted passageway from his private study flanked by his permanent secretary who was hurriedly scribbling Haversham's ministerial ramblings on to a notepad. Brian Chance, walking a step behind the rest, caught the Prime Minister's eye as they paused at the balustrade on the landing. They were standing beside a portrait of the Duke of Wellington when Haversham gestured for them to descend the east-wing staircase leading down to the Cabinet Room. The others walked on ahead whilst Haversham deliberately hung back, Chance reaching him just as the others started down the stairs and looked up at the famous foreboding grimace of Napoleon's nemesis staring down at them.

'The Attorney General wasn't by any chance educated at Eton?' he asked.

'No, we were both Ampleforth. Why do you ask?' replied Haversham.

'Wasn't it Wellington who said that the battle of Waterloo was . . . ?'

'. . . won on the playing fields of Eton,' Haversham interrupted, finishing the quotation as he turned down the staircase. 'I see what you're getting at. Don't worry, Geoffrey's made of stern stuff, you can be sure of that. We were taught by Jesuits and they could be worse than any Eton master when it came to discipline. That's why he ended up so damned stubborn and argumentative.'

'I suppose they're pretty good qualities when it comes to being a lawyer, but what he needs in this situation is very different.'

'I'm sure he will cope, it's just a question of how long.'

'Time is a precious thing indeed, Prime Minister; it is blissfully obedient to the laws of supply and demand,' Chance said in a cryptic reference to the politician's own background in economics.

'What do you mean?'

'It becomes more valuable the less you have left.'

'Quite profound, Chief Inspector, I've never thought of it like that before and you're absolutely right, of course, but is there any way we can guarantee him more time?'

'First job is to get this contact over. We'll know exactly what they want then.'

'How do I approach it?'

'Non-confrontational; listen and don't argue: encourage them to understand that you are there to co-operate, above all make sure you convince them that you are not interventionist.'

'Not easy.'

'Never is, but what part of your job could ever be described as easy? One last thing.' Haversham raised his eyebrows in antici-pation.

'Keep control and stay calm no matter what. It may not seem like it just at this moment but you are in control, whether you're dealing with terrorists or those a little closer to home.' Chance concluded by raising his eyebrows and indicating the others just ahead rounding the corner. Elizabeth Arlington was still obviously dictating her views to the incident commander in animated fashion. Haversham looked at Chance with growing respect. They both knew that as far as Arlington was concerned, and perhaps a number of others in Whitehall, if anything went wrong it would be down to him and him alone.

'Thanks for the vote, Chief Inspector.'

'I'll be listening to everything and you'll be able to hear me. Don't feel obliged to pick up on my comments but I'll be with you every step.'

They walked into the Cabinet Room with exactly thirty seconds to spare before the technical team were to make contact with the hitherto unobtainable Internet number. As Haversham sat down in front of a glowing computer terminal the room was perfectly still. He removed his jacket and slung it unceremoniously on the table in front. As he looked around for a brief moment, unfamiliar faces

staring back at him, an underarm sweat gland broke into activity
and deposited its load in a trickle that ran the length of his ribcage.
Chance was sitting to his left in front of another monitor and gave
him a slight nod as he too settled into position and adjusted the
brightness on his screen.

In thirty seconds his brother could be dead. The heaviness he
had felt earlier suddenly returned to Haversham like the dense, dark
moments before a rainstorm, as a young officer at the back of the
room called out fifteen seconds to contact. Inside, he could almost
taste the awesome weight of his office competing for space against
the love of his brother. It was as if everything around him could hear
his turmoil: the furniture, the portraits, the delicate silverware and
especially the walls of this ancient room. They had all listened in
on the most important decisions in history, good or bad. Suddenly
he didn't want this, any of it, not the job, not the status, not this
chapter in his biography. 'Prime Minister, could you please position
the earpiece,' said the young man. 'Five seconds and counting. Four,
three . . .'

Too late to turn away now. Keep calm, keep cool, his inner voice
battered his brain. Haversham nervously positioned the delicate
earphone and could hear Chance whispering good luck into his
right ear. He braced himself against the back of the chair. Cool
or fool. Cool or fool, the mantra chanted inside his head.

'Two, one and modem initialised . . .'

'Tracer activated and following . . .'

'Computers now shaking hands . . .'

The jargon trundled on, rolling into one long continuous drawl;
he was unable to distinguish the voices. The palms of his hands
were wet as the technical team clicked furiously at their keyboards
around him. Chance shot him a reassuring nod. Arlington and the
rest were crowded over another monitor at the other end of the room
in grim silence. And then he saw it. They all saw it.

'Jesus Christ,' Haversham blurted as he stared at the still picture
on the screen in disbelief. 'Somebody tell me that's not what I
think it is.'

'Hold on, sir, it could be a montage: they could have morphed
his head on to a pre-programmed image.'

'How's the trace doing?' Chance snapped.

34

'Blocked at a Vodaphone transmitting station. We think they're bouncing the signal off a communications satellite.'

The screen in front suddenly snapped into action; the picture was as clear as if his brother were sitting right in the same room. Only he wasn't. No sound accompanied the vision before them and Haversham knew then that this was no hoax. He watched mesmerised in abject horror as the camera panned slowly across the body of the Attorney General wearing a waistcoat made entirely of plastic explosive.

Just as the entire room was collectively trying to comprehend the possibilities of a bomb that size it dawned on Haversham that they still didn't know what the hell this was all about. He didn't have to wait much longer, for slowly creeping across the bottom of his screen was his answer.

Who really murdered Charles Easterman? Not Jenny Fox. That is your task: the true killer in exchange for your brother's life. I'm setting my watch by her jury; I suggest you do the same, Prime Minister. The rules are simple. You have until the jury returns their verdict to tell the truth. Don't call us . . .

1.18 p.m., The Jury Room

Jayne Pitt, or the 'Mouse' as Alex knew her, continued to twist her wedding ring nervously. The other ten waited patiently for her question. Small and slim, brown hair, eyes rooted to her own hands where her nails were gnawed down to delicate finger ends fluttering in panic. A silver crucifix dangled from the demure dark suit, cut slightly above the knee, and gave the impression of religious devotion. But Jayne knew it was a lie. Her year-long affair with her brother-in-law was the sacrilegious reality and was tearing the former convent-school pupil into self-loathing shreds. It had taught her one important reality: the roads we walk are not always the ones we would choose. She suspected the same of Dr Jenny Fox.

Uncle Bob whispered gently, 'It's all right, Jayne, really it is, we are friends here, but it's vital we do the job properly.' He glanced meaningfully at her shining cross. 'We swore an oath before the trial began, a holy promise.'

Skilfully he left his remarks there and smiled benignly as her hand deserted the much-twisted wedding band and clutched at her necklace like a lifebelt.

'Yes, I'm sorry, just nervous.'

'We all are, dear,' Pearl clucked quietly, pausing from her knitting and smiling warmly.

Alex watched the Mouse clear her throat of nerves.

'You may think me shy and silly . . .'

Stalin snorted but was silenced with a glance from Pearl that would have terrified a bare-knuckle fighter.

'But,' she continued, 'I think myself a good judge of character, and whilst I abhor clichés, what *is* a nice girl like Jenny Fox doing in a place like this?'

Next to her, at number one, Stalin slumped forward and exhaled in obvious exasperation; to his left at three Eleanor Smeaton, or 'Kaftan' as Alex referred to her, whispered to him, 'You have some very negative karma coming your way next time around.'

'Jesus,' Stalin muttered.

'Jesus, Buddha, Mohammed, whatever the name, the result's the same,' Kaftan replied.

This wasn't the first time Alex had seen how flaky but well meaning the bangle-wearing, Kaftan-billowing, tarot-reading forty-six-year-old was. Thin to the point of anorexia, dark eyes recessed in unnatural hollows, she possessed an otherworldliness that made Alex uneasy, but she had bottle, he had to give her that.

'We agreed on the rules,' Uncle Bob chided, glancing between his early afternoon clock counters. Kaftan shrugged whilst Stalin scowled. Alex saw Princess Grace smile slyly, royalty amused at the excesses of the peasantry. Bob swivelled his attention back to the Mouse. 'Can you explain what you mean by that?'

The Mouse nodded twice. 'Yes, yes, I think I can. It was during the first week of the trial. I remember feeling sick when they showed us the video of the killing.'

'The murder, you mean,' said the Prof at number four on Uncle Bob's human timepiece. His thin face was unreadable, blanked of expression, and sharp grey eyes, enlarged by a battered pair of NHS half-rimmed glasses, never wavered. Alex had spotted the tell-tale collection of motley Biros in the retired physics teacher's pocket on the first day of the trial: they had remained there ever since, the badge of a lifetime spent in bad schools educating disinterested children. 'We must be precise,' he continued. 'This is a murder, the defence accepted that; what we have to decide is whether the defendant committed it.'

'Sorry,' the Mouse said meekly. 'You're right, it couldn't be anything else.'

The Prof nodded evenly, a precise man in a chaotic world.

'The murder was horrific,' the Mouse continued, 'so wicked and cold, yet everything we heard about her . . . it just didn't add up.'

'What in particular?' Bob asked.

'When they went through her life, a good life, spent in the service of others.'

Alex clasped his hands together and rewound the spool of his memory to the introduction of the past and politicisation of Jenny Fox.

Court Two, The Old Bailey, Day Three

They were three days into the prosecution case. The Attorney General, with a team of eager, white-wigged Treasury counsel scribbling notes furiously behind him, led a senior officer from the anti-terrorist squad through his evidence.

'Commander.'

'Sir,' the grim-faced career policeman replied.

'I would be grateful if you could tell us something of the defendant's history, who she is, who her family are, what she has done with her life.'

The commander reached for a file which lay in front of him in the witness box. 'May I, my Lord?'

The judge's heavy lids raised momentarily towards the casual figure of David Milton, QC, leading counsel for the defence, who nodded. The witness shuffled through the file and began.

'Jennifer Jane Fox, Doctor of Medicine, thirty-five years of age, born in Surrey, daughter of Sir Marcus and Lady Fox, themselves eminent neurosurgeons.'

The judge spoke quietly. 'Their reputations are well known to this court, let us not dwell on them.'

'My lord,' the witness answered. 'Qualified from St Bartholomew's at twenty-two, and worked on the paediatric ward until 1986, when she volunteered for overseas service with the Red Cross.'

'And where did that take her, commander?' the barrister continued.

'To Chernobyl, sir, to work with irradiated children.'

The judge placed his pen carefully but with some force on to his highly polished bench. The officer hesitated, the Attorney General turned his head questioningly.

'My lord?'

'This is all very interesting, indeed laudable so far as the prisoner is concerned, but I fail to see where these matters take this case. Would you care to explain, Mr Haversham?'

'Certainly. The Crown's case is clear. It is our contention that during her trip to Chernobyl the defendant became a radical and on her return to this country became a political agitator; this led her into conflict with the deceased.'

'You mean motive?'

'Precisely, my lord.'

'Very well, continue.'

But it was the subsequent cross-examination by the Defence QC that stuck in Alex's memory more solidly.

'Commander,' he began, 'let us not call a spade a gardening implement.'

The witness appeared puzzled.

'Let's call a spade a spade, shall we?'

'Sir?'

'Jenny Fox, Dr Fox, my client, has always accepted that she was involved with radical eco-groups.'

'Eco-terrorists.'

'Semantics,' the barrister retorted.

'Reality, sir.'

'You are aware that my client has long been a target of your department?'

'We watched her with interest.'

'You are aware what her field of research is?'

'Pesticides, I believe,' the officer answered flatly, saying no more and no less than was permissible.

'What is the Circle of Poison?'

The question seemed to nudge him out of his confident stride.

'Circle of what, sir?'

'Poison, Commander. Now think hard, remember your lengthy and numerous interviews with the defendant.'

'I do recollect something about it.'

Milton smiled like a pin-striped tiger.

'Then pray enlighten us.'

'It concerns the international trade in pesticides.'

'Why the circle?'

'It is alleged that it begins with chemical workers in the West who make the product, travels around to third-world countries who use the pesticides to produce basic foodstuffs, and ends back with the Western consumer, but it is only a theory.'

Milton appeared satisfied with the answer then he leaned forward, his voice a low deep whisper and asked, 'And the poison?'

At this the commander glanced towards the judge who nodded for him to continue, and with obvious reluctance he did.

'People like the defendant believe that the produce yielded by the third-world workers is carcinogenic.'

'You mean, for the ordinary folk like me, that it causes cancer.'

'There is no proof of that.'

'Dr Fox's researches concerned the intolerably high incidence of leukaemia amongst children in areas close to chemical pesticide plants,' Milton continued.

'I understand her papers were dismissed as alarmist and unbalanced, sir.'

'The trade in these pesticides is very big business, Commander, millions, billions at stake.'

The commander stuck out his chin firmly. 'I would not like to speculate, but I would like to point out that it was the deceased who . . .'

'Please listen to my questions,' Milton interrupted abruptly, 'and kindly do not point out anything that is not directly relevant to the question.'

Rebuked and red-faced, the witnesses eyes narrowed, but he remained silent.

'She has done much to help and ease the suffering of dying and deformed children?'

'So I believe.'

'Yet you stand there in front of this jury and attempt to persuade them that this doctor, this healer of the sick, is capable of taking human life in so callous and brutal a fashion?'

41

'That is for the jury to decide, Mr Milton,' the judge whispered menacingly, but it was a point that troubled Alex deeply.

It was later when Jenny Fox returned to the issue in her evidence that Alex saw the problem: she was committed, totally, utterly and irrevocably. He recalled her slight trembling figure in the witness box as she dealt with her barrister's questions. As they dealt with the topic of the pesticides her grave eyes took on a zealot's shine, her voice became more strident as she spoke.

'There is a code of conduct issued by the United Nations Food and Agriculture Organisation that attempts to regulate banned pesticides, but lobbying from the government ensures that it has no legal force. It really is very simple and very deadly. Banned pesticides still cost money to produce. They have to be used somewhere. That somewhere is the third world. *They* have no legal protection from the carcinogens the pesticides contain. The pesticides are then used on crops to produce grain and other basic foodstuffs. Those crops are exported and we, along with other Western countries, import them. It amounts to the fact that we are buying back death-foods for our own children to slowly choke on. My own research proved it. I was of course discredited.'

'Why?'

Jenny Fox smiled wryly. 'Can you imagine the pesticide industry admitting it? I mean, what about share prices? What about the investors? Can you imagine the law suits, the crippling compensation? It can never be that way as far as they are concerned. Profit is everything and people are nothing to them.'

'Is that why you sought out others like yourself?'

'Committed people who care, yes.'

'Eco-terrorists,' whispered the Attorney General but the word carried across to the jury as was his intent. 'Were you willing to breach the Official Secrets Act in order to do this?'

'Most definitely.'

'But were you willing to murder?'

The court waited for her reply. Alex noted her hesitation that might well count against her case. Eventually she responded.

'I save lives, I do not take them.'

Her barrister nodded solemnly, adding unneeded gravitas to the weight of her words.

'What did your contacts with these groups teach you, Dr Fox?'

She blanched slightly, turned her head towards the jury and fixed on Alex before replying, 'All I can say is the more I learned the more terrified I became.'

And Alex believed her, but her honesty was a double-edged sword: it elevated her personal commitment to the cause but harmed her own case.

Alex turned his attention back to the jury room: the debate had ticked by, each volunteering their own view of Jenny Fox to the others. The air was heavy with pipe smoke from Uncle Bob's crusty briar, which he continued to puff at despite complaints. Kaftan was contributing her own odd insight.

'I've seen a lot of very heavy, very committed people in my life.'

'You should be committed,' Stalin whispered.

'Bad karma again,' she replied sweetly. 'But that girl is deeply into her own thing, like she really cares, perhaps too much. It really cuts both ways, but whichever way you look at it, it is very weighty cosmic badness, someone saw him off to the next cycle.'

Alex knew Kaftan was right. Whichever way you viewed it things looked bad for Jenny Fox. You just had to look at the wealth of prosecution evidence to see that, but he also remembered the look on Jenny Fox's face when she had said quite flatly and without any real anger or emotion, 'They had too much to lose, too many profits, too many vested interests, that was why they set this whole thing up. That was why I was framed for the murder of Charles Easterman.'

He wanted to believe her but the evidence – oh, the evidence, they would come to that soon, perhaps too soon for Jenny Fox, the prisoner at the bar.

1.43 p.m., SO10, Tenth Floor, Central Communications Complex, Scotland Yard

Ray Prince looked dishevelled when he arrived at the briefing with his team of analysts at the counter-terrorism contingency planning room. The group watched him closely, carefully trying to judge his mood, wondering what they were about to face. The whole ethos of CTCP demanded that everyone adopt a calm and dispassionate approach, despite the often critical advice they had to offer to the incident commander and the Cabinet Office Briefing Room. They dealt in facts, and facts alone.

As Ray Prince connected his notebook and logged on to the network of computers already humming among the six-strong unit, he felt the first twinge of uneasiness, something alien to him. He was tired but it wasn't that: an unfamiliar tension had crept in. He felt deeply apprehensive when usually he relished the challenge of out-manoeuvring his opponents. He'd known pressure before, but nothing like this. He looked around at his young team: there were five men with regulation haircuts and keen, bright eyes, each one sporting a brightly coloured necktie the bottom half of which was festooned with an assortment of Loony-Tune characters hidden when jackets were buttoned. A tradition he had started, it had been meant as a gesture of secretive solidarity echoing their special status within the Met, but met with disapproval from the sceptics. It was no more than a touch of light-hearted anarchy within the starched collar regime of the force, designed to remind them all that the surreal world they were forced to deal with was equally surreal as that created by Warner Brothers. Forget the real people on the ground and concentrate on the data, that's how they functioned, crunching the numbers.

As he focused upon the only woman in the team – no tie but, not wishing to let the side down, her dark shoulder-length hair slightly obscured a Daffy Duck brooch – Prince began to wonder whether his wits would be anywhere near as sharp as the adversary who was currently about ten steps ahead of the game.

'Afternoon, everyone. Listen up,' Prince opened to the expectant faces fixed upon him. 'The Attorney General, Geoffrey Haversham, has been the subject of a kidnap. He was abducted some time yesterday evening, probably from Hyde Park . . .'

'What, you mean one of our dinosaurs is missing, sir?' joked one of the team to a ripple of giggles, which soon disappeared when they realised Prince's expression had not altered.

'You could put it like that, John, but I doubt whether the rest of the country will share your sentiments if this goes the wrong way. Now, we have a situation which carries code red status. This is not a training exercise.' He looked around until satisfied that he had made his point. 'Our systems are live and on-line to the Cabinet Office Special Emergency Unit as of . . . now.' He quickly depressed a button on the grey laptop in front of him. The screen's liquid crystals quickly formed a recognisable shape. All present watched as the electronic logo bearing the Queen's coat of arms slowly phased into focus. Moving into the centre of the screen from the left was gold lettering which read C.O.B.R.A. Cabinet Office Briefing Room Annexe.

'I am network administrator for the operation. In a moment we will adopt our routine parameter configuration and establish the first database from the information I am about to download on to your screens. You will split into three cells of two starting from my left. Your passwords are Alpha, Beta and Gamma respectively.' He pointed to each pair in turn, then continued. 'In section one you each have a general outline of the intelligence, which is very limited: nevertheless, it's all we've got. Section two includes a copy of the recent web-site contact. In section three you will find the specific tasks allocated to each cell. For the present these tasks are independent. We collate and share information at fifteen-minute intervals starting from now. Go to it.' He quickly retrieved the notes he had made at Downing Street from the computer's hard drive and copied them into the server file. 'OK, you can access now.' Within seconds the six monitors sprang into life around him and the analysts began to read the initial assessment in total silence.

For the next quarter of an hour Prince paced the room looking over shoulders and occasionally catching the eye of one or two of his team as they hacked away at their keyboards and generated a growing pile of paper from the bank of printers in the corner of the room. Although the team gradually became more animated as they digested the information, Prince hadn't been mistaken when he'd felt that earlier twinge in his stomach. He could tell from the looks he was getting that the team felt exactly the same; it didn't get any closer than this. He glanced at his laptop and could see the onscreen timer counting down to the first checkpoint. He swiftly resumed his position at the head of the table and called time.

'All right, let's see what we've got,' he said, adjusting his glasses. 'Alpha team were designated to look at the explosives situation. Take us through it, John.'

'OK. I'm patching up a still taken from the video of the victim *in situ* and running a program to get an accurate analysis of the amount involved, but as you can see, the waistcoat itself is only partially visible. If the explosives are packed all the way round we are dealing with one huge mother of a banger.'

'What do you reckon on the type: is there a chance it's a hoax?'

'Doubt it, the amount of wiring going into the timer attached to his chest looks like a plate of spaghetti. It has to be Semtex or some derivative plastic explosive. There don't appear to be any markings on the packets that we can see but the colour is unusual, certainly different from the type used by the Provos.'

'That could be the quality of the picture, couldn't it?'

'Doubt it again, sir. Even taking into account the fact that the pictures have come through a telephone link, the hardware used would still give us a decent pixel resolution. In fact, it doesn't break up that much on enlargement. See.' He flashed a command to his terminal and instantaneously the picture grew, focusing on the timer device. 'If you look closely you can pick out some of the blue and red wiring to the detonator. There you go: crystal clear.'

'OK, let's get that segment blown up to maximum and sent to the Explosives Office, see what they come up with. Now what about the quantity?'

'As I said, sir, it's going to be fairly rough, based only on what we can see, but at least fifty kilos, possibly more: the numbers are still crunching.'

'Jesus Christ,' Prince hissed through his teeth. 'Right, look at giving command some idea of the potential damage. I want estimated first-impact outlook, casualty counts, and secondary damage calculations on a worst-case scenario: built-up area with maximum human occupancy.'

'How do we know the stronghold is in a city, sir? He could be anywhere by now if the abduction was last night.'

'You're right, we don't for sure but I'd say it's highly unlikely that our hostage-taker would waste that much firepower on anything else. I'm hoping Beta may be able to shed some light on the matter.' Prince looked over at the woman expectantly. 'What have you got for us, Jessica?'

'Not looking good, sir,' replied the woman.

'Does it ever? Dish it up. How have you approached the problem?'

'Trying to get a fix on the location by narrowing down the trace on the last contact to Internet exchanges: nothing as yet.'

'There must be something to go on.'

'At first sight, it looked like they had utilised a conventional web site – but there's something very odd about it.'

'Go on.'

'The signal was piggybacking a Vodaphone line.'

'So he's using a mobile phone to hook up to the net: there's nothing unusual about that.'

'Maybe not, but it is very unusual for any cellular line to be inaccessible to our tracking devices. They were cut off every time at a specific point. It looks like a phantom web site.'

'Keep working on it; we need to find that location. Contact the web-servers. He must have set up the web address through one of them: surely they'll have some sort of record.'

'Already done: the address used is a Domain name system using secure hypertext transfer protocol, although he gave us seemingly ordinary HTLP.'

'So?'

'A scrambler was used. It converted the characters he gave us into an anonymous location using cryptographic algorithms, the same sort of thing used by the credit industry.'

'I don't care if it's used by the Bank of England, get me that location: that's our number one priority.'

'Encrypting will take some time.'

'That's the whole point of using it. What's the best estimate you have on the jury in the Fox trial, Gamma team?'

'Could be anything. Basically, the case has lasted just over four weeks of court time. The prosecution case lasted fourteen working days, the defence three, counsels' speeches and the judge's summing up took them to last Friday. We know they were late sitting this morning: the judge did a little tidying up, then golden words and the jury were sent out just before midday. The Crown called forty-eight witnesses so there's a lot of evidence for them to go through – that's assuming, of course, they haven't made up their minds already.'

'The way the press have been running it, you wouldn't bet against them coming back this afternoon with a guilty verdict,' remarked Jessica.

'On balance I doubt it,' replied Prince. 'You have to remember she's called a boatload of character witnesses that the jury have to take into account as well as her own evidence. I think it's more likely they'll be out overnight. What do you think, Graham?'

'We need to run some research programs from central statistics at the Royal Courts of Justice for details of similar-length hearings, but really it's anyone's guess how long they'll be out.'

'The incident commander will need our best guess, so let's give him a working model. I'm going to report that worst-case is they come back with a guilty before close of play today. The judge won't let them sit longer than four thirty and I doubt whether he'll give a majority direction in a case this big today. That means he'll have to send them to a hotel overnight if they haven't reached a unanimous decision, taking us to tomorrow morning, ten thirty. So, best-case scenario on present knowledge is that we have twenty hours to find them. Now get back to it.'

2.25 p.m., 10 Downing Street

Edward Haversham walked along the long green-carpeted corridor of the wing linking the front and back houses that make up the Prime Minister's residence. As he passed by the private office he could see a couple of duty clerks glance at him through the window next to the press office. The flat look of desperation in their eyes mirrored his own. What training could ever have equipped him or any of the staff for a situation like this?

He knew that the press secretaries would be fielding a thousand enquiries from the media and the opposition spin-doctors. The rumour-mongering would be in full swing by now, precipitating all sorts of unwelcome speculation, but for the moment he didn't care so long as Geoffrey was still alive.

Haversham kept his head down as he passed the glass-walled 'garden room' at the foot of the staircase to his private flat. It was full of yet more secretaries trying their best to carry on with the ordinary business of the day and he didn't want to risk any of them detecting his anxiety. He welcomed the almost family-like atmosphere that he and his wife had instilled since their arrival. He felt strangely enough like a worried father waiting for a wayward son to return whilst the other children watched on.

In many ways, Downing Street was an extraordinary home. Gilt-framed portraits and stony-faced busts of Great Britain's most celebrated leaders could be found all over the building, serving to remind the current incumbent of the quarter of a millennium of political history that preceded him. Gladstone, Pitt, Wilberforce and Disraeli all looked down at him as he slowly climbed the staircase, and he wondered unnecessarily whether he would ever be worthy of a similar distinction.

Words began to play tricks in his mind: venerable or vulnerable, which was it? For, despite being blessed with an unassailable confidence, the self-doubt born of years of attempting to persuade the unpersuadable of his worth was swelling with every step.

He arrived at the landing just outside the flat which was literally in the rafters of number 10. He knew his wife would be inside waiting for news, but instead of walking straight in he slumped into an armchair and held his head in his hands. It couldn't have been more than a couple of minutes before he heard the door behind him swing open with a gentle groan. There was no need to look up. He felt her familiar hands running through his hair, then softly caressing his face down to his tight shoulders. He pushed hard against them, stretching the muscles in his neck like a lonely tomcat in dire need of a human hand.

Emma stepped round the chair and knelt down in front of him, her exquisite blue eyes searching his own, frantically yearning to share the burden just as she'd always done.

'Whatever it takes, Edward, do you hear me?' She pinched the flesh on his cheeks between her fingers, forcing him to look at her as his gaze wandered away. 'We will get him back, do you know why? Because we have to.' He felt his lips break into a smile for the first time in what seemed like years. He immediately recognised his own words, the ones he'd used on her so many times in the past. She'd always been the one who had selflessly urged him forward, forever questioning but never complaining even when it seemed that he would never crystallise his ambition.

He slipped her hands into his and opened his mouth to speak but the words wouldn't come.

'I know, I know,' she said for him. 'Don't talk now. Come on, let's go inside, take five. Everyone's doing everything that can possibly be done. They won't get away with it.' But he couldn't move. Was it the will or the way he was lacking? Or maybe both? He couldn't be sure – those damn wordplays again.

'They've got him trussed up, Emma, trussed up like some sort of

51

bloody freak,' he croaked, 'and we don't even know what they want. The truth! What truth, for Christ's sake? What do they mean?'

'We'll find him, wherever he is.'

'In a million pieces, maybe.'

'Don't talk like that, Edward.'

'I should have listened to you, I should never have sanctioned his appointment. It's all my fault.'

'For God's sake, your arrogance is sometimes staggering. This has nothing to do with you or me or the choices we've made, this has to do with some sick individual who thinks he can change the world with violence. If it hadn't been Geoffrey it would have been someone else; it could have been one of the children. Now come on, Edward, get a grip of this situation.'

'I know, it's just I can't help but think that way. He was always going to be easy prey: he wouldn't entertain protection, so bloody stubborn, and so he's a target which was just too attractive to pass over. You said it, most of the Cabinet said it, even that woman Arlington predicted it and I could have stopped it.'

'What, and ended up with a brother who hated you for the rest of his life? Look, you made the right decision; the rest of us were wrong. Remember the night you told him how happy he was? You both were: remember the toast to the Kennedy brothers and the Haversham brothers?'

'Let's just hope it wasn't too prophetic,' he said clearly but heard the words' pathetic ring in his ears in time with the half-hour chime of Big Ben.

As the last chime was fading into the Westminster sky Haversham heard footsteps clambering frantically up the staircase behind them. Emma quickly stood up just as a breathless permanent secretary emerged on to the landing area.

'What is it, Donald, what's happened?' Haversham asked warily.

'The police, sir, they have a contact on a location: you must come at once.'

2.34 p.m., The Jury Room, The Old Bailey

Almost three hours in and it felt like three days. Alex Parrish laced his long fingers together in front of his flat stomach, leaned back and crossed his black-jeaned legs at the ankles. Next to him, Uncle Bob had slackened off his primly knotted tie, unbuttoned his frayed cuffs and rolled them back, exposing surprisingly muscular forearms. Alex watched as Bob produced a small bottle of tablets and swallowed two of them.

'You OK?' Alex asked.

'Heartburn,' he explained, though as Alex was well aware, antacid capsules normally came in a packet.

At five and six, Pitbull and Danno nudged each other and whispered a joke, but stifled their shared amusement as their foreman did no more than flick one eyebrow in that general direction.

The Prof, at four, scribbled some notes on a pad, then underlined a particularly pertinent point with a pen with a red cap; one to watch for later, Alex mused.

Stalin leaned forward, thick arms folded defensively across a barrel chest, staring intently at Princess Grace who only had eyes for handsome number nine, Denzel. Perhaps that was the problem, Alex thought; the reason for Stalin's hostility.

Pearl continued to click away, unperturbed and unshakeable in her task. Alex turned his attention to Kaftan: it was her strike of the clock, her place on the dial of jurisprudence, yet she too seemed focused on a private horizon. Alex coughed, breaking the fragile peace of the jury room. From the corner of his eye he could discern Uncle Bob turn slightly towards him.

'Just coughing,' he explained unnecessarily, in a whisper. The hum of the air-conditioning droned monotonously: a steady, dull accompaniment to their deliberations. In front of him, Alex had his own pad, now rich with architectural doodles, but the flip-side revealed his real interest – how he believed the jury would vote in the end – and thus far it didn't look too promising for the lovely eco-warrior. At number eleven, where his own vote would be counted in the general election of her life, he had merely placed a cowardly question mark and he felt uneasily guilty about his life-long inability to commit. By the grimly barred window Kalsi stood gazing idly at the teeming life of London in the street below.

'Kalsi,' Uncle Bob murmured kindly, 'I think breaktime's over. Let's get on with it, shall we?'

'About time,' Stalin muttered, but his recent shaming by their jury foreman had stolen the swaggering volume from his thick-set voice. Kalsi shrugged her shoulders and returned to her seat next to Alex. He turned to risk a light smile, but the set of her features wiped it quickly away. He waited instead for Uncle Bob to begin.

'Now then, we're ticking around our little timepiece nicely, but I must say at this rate we'll have to come back in the morning.'

A low collective groan found its voice, wobbled then died away. The same problem had occurred to Alex. This case had robbed each of them of a month of their normal lives. He had believed that today would be the last day of their onerous public duty but felt uncomfortable at his own selfishness in wishing it so; it could also be the last day of Jenny Fox's hope of freedom.

'Just means we have a lot to talk about, Robert,' Pearl said chirpily to Uncle Bob. 'If people are talking it means there's something worth talking about, stands to reason. We wouldn't bother otherwise.'

Not in my line of work, Alex thought. He could remember a thousand deep, meaningful discussions with clients at tender, each of whom had appeared sincere during technical debate, each of whom had plumped for cheaper, shoddier specifications.

'I mean,' Pearl continued, as she finished a dangling sleeve in baby pink and held it up for general inspection, 'when we adopted your clock, a fine idea I might add, it was always going to take a wee time, wasn't it?'

It was the first time she had looked up from her handiwork during the digression but her peachy smile was clouded by fierce eyes. What is this, Alex wondered, pensioner power? Uncle Bob nodded reasonably.

'I wasn't suggesting for a moment that we cut anything short, just that we keep an eye on what's important. Do we all agree on that?'

He turned from head to head as each nodded their agreement until he came to Alex who hesitated before speaking.

'With one proviso,' he began.

'Thought that was part of the IRA,' whispered Pitbull to his friend Danno, who snorted appreciatively. Alex ignored them.

'Everyone has the right to ask their question whatever its content: however long it takes to talk through is another matter.'

'Seems fair enough to me,' Bob responded quietly, too quietly for Alex's liking. 'But let's move on.' He raised his eyes to number three, Kaftan, and nodded for her to begin. Alex watched as she swept her hand, bangles jingling gaily, into her environmentally friendly rattan handbag and produced a thin black waxed rectangular box. Alex exhaled more noisily than he had meant but his dismay was masked by the Prof who tutted loudly.

'Tarot cards will not help to determine the facts,' the Prof continued.

'Perhaps not for you,' Kaftan replied calmly, removing the pack of cards and beginning a spread, 'but we all have our own ways of divining the truth. This is mine.' That and a couple of joints, she thought.

'Mystic Meg's off again,' Pitbull whispered, shaking his head. Alex shared their frustration, but the lady was not for turning, only the cards. Stalin stared imploringly at their chosen foreman who raised one hand, inviting patience.

'I know the question I want to ask: this will tell me if it is the

55

correct one,' Kaftan muttered, concentrating hard as the spread grew and finally became complete. She screwed up her eyes, as if seeing beyond the waxed cards with their arcane and colourful characters. Stalin's hands had moved away from his chest and now fingered a wry drum-roll on the table-top.

'For God's sake,' the Prof said, exasperated.

'Yes, exactly,' Kaftan answered. 'It is correct,' she continued, scooping the cards up methodically and replacing them carefully in their container, like tucking a duvet around a sleeping child. 'It's a lot to do with karma. What we do now, we will live with, not only now but for ever, eternity, like that circle of poison we've heard about: sow and reap, cause and effect.'

'Simon and Garfunkel,' Pitbull shouted.

'Abbot and Costello.'

'Or you two,' Alex said, glaring at Pitbull and the sniggering Danno. Pitbull measured him up and down, all amusement lost in the confrontation. Alex held his bully-boy stare. Funny boys never liked to be laughed at, hard funny boys especially. But Uncle Bob let it ride, as if he found some justice in Kaftan's humiliation, though she just smiled, raised both of her palms flat and said, 'Lilas.'

Alex had no idea what she meant, but her demeanour suggested strongly that she was unmoved by the occurrence.

'As I was saying, if she did do all that wicked stuff on the video, then some very heavy karma is coming her way. But she said it wasn't her on the video, that it was someone else with the same build and shape. The judge told us that it's up to the prosecution to prove the case, not Jenny.'

'The defendant,' the Prof reminded her. 'This is not a personal matter.'

'She's a sentient human being; of course it's personal,' Kaftan replied sweetly. 'Anyway, you call her that and I'll call her Jenny.'

'I'd prefer to call her guilty,' Pitbull chipped in, still bullish after the previous stand-off with Alex, who put a mental tick against his jury form guide on the back of his doodle pad.

'Could you put your question a little more simply for those of us who don't understand the laws of karmic causality?' Uncle Bob asked, then appeared to hear his own words as if for the first time and added, 'If that's what it's called.'

Bloody good guess, Alex thought: not bad for a retired watch-maker from the Smoke.

Kaftan nodded two or three times before speaking again.

'Everything we've heard about her proves she's done nothing but good in her life, then wow, like a mega explosion of evil, it's there: Kali, the devil.'

'Everyone has their breaking point,' the Prof answered dreamily, then pulled himself together with a mental snap. 'We saw what she and her two dead friends did with the others in the research centre that night on the security video.'

Alex remembered the video the Prof was referring to.

Court Two, The Old Bailey, Day Four

The large-screen monitor was dragged across the wooden court floor, its rubber castors squeaking in annoyed protest, and placed once more before them. The Attorney General thanked the ushers then turned his attention towards the judge.

'My lord, may I?'

The judge nodded gravely, a button was depressed and the visions from the VCR transferred on to the screen. At first, the whitewashed corridor was silent and eerily abandoned, then off-camera the in-built microphone began to pick up sounds.

'Get the fuck along there.' It was a man's voice, a harsh rasping voice that invited no debate. Several whimpers could be heard as four people, two women and two men, in lab technicians' coats were herded into focus by the two male accomplices. Behind strode the woman, again utterly in command, as her lieutenants flanked the captives, ushering them towards the camera and jabbing with their assault rifles at the stooping shoulders of the terrified four.

One of the women fell to the floor and began to crawl, snuffling and crying. Alex watched in horrified fascination as the female terrorist began to kick her from behind, right in front of the video camera: then she looked up into it and smiled. Heat sensitive, it panned to follow their violent progress to the end of the corridor where the sprawling, now screaming woman was dragged around the corner by her hair. The prosecution alleged it was Jenny Fox who manhandled her so viciously. Whoever it was was not afraid of the camera; indeed, appeared to relish the recording of her every crime. Another camera then took up the sickening progress of the group.

According to the prosecution this was a refrigerated holding area on the second floor. Alex had checked this against the floor plans of the research centre provided in the jury's bundle of documents; it corresponded. One of the captives had struck out as he was clubbed along and was rifle-butted in the teeth before being helped along by the other three prisoners: more blood. He was lucky to get away with a broken jaw. They were then sealed in. This was five minutes before the execution of Easterman.

'Vicious that was,' Pitbull said, eyeing Alex in the jury room. 'Turned my stomach that did, hitting women; well, a woman. Deserves a good slap. If they weren't dead, and she wasn't in the dock, I'd do it myself.'

His eyes stayed firmly with Alex. All forehead, shaved hair and flat nose he should have been subject to the regulations of the Dangerous Dogs Act, hence Alex's nickname for him, but the jokes had disappeared and the real nature of the beast was now on show to them all, particularly to the bestower of his secret tag.

'She was building herself up to the killing,' the Prof pronounced.

'Didn't seem as though she needed to,' Denzel at number nine added. All the other members turned towards him in slight surprise. He had been the most reticent of the jury throughout the last month, and, when he did speak, he was concise, quiet and methodical in delivery. 'We saw what she did when she popped Easterman: it was quick, not a moment's hesitation,' he continued now, finding his verbal stride.

'Popped!' Pitbull snorted. 'Popped! Who are you, then, Quentin Patel-Tino?'

Alex watched Denzel's muscular frame swell as he turned to Pitbull: just a couple of hours on the jury clock and already they were at loggerheads. Only an alarmed Princess Grace and a calmly knitting Pearl separated them. It was Pearl who spoke.

'Hold this for me, will you?' she said to a confused Pitbull, as she handed him her knitting, needles and ball of pink wool. He took them, but continued to glare at Denzel, who pushed back his chair noisily. Pearl glanced towards him and smiled sympathetically, but shook her head, then turned quickly and delivered a stinging slap to the stunned Pitbull's face. His mouth dropped open like a surprised cod.

'I don't know who this Quentin man is,' she said in a low voice, 'but I know racism when I hear it. My Kevin ran with those National Front people for a while and I gave him the same treatment as you. Hatred: it eats you up whole in the end, young man; learn to live *with* people, not against them.'

She looked into his face, where a single tear of humiliated impotence had pooled in one eye, nodded, then reclaimed her knitting and began again. Pitbull shook his head in disbelief, looking to Danno, whose own eyes were averted from his friend's shame. Denzel, satisfied that honour had been restored, shrugged and pulled his chair back into line. Alex had never before seen such a display of foolhardy heroics. It was as if a street thug had been mugged by his intended victim, but all she had stolen was his pride. All! He reminded himself that it was probably all Pitbull had.

Uncle Bob coughed loudly, as if bringing a union branch meeting to order.

'We are all under a tremendous amount of pressure in this room, but an unhappy workshop never gets the work done. We were told by the judge to try the case on the evidence and by God that is what we will do, or you will find yourselves another foreman.'

The command and determination in Bob's voice impressed Alex hugely: that and his threat to resign could have graced many a boardroom coup and consigned its plotters to the dole queue. Bob's lined face appeared wreathed in dignity but also stung by his comrades' disloyalty and, though he had played no part in the recent confrontation, Alex was forced into a reluctant communal shame.

'I'm sorry, Robert,' Pearl announced quietly. 'Don't know what came over me.'

Bob nodded, still smarting, then all faces turned to the disgraced Pitbull who still hadn't moved. Eventually their stares seemed to pull him out of his state of shock.

'Yeah, out of order here too. Er, sorry like, Uncle Bob.'

The apology's recipient appeared satisfied that the verbal affray was over, and turned once more to Denzel.

'You were saying.'

'Yes,' he replied. 'The murderer never hesitated: it was like a mission or something; had to be done. Or she hated this man so much that any thought of mercy never once entered her head.'

His words stuttered to an embarrassed halt, then Princess Grace's brittle vowels came to his rescue.

'She said that if it wasn't for Easterman then hundreds, perhaps thousands, of people, particularly children, would still be alive, not dying in agony. Fox clearly holds him responsible for their deaths; why would she show him any mercy?'

'Because she's a doctor,' Alex said wearily.

Princess Grace fixed him with her glacial eyes. 'Have you ever heard of a mercy killing?'

2.41 p.m., Cabinet Room, 10 Downing Street

Edward Haversham rushed into the room through the double doors, barely managing to stay upright as the highly polished parquet floor nearly took his balance away. In the short time he'd been upstairs with Emma the amount of computer equipment and telephones had clearly multiplied. There was barely any space on the floor behind the conference table as wiring, extension sockets and grey boxes had colonised the area. Everything now was linked in to the mobile incident van ready to respond to any location and a closed network had been established with Scotland Yard central communications complex. Haversham recovered just in time to hear the telephone's sharp insistent beat. Once, twice, three times it rang. What were they doing? Answer the damn thing, he wanted to shout, to scream, but he didn't. No one, it seemed, wanted to acknowledge his presence apart from Elizabeth Arlington who cast a quick but solemn glance in his direction. He watched as Brian Chance calmly put the headphones on and began counting down, his fingers aloft, curling them in descending order from the thumb inwards. Five, four, three, two, one they went down in perfect synchronisation with a young technician at the far end of the room who was about to start the trace. Chance lifted the receiver as the rest of the room went still. Haversham felt utterly inadequate as the hiss of the loud-speaker reverberated around the room . . .

'Hello, this is Chief . . .' Chance started.

'I don't particularly care who you are,' the voice interrupted sharply. 'So long as you and your colleagues appreciate who is in control of this situation. You see, it may not seem it at present given the circumstances but I am a fair man. A very fair man indeed; it is however vital to our relationship that you acknowledge the balance of power here is not in your favour. Regrettably I have learnt over the years there is no other method of gaining people's full attention. Do you understand me?'

'I understand you perfectly.'

'You tell me then, Mr Policeman. Say it to me. Who is in control?' The accent was foreign, an intonation that Chance couldn't accurately identify but certainly not Middle Eastern or Irish.

'From where I'm sitting that sounds very much like a rhetorical question.'

'Say it,' the voice demanded.

'You are in control,' Chance parried quickly.

'You guess correctly, Mr Policeman. If you continue in this manner I see no reason why our relationship should deteriorate. On the contrary I expect that we can both achieve our objectives.'

'I'm pleased to hear that, but you must understand that I am here purely to ensure that you have the opportunity to communicate with those who can make the decisions. I personally have no authority to make deals.'

'And you on the other hand must understand that I am not interested in deals nor am I the slightest bit concerned as to how you go about your business. I seek only the truth.'

'You say you seek the truth about Dr Jennifer Fox but we have no way of knowing how to help. What information do you want?'

'The information that the jury and the public ought to have had in the first place. The information, Mr Policeman, that your so-called fair system has deliberately withheld.'

'It has been a long trial, with a great many issues ventilated before an experienced judge and, as far as we are concerned, it has been a fair one. If your complaint has some genuine foundation then surely your demand will be better addressed to the Appeal Courts with the assistance of Dr Fox's lawyers, should she be convicted. I am not a lawyer, therefore I am not in a position to comment on the evidence or proper procedures but I doubt whether violence is the answer or whether, ultimately, it will help Dr Fox.'

'Violence, lawyers, Appeal Courts, hah. What is this doubletalk? Your first mistake is to patronise me. For a moment you had me believing that we had established the parameters of our relationship but no, it seems you lie. How short-sighted. Have you forgotten so soon? You acknowledge that I am in control, yet your words suggest otherwise. What is it with you? Do you not respect me?'

'I have to respect you, it's my job to respect you, but it appears that you're fighting a system not me. I have no control over the system.' Chance dropped his own voice trying to mimic the tone of his adversary. He glanced over at the technicians at the far end of the room. One rolled his hands over indicating the trace hadn't found its source yet.

'Do you seriously believe that I would have wasted my time, your time even, had I one iota of confidence in the integrity of your establishment? You must have confused me with someone who cares for your precious system of justice. Be under no illusion, it means nothing to me. I said I was a fair man, further than that I am a man who embraces the concept of compromise, but now you are beginning to stretch my patience, not to say insulting my intelligence.'

'Now it is you whose words betray your actions. How can you believe in compromise yet spread terror and violence?'

'These are desperate times dictating desperate measures. Your refusal to listen to my cause forces the extreme gesture. Those who govern will not hear me at their table so they must witness the effects of their own belligerence. I need no justification for my actions for they are simply the results of cause and effect.'

'It is difficult to gain the confidence and trust of orderly society when the safety of her inhabitants is at risk from those actions. You must agree?' Chance pushed, conciliatory but firm, while frantically waving for an update on the trace. A scribbled note telling him the terrorist was using a different mobile phone to the one used for the weblink earlier meant he had to keep going.

'Trust and confidence!' the voice snapped. 'Your hypocrisy is astonishing. For the sake of clarity allow me please to enlighten you in the spirit of understanding, hopefully then your ignorance may be liberated. Hear me well, Mr Policeman, for I will not repeat myself. I do not adhere to the collective intellectual dishonesty displayed by your governments nor do I respect your fragile democracies. My world has no borders, no boundaries and no rulers, only the natural common denominator of the planet which supports us. You speak of my fight! Dismissing it as some petulant squabble with authority. I implore you to re-evaluate that assessment. What do you know of my war? What can you ever know of my war? Your governments in the brutally overrated and so-called civilised Western world consistently lie to and mislead the people they should protect. Their fingers are stained with the blood of Mother Earth and their pockets lined with the proceeds of her rape. My war is my reality, Mr Policeman, and that is far greater than the limits of your imagination.'

'I do not doubt your conviction, only your methods. There can be no compromise while the Attorney General's wellbeing is in jeopardy. You must be aware that it is an inalienable policy. No co-operation. No horse-trading. No deals. If you release him the dialogue could continue.' Chance offered just a touch of authority resonating in his tone. Hard and soft. Twisting and turning. Where's that damn trace, he thought, realising that they could be close. He didn't want to lose the moment and was about to push further in the brief pause as his opponent considered a response. But the terrorist spoke first.

'So be it. It appears that we have very quickly reached the unenviable position where an irresistible force meets an immovable object. In those circumstances you will appreciate there can only be resultant chaos according to the laws of nature. I can only hope that your conscience is as repairable . . .'

'No, stop it. Hold it right there. I've heard enough, you sick bastard. It's my brother we're talking about here. You will never escape.' Edward Haversham suddenly jumped to his feet and shouted across the room into the empty airspace. His face was a contorted mask of confusion and anger. 'If you harm him I will not rest until . . .' He realised that he had crossed the line but he could stand the sheer impotence no longer. He stood alone, his words echoing somewhere down the phone line, threatening a voice with no face. He felt pathetic and he knew it would do no good but he had to do something.

Elizabeth Arlington glared at him, fury burning in her eyes, which sought out and locked in on Haversham's pupils like a pair of heat-seeking missiles. All her earlier reservations concerning his reliability slithered across the void between them and hung tightly around his shoulders like a dense black shawl. He managed to break the spell and almost like a helpless child searched the surrounding faces for the slightest sign of support. He found no joy from the professionals, the entire room looked shell-shocked at his untimely and indelicate interruption. The line was silent. Perhaps a momentary signal failure, more likely gone for good. The tracer was down to a one-mile radius; just a moment longer and they would have had him. But that was the secondary concern now. They'd all listened to a hundred finely balanced hostage negotiations before, but never one like this. For, despite the threat of chaos and certain loss of life, most of them knew by experience a standoff had been achieved before Haversham's outburst. The end of round one only. Chance had done well during the exchange, parrying and cajoling his foe, inviting debate, building that bridge but never relinquishing the party line. Unlike Haversham they knew that Chance had bought them time. They hadn't given in and the hostage-taker hadn't got what he wanted. Round two was still to come in this perilous game of psychological snakes and ladders. But what now? How many lives would be lost if the dice that Haversham had just thrown upset the playing board for good? There was no way of predicting the response of a control freak with his finger on the pulse of a detonator. Affronted and insulted, the thin veneer of respect so essential to him being stripped away, the unknown kidnapper might do anything. New territory, dangerous territory. Could it be that somewhere their own loved ones – children, wives or parents – innocently walking the streets of London would be suddenly blown apart?

The line hissed ominously in the background as they all waited for a reaction. Surprisingly it was only Brian Chance who truly understood Haversham's anxiety. He responded to the bristly nervousness vacillating through the room by waving a calming gesture: both palms raised he circled around, urging the rest of the team to relax. But as the line was still dead, that nervousness was replaced by an uneasy heaviness which crept stealthily into the atmosphere like an early-morning sea fret.

Then suddenly the loudspeaker crackled into life once more. Chance snapped his fingers furiously at the technicians to continue the trace.

'I must say a degree of control over your own personnel would be helpful, Mr Policeman. I do like order but I anticipate you have a difficult task with Mr Haversham. Am I correct?' the voice mused. 'Perhaps I can assist. Listen carefully, Prime Minister.' A slight pause, and a muffled shuffling followed before the voice returned. 'Alas your brother is still asleep but when he wakes I'll be sure to tell him this was all down to you. This little piggy is for your insolence' – a loud crack rang out over the speaker, a sick, dull sort of crack, the sort of crack that you heard when someone was having their fingers broken. The scream that followed caused several people to thrust off their headphones: it was pitched like the squeal of rubber tyres screeching across hot concrete roads. To hear it once was bad enough, to hear it five times was more than some could bear.

Haversham held his hands over his ears but couldn't stifle the rhyme: 'This little piggy for your arrogance' – crack . . . screech – 'This little piggy for your ignorance' – crack . . . screech – 'This little piggy for your stupidity' – crack . . . screech – 'And this little piggy for your . . . your . . . Oh, what a dreadful shame, he's passed out again . . . I'll talk to you soon, think about things why don't you?' CRACK . . . silence . . . click.

The connection was severed just as the tracer program blurted its message across the screen.

'Got the bastard, North-West One, New Synagogue, Woodbridge Road, repeat New Synagogue Woodbridge Road. Go, go, go!' the young technician shouted euphorically down the line to the incident van whose occupants responded with a cheer.

In the Cabinet Room Brian Chance was slightly less optimistic. Why, he asked himself, had the kidnappers moved their communication link from a seemingly impenetrable and basically untraceable internet address to an insecure and easily locatable mobile telephone?

3.03 p.m., The Jury Room, The Old Bailey

The Prof gazed down lovingly on his notes. Alex craned his neck to the right-hand side in an effort to read them across the table-top, but could only see that his jottings were colour coded. Alex had an irrational fear of people who were multi-hued with their scribblings. It was evidence of a highly organised mind, and often indicated a reluctance to see any other person's point of view, as if the argument was there, on the paper, in black and white, purple, green and red. The Prof picked up the sheaf of paper, tapped and squared it on the table-top, then laid it flat. Christ, he's going to give us a seminar, Alex thought, then chided himself for his lack of charity. He was, however, accurate.

'How do we know that something exists?' He scanned their faces as if transported to an invented past, where the pupils cared and hung on his every equation. Several, including Alex, shrugged. The Prof was obviously encouraged by their show of ignorance and smiled with what he believed to be engimatic charm. He continued.

'Because we have the proof. Every scientist needs proof in order to come to a clinical conclusion; without it, any finding is no more than idle conjecture.'

Alex quickly glanced around the other ten, but their mutual embarrassment forced eighteen eyes to the table-top. Only Uncle

Bob listened intently, his glistening brown orbs riveted to the speaker's face.

'We as the jury in this case must act as scientists act, with no reference to our hearts but solely to our minds in order to scrutinise not what we feel but what we know.'

This would have been impressive stuff had he been collecting the Nobel Prize for Physics or joining the Royal Society. Alex thought that patience might well be at drought point.

'You mean look at the evidence?' Alex asked, raising his voice an octave, as if it were a revelation. The Prof looked ecstatic.

'Exactly, young Alex, we must look at what, scientifically, the prosecution can prove, so that we are sure about it. Remember, that is the test, the only test.'

'What part of the scientific evidence do you mean in particular?' Uncle Bob asked quietly, in a gambit to pin their lecturer down to a specific topic. The Prof, to Alex's dismay, spread his large sheaf of notes over the table-top.

'Why, all of it, of course.' He looked quizzically at Bob as if it were the foreman's lack of insight that was causing the problem. Bob smiled broadly.

'But that wouldn't leave anything for the rest of us to talk about now, would it, Eric?'

Alex had forgotten that Eric was the Prof's Christian name.

'We'll be here for days,' Stalin groaned, and for once Alex had to agree with him.

'But I'm a scientist, the right man for the job. I can explain what all that jargon means.'

But Bob forged on.

'What particular piece of the forensic really grabbed you? I mean, when we went for a pint a couple of weeks ago, you were fascinated with the DNA stuff.'

'You mean the hair samples?'

Bob nodded encouragingly. 'Yes, I got a little bit lost with that,' he replied cheerfully.

'Amazing stuff,' the Prof answered brightly, then shuffled through his notes until the appropriate page was recovered. Alex could almost discern a collective sigh of relief from the round table:

somehow Bob had averted a minor crisis whilst still allowing the Prof to retain his dignity.

'Deoxyribonucleic acid,' the Prof began, 'or DNA to the rest of us, otherwise known as the "blueprint for life". Every human cell contains all the information required to create a whole human body, but samples of any tissue – be it semen, blood, skin or, in this particular case, hair – can be used to identify whether the sample came from a particular person.'

He was warming to his topic and, Alex could see, enjoying his place in the sun.

'That is why it is also known as DNA fingerprinting. As we know, when the ski mask worn by the woman killer was taken away for analysis several strands of hair were found. These were matched against a control sample from the defendant's own hair and found to be identical, not only in root growth and colour but also in its DNA.'

'Settles it for me,' Stalin added.

'Don't we have to look at the circumstances and what Jenny Fox had to say?' Alex asked, but the Prof continued.

'The odds against it being anyone else's hair are over three million to one.'

'Alex,' Princess Grace interrupted. 'The ski mask was removed from Dr Fox's head at the scene. How on earth do you explain that?'

Alex shrugged. It was insufficient, he knew that, but all he could do: the facts in this case bore down like a thousand tons of sea water on a scuba diver beyond his depth.

Court Two, The Old Bailey, Day One

'And you were the first police officer on the scene, Inspector?' the Attorney General asked.

'I was, sir. An alarm had been sounded at the research centre and we responded to it.'

'Your response time?'

'Five minutes,' the witness replied proudly, highly polished silver buttons dimly reflecting the hazy overhead lighting.

'So this alarm could not have been triggered by the initial break-in?'

'Correct. The external alarms had all been foamed on arrival: this alarm was an internal, manual one.'

The prosecutor waved his wrist limply in circles.

'We have seen some plans of the installation, also photographs of the site and the deceased. Could you supply us with a more general description of the place?'

'A bleak place, sir, five miles from the nearest town, set in a small valley which cuts out most of the sun. Access is by one road, a B road, that leads on to a clearly marked private road then to the compound itself.'

A bad place to die, Alex thought, but then again there was no such thing as a good one.

'The compound,' the witness continued, voice flat, unemotional, as per police training technique, 'is one mile square, surrounded by razor wire and clearly marked as government property. We later found that the wire had been cut on the western perimeter.'

'Very good. Now tell us what you saw on arrival.'

'I was in the lead car of three, all marked with police signs and sirens operational. The stop barrier was in the upright position allowing us immediate entry. The main compound, where we later found Mr Easterman, was straight ahead, the front door of the building wide open.'

'Did you enter the building then or did something attract your attention?'

He cleared his throat.

'I could see them lying on the grass, about twenty yards from the door.'

The prosecutor turned his head to watch the jury and, though in his opening address he had outlined the facts of the case to them, he now emphasised that this was the first live evidence of the grisly discovery.

'Them?'

'Yes. Four people, three men, dead, and,' he swept his eyes to the defendant, 'Dr Fox, who was unconscious.'

'Did you learn the identities of the deceased?'

'Deceased one and two were Peter and Piers Cresta, friends of the accused, the third was a security guard employed at the installation: Derek Philips, a very brave man, sir.'

70

Alex heard the low grumble of objection from the defence ranks until the judge intervened.

'The officer will restrict his evidence to what he saw, no matter how understandable the temptation.'

Both witness and prosecutor nodded their acknowledgement.

'How had they died, officer?'

'Gunshot wounds.'

The Defence QC rose to his feet.

'My Lord, there is no dispute as to how they died. My learned friend may lead the witness on his observations. But let me be plain, the defence case is that whilst the bullets came from the various firearms found at the scene, who was pulling the trigger is another matter.'

At that stage, Alex and the other jury members had no idea what the oblique speech meant, but the prosecutor smiled grimly, before asking his next question.

'Who had shot whom? No, do not answer that, let us keep my learned friend for the defence happy: which weapon was used to kill which person?' He grinned like a great white shark about to strike.

'Mr Philips' automatic weapon was used to kill the raiders, a semi-automatic machine-gun, found next to the deceased Piers Cresta, killed Mr Philips.'

Alex turned to the back of the court where Jenny Fox shook her head from side to side slowly and certainly.

'It's all in the ballistics report from the Home Office, sir.'

'And what was Dr Fox wearing when you discovered her, officer?'

'A black combat suit and ski mask.'

The prosecutor raised one finger and instantaneously a plastic exhibit-bag was produced by one of his junior barristers. It was transported by the usher to the witness who read the yellow exhibit label carefully before speaking.

'That's the one, no doubt about it. That is my handwriting.'

'And was this item forwarded to the Home Office laboratory?'

'Admitted, my lord,' the Defence QC interjected in order to speed the trial along.

71

'Why did you send it there? After all, it was recovered from the defendant's person,' he asked the witness.

'When we spoke to the accused, she claimed that the first time she had ever seen the mask and clothing was when she regained consciousness outside the institution.'

The prosecutor snorted, 'Yes, of course she did.' Then added quietly, 'Had to say something, I suppose.'

'Of course she had to say something,' Stalin argued. 'Her terrorist mates were dead, so was the poor bloody security bloke and Easterman was spread down the corridor.'

'Please,' Mouse next to him implored, her hand going to her mouth. Stalin tutted.

'OK, sorry,' his tone flat with insincerity. 'But even the world's best thieves get caught with the hooky gear sometimes, and they always have a back-up story.'

Expert evidence or opinion, Stalin? Alex wondered.

'And her story stinks. I mean, for God's sake, is that really the best she could come up with?' Stalin raised the pitch of his voice and successfully imitated an upper-middle-class accent, staring at Princess Grace as he did so. '"He was dead when I arrived, we panicked, ran outside, then I was hit with something. When I woke up,"' he began to sniffle theatrically, '"Piers and Peter had been executed, the other man was dead, I . . ."'

'She never cried,' Alex said, more angrily than he had any right to be. Stalin smirked.

'No compassion, your middle class, just greed and arrogance and also no imagination. Her story is cobblers and we all know it.'

'The world is a strange place,' Kaftan said dreamily.

'Yours more than anyone else's,' Stalin replied.

'Can we decide what we make of the DNA?' the Prof asked.

'Of course it's her hair,' Alex responded, 'that's not the issue.'

'Isn't it?' Uncle Bob asked reasonably. 'Forgive the wanderings of an old man's mind, but I thought it was. I mean the samples were found inside the ski mask, that came from her head, twenty yards away from a murder, recorded on video.'

'He has a point, dear,' Pearl chipped in.

'Top point,' Pitbull added, with Danno's nodding agreement.

72

'He's right, man,' Denzel remarked kindly.

'Her story's too weird.' Princess Grace smiled indulgently at him.

'Lots of weird stories are true,' Kaftan said.

'Not this one,' Stalin concluded.

Alex glanced to Mouse, who shrugged, and Kalsi, whose face remained unchanged, then to Uncle Bob, who nodded gravely.

'Well let's move on, shall we, Alex? Let's see if we can't get this thing sorted out and get you back to your architect's office.'

It sounded reasonable enough, but Alex, try though he might, could not remember ever telling their remarkable foreman what he did for a living.

3.24 p.m., Incident Command Vehicle, Travelling North-West on Farringdon Street, London Short-wave Radio Transmission, Secure Frequency

'Gold to Central Traffic. Gold to Central Traffic.'

'We have you on the monitor, sir. Please confirm status.'

'Approaching junction with Stonecutter Street. What's ahead?'

'Copied, Gold. No problems for next three minutes: you're clear until Farringdon Station which is heavily congested. Alternative routes to rendezvous point suggested, sir. Traffic patrol now clearing pedestrian area at Smithfield market: you have access to Charterhouse Street through East Poultry via Smithfield Street. The lights have been disabled at the junction and the eastbound lane has been dedicated in your favour.'

'We copy, Central Traffic. Over . . . Central Casualty, come in please.'

'This is Central Casualty, Gold, we copy.'

'Hospital Status Report?'

'Barts and Moorfields both alerted and now initiating major incident procedures. Shoreditch General is bursting at the seams and moaning about a written cost indemnity from us for recalling staff on holiday but otherwise we can cope up to a level three major injuries scenario: anything after that we would have to look at bringing facilities south of the river on board. What is your current casualty estimate?'

'We do not have visual contact with potential first blast sector yet but it's a densely populated area. CTCP have identified at least seventeen hundred civilians who ought to be within range from analysis of the plans. One way or another if it goes up they're going to be right in the way. They'll be caught either by the initial explosion or secondary building damage and flying debris.'

'Jesus Christ . . . seventeen hun— Sorry, sir, but that's a level one.'

'I know what category it is, son, just keep your mind on the procedures. Breakdown is seven nought nought severe trauma or life-threatening situations and a further one thousand victims with minor injuries.'

'Yes, sir.'

'Now, best case is that we may be able to reduce those numbers considerably after a covert op to evacuate the sector but I cannot confirm until we have visual.'

'We need to be targeting at least a seventy per cent reduction in the figures to give the medics half a chance.'

'We'll do our best but I can't rule out the worst-case scenario, so get moving on overspill estimates from the closest three hospitals with A and E facilities and spare capacity totals at the others.'

'Yes, sir.'

'If our trace is correct, looking at the street plan our major problem is going to be the proximity of the schools on either side of the square. This one knows exactly what he's doing; he's picked his spot for maximum containment. We won't be able to establish whether evacuation routes for the children are out of his sight lines from the stronghold until we survey. I'll update you from scene, over . . . Silver, come in Silver at CTCP. Ray, are you there?'

'I hear you.'

'Did you get that?'

'Yeah, we reckon that he could be using the schools as some kind of early-warning system. Chances are that when you get there he'll have a way of knowing it. Risk factor has to be high either way. If you file the kids out and he sees them, then it's a clay pigeon shoot with us loading the firearm. Throwing the possibility of an automatic weapon in there would justify a decision to alert the schools but keep them *in situ* for the time being. Catch twenty-two is that leaving them in place means he gets to increase his hostage factor big time once he knows we're in position. There's no easy way to call this one,' Ray Prince concluded.

'I know, Ray. How do you see it from there?'

'OK. The major priority as we see it is buying some time. We don't think he'll pull the plug as soon as he sees a blue flashing light: no point yet as the jury hasn't come back so there is no resolution of his demands.'

'Have you listened to the dialogue from the last contact?'

'Yeah, just reported in to COBRA with our thoughts on it. We have to give him some latitude; he has his own timetable, which is by definition incapable of accurate computation. What we have to work on are ways to steal some time off him – that way we get to redistribute some of the pressure his way. Basically the way it looks from our angle now is that he feels he's in a no-lose situation and cruising to victory.'

'What do you mean?'

'That he's intelligent like most control freaks but that gives us some flexibility in predicting the moves. He has to have a plan which has to be played out at its own pace and we don't believe it's time for the endgame just yet. It's been too well executed so far. Best guess is, even if the jury does come back today and he was penned in with a guilty verdict, he'll sit it out for the publicity until he can bargain for Fox's release. In other words his two objectives are being satisfied at present: first he gets to plaster 'ecoman has arrived' posters all over the world, and second he is moving towards his real goal to get the girl. It may sound crazy but I honestly think that he doesn't want to kill people; injure them if he has to, maybe, but kill them, no. Remember, he has the overall cause to think about and when it comes down to it, you don't get much sympathy for blowing kids up even if you do want to save the planet. The longer we let him go on talking the better the opportunities become.'

'I hear what you say, Ray, but I don't agree. Look, he doesn't know we're coming yet, if we can get on his blind side and then wake him up with a call he's not expecting, he's sure to panic.

77

Never mind the cause, what you have to remember is that his best asset so far has been his invisible location: with the stronghold identified we have closed down his escape routes.'

'So he blows it where he stands, if there's no way out for him.'

'Not if he doesn't know it's coming. Strikes me that he may lose a lot of confidence when we're up close, and who knows? if we can get real close it's only a short step to take him out. Odds from the front line, I'm afraid, are stacked against a stakeout siege. I've got to get those kids out of the way without delay.'

'I hope you're right; we only get one chance.'

'Ray, this is all about damage limitation. We both know there's going to be a bill when it's all over and, call me gung-ho if you wish, but one thing's for sure: I don't want to be the one who contributes several hundred small body bags to the bottom line when there exists the slightest possibility that we could have done something to reduce the odds. I mean, how can you be so sure that if we let him, he won't just wait until every TV station in the world is watching, make his predictably right-on anarchic statement and then blow the godforsaken roof off? How about that for a finale, Ray? Look, what I'm trying to say here is I need some support on this. We have to try.'

'But what if he blows it anyway? How's that going to look on the front page? Think of the headline. "There was still time to talk and no one could be bothered": just think about that one.'

'Like you said, Ray, it's no easy call. COBRA have dispatched a separate military initiative with orders to liaise with me and, after their assessment, if it's two green lights from this end then we go in on the nod.'

3.31 p.m., Cabinet Office Briefing Room

'Statistically our best information tells us that between three-and-a-half and four hours is the optimum time for any jury to return a verdict in a case of this weight and complexity. It is no guaranteed window because the range is so diverse. In fact, the percentage of cases concluded in that time is only marginally more than the next category we analysed, but it means we're now on maximum alert. If the jury go past four p.m. the judge is sure to send them out overnight and you may as well say it's anyone's guess after that. We have to consider a military assault,' the Home Secretary summarised to the team at COBRA.

'What about the possibilities posed by Prince at contingency planning?' Edward Haversham countered quickly.

'I agree that so long as the jury is out he is unlikely to press the button, but that's as far as I would go in trusting any armchair analysis of this character's make-up. He's holding a bomb and the longer this goes on the more chance there is that anything could happen to make his fingers twitch. We have to accept that in reality we don't know when or even if he might decide to detonate it. But in all conscience how can we even begin to think about some sort of gamble with the lives of those children? We have to risk an attempt to evacuate without further reference to him and simultaneously launch an assault on the stronghold. If he kicks off whilst it's in progress then God help us but we aren't holding the country to ransom, are we?'

'No, but we are responsible for its people and that means all of them, not just one group or one gender, every one of them individually and that includes the Attorney General.'

'You're not seeing this clearly, Prime Minister. With all due respect, the Attorney General is already involved and our only true criterion now must be to eliminate the danger to others. We have to act positively; if we do, then any criticism of the decision to evacuate the schools even under threat of sniper fire would be unwarranted. This, lest we forget, is a situation created by a madman: if we don't evacuate immediately when the alternative is potentially much worse, we will be crucified at the inquiry. There can be no more effective message sent around the world, to terrorists of all persuasions, that they will not be tolerated or pampered by this government. I am deeply sorry that Geoffrey has been caught up in this and if there were an answer capable of justifying it all then, believe me, I would dearly love to give it to you. But I can't, Edward, and what's more, you know it. The strangest thing about it is that Geoffrey would understand probably better than the rest of us. It's called the greater good, remember?'

'We might as well be signing his death warrant. How can you expect me to do that, for God's sake.'

'You're forgetting that the SAS are the best in the world at this. It doesn't necessarily mean that he will lose his life.'

Before Haversham could reply, the PPS bustled into the room and walked directly up to him at the far end of the long table. 'I'm sorry to disturb you, sir, but I think you may now want to reconsider giving a statement to the press. The Director General of the BBC has called three times seeking verification and guidance. He's on to the story personally and is insistent that he'll run it in the absence of any comment.'

'How the hell has that happened?'

'The political editor received a call from a woman claiming to have kidnapped the Attorney General; at first he dismissed it as a hoax and passed it on to a junior reporter to verify with us. We, of course, denied any knowledge in line with your instructions; this was just after two o'clock. He was called again it seems prior to the last contact made here, and this time the caller was a man styling himself the Liquidator. Apparently the details given to verify his credibility have all checked out with BBC researchers.'

'That's all we need. Is it some kind of joke? The Liquidator? Who in God's name is that?'

'Yes, sir, that was the title given. But the BBC are taking him seriously. It seems he is also claiming responsibility for a number of other terrorist incidents related to ecological issues.'

'All right, first thing is to pass this information on to Ray Prince at Contingency and the collators at Central Intelligence: let's get digging and find out exactly who this is,' suggested Elizabeth Arlington. 'But what shall we tell the press?'

'Get hold of the Director General and issue a holding statement backed with a D notice. We have a situation developing and in the interests of public safety we are unable to release details at this stage without risk to the delicate operation which has been mounted. There is no connection with the trial of Dr Jenny Fox, if he happens to ask, and we are assuming control of the matter in a way which will ensure the safe return of the Attorney General. I am, of course, unavailable for comment until the situation is resolved. Tell him we guarantee the BBC first inside interview.'

3.35 p.m., Incident Command Vehicle
Mount Pleasant Post Office, Phoenix Place,
Radio Transmission

'COBRA, come in, please, this is Gold.'

'We receive you, Gold, go ahead with status report.'

'Stationary at rendezvous point. Reconnaissance is complete. Units deployed at roadblocks on Aylesbury Street, Sekforde Street, St James's Walk and Rosoman Street. He can't go anywhere without passing us. The stronghold is a Synagogue in St Anthony's Square: no signs of anyone inside the main building. We think they are holed up in the caretaker's accommodation on the first floor at the back in an annexe.'

'What about the schools?'

'If he is positioned where we think then he has a grandstand view of the entrance to Woodbridge Comprehensive but can't see the back fire escapes leading on to the playing fields. We can lead them out to Wilmington Road on the edge of the secondary damage zone. The smaller infant school in Clerkenwell Close is covered front and back from his position so no chance of a covert evacuation there. I propose therefore to proceed with clearance of Woodbridge immediately and estimate they can be out of the first blast sector within twelve minutes. Do you confirm authorisation to proceed?'

'What do the Bomb Squad say?'

'They have an idea that the explosive is some sort of Semtex derivative. They have seen it on a few occasions in the past though never in this country. Probably manufactured in the former Yugoslavia or Russia, it's a lightweight plastic type capable of rapid velocity chemical change. The whole thing is encased in nitroglycerine which acts as an accelerant. Two things have emerged from the enlargements of the internet pictures shown at the first contact: firstly it seems the timer mechanism is not set and secondly the whole set-up is the type normally associated with remote-control devices. If that's still the case then before he can blow it he would have to set the timer, otherwise he goes up with it. That certainly expands our time-slot to a lot more than we first thought. If we work on the basis of a military assault on the building taking less than sixty seconds we can take him and his sidekick out without giving them a chance to key in the sequence.

'The thermal imager is picking up three sources from the location. One is highly mobile and moving between front and back rooms as if on the lookout. We can't get close enough for the radio-mike to pick anything up on audio but it looks from the imager like we have one source prostrate possibly in a bedroom on the eastern side. The other is close by, seated and probably keeping watch from the corridor to the side entrance. It looks like a golden opportunity from here. I repeat, request for authority to clear the schools and sign over to the military.'

'Stand by for instructions, Gold.'

Arlington and Haversham locked eyes across the room once more. 'We have to send them in, Prime Minister. I'm going to give the authority and may God be with us.'

Haversham dropped his gaze to the shiny redwood of the table to see his own reflection staring back at him like a powerless mirage. The time had come to face reality: his protestations would be futile and unjustifiable in the face of the risk to the children. He could feel the entire room waiting upon his sanction but, just as he lifted his head, a voice announced, 'The judge has decided to give them the majority verdict direction at some stage between four thirty and five.'

3.36 p.m., The Jury Room

'But her fingerprints were all over the gun.' Danno's almond
Eurasian eyes flicked to Pitbull for support. Theirs was a
curious relationship, inconsistent, like many things in life,
Alex thought. There was Pitbull, no more than an hour before,
spewing racism like a mantra, almost coming to blows with Denzel,
yet his friendship with the half-Chinese seemed real enough; maybe
it was just a black thing, who knew? But he supported his friend
with a stern nod of his bullet head.

Alex had Danno down as aspiring second generation. His accent
was southern, but with none of that region's dragged vowels. Tall
for a Chinese and bulkier than was usual for a preternaturally slim
people, the Oriental in him had granted his face exquisite cheekbones that jutted either side of pleasant open features. A black polo
neck matched expensive, well-cut baggy trousers, a glint of gold
from his wrist indicated there was money in the family.

'Just all over it, like she didn't care,' Danno continued. He
wanted to make his point and make it well. His parents, and
numerous uncles and cousins, who had made their mark in this
land of opportunity, would have expected it of him.

'I don't care,' said Stalin, head in his hands, the overhead lighting
reflecting off his balding pate.

'Feels like we've been here all day, isn't anyone else fed up with

83

this charade?' He made it rhyme with parade. Bob reached inside the pocket of his waistcoat and produced a burnished, brass pocket watch, flicked its thin circular cover with a well-practised thumb, looked at the dial and pursed his lips.

'Right enough, twenty to four. I wonder how long his lordship expects us to sit here?'

Alex scanned the glum faces opposite and alongside him. Each in its own way reflected his own tiredness and frustration.

'Let's have a vote,' Stalin suggested. 'Knock this nonsense on the head once and for all. All those for guilty raise your . . .'

'Steady, Dave,' Uncle Bob warned. Stalin's hand was halfway to its full extension, where it hovered uncertainly, whilst a number of other arms had also begun their ascent to Jenny Fox's guilt. 'It was your suggestion that I be foreman; have you changed your mind?'

Stalin dropped his arm heavily on to the table-top.

'Just trying to speed things along, Bob, no offence.'

'And none taken. Finding out where *we* stand, that's all.'

The challenge to Bob's supremacy had been defeated, at least for the moment. Stalin shrugged whilst their foreman continued to stare hard, his tough little face stern and unforgiving.

'I hate to agree with him,' Princess Grace said, indicating Stalin with a nod of her fine head. Stalin smiled thinly in response, 'but isn't it about time we discovered where the land lies? At my squash club any dispute is handled quickly by means of a vote. As Ladies' Captain, I fulfil a similar role to yours, Bob, but the talk can only go on so long.'

'I agree,' the Prof chipped in. 'We need a benchmark, we need to count the numbers, identify the problems, then solve the equation; i.e. is she guilty or innocent?' It appeared as simple as an algebra test to him, but not to Alex. Bob listened patiently as the others, by nods or a simple 'yes', gave their blessing to the suggestion, until it came to Alex.

'Well, number eleven, what do you say?' Bob's voice was flat, but he was still unable to mask his irritation at the minor revolution. They all watched Alex's face which was propped sideways on the palm of his hand.

'A vote, yes, but not by a show of hands. A secret ballot.'

'What are you afraid of?' Stalin asked.

'Yeah,' Pitbull added, 'haven't you got any ba—'

A cough from Pearl terminated the last word.

'It's not that,' Alex replied, raising his head and linking his fingers together. 'It's just that some people might be intimidated by a show of hands.'

All eyes swept to Mouse, whose own were fixed across the table on Pearl's knitting. Alex could see the colour rise up her cheeks as a fluttering hand rose halfway to her reddening right ear, then moved uncertainly to her silver crucifix. But it was Pearl who broke the uncomfortable silence.

'That's what they did at my old man's Union meetings at the docks. He used to say, "A vote's a vote, however it's done. Lose too many friends and make too many enemies by a show of hands." I think he was right, don't you, Bob?'

'Perhaps,' the foreman answered unsurely. Nice move, Pearl, Alex thought, become the voice of reason then forge a power block with the head man.

'But we agree that it's time to vote?' Bob continued.

'What about the fingerprint stuff?' Danno asked. 'I was just geting into that, and you said we all could have a go.'

'We may not need to go any further, man,' Denzel responded. 'Depends on the vote.'

'The secret ballot,' Alex added, still tenaciously forcing the point to mutual agreement. Bob flicked his eyes around the other jury members. Mouse hadn't yet raised her eyes, Kaftan appeared puzzled. Stalin, Prof, Pitbull and Danno were all shaking their heads, Pearl nodded hers, whilst Denzel and Princess Grace shrugged non-committally. Kalsi's face was, as ever, unreadable.

'I suppose the vote will be the same,' Bob said eventually, though clearly unhappy that Alex's amendment had found support. 'Alex, if you will do the honours.'

From the inside page of his notebook Alex quickly removed twelve identical slips of white paper.

'One you prepared earlier?' Bob asked sardonically. Alex shrugged.

'I was a Boy Scout,' he replied, handing the papers around their human clock. When each of the twelve had a slip and a blue Biro, Bob resumed command.

'Guilty or not guilty, that's what his lordship said; no middle ground. If it was her, then it's murder.'

'And if we're not sure it was her?' Kaftan asked.

Stalin whistled loudly.

'We know what your vote's going to be, don't we, darling?' She smiled sweetly.

'Like Plato, the only thing I know is that I know nothing.'

'That's bleeding obvious,' Stalin replied smugly.

'Look,' Uncle Bob spat, 'I'm becoming more than a little tired of this bickering. None of us want to be here, but we are, so let's at least try to get along. Just write the word.'

'You mean word or words,' Alex pushed. Bob tapped his index finger angrily on the table, breathing through flared nostrils.

'Just do it.'

As each one of them applied pen to paper, Mouse cradled her slip with a defending arm; Pitbull and Stalin clearly wrote one single word with a flourish; the Prof deliberated before adding his verdict to the tiny document, folding it in two and pushing it back into the middle; Denzel and Princess Grace appeared unhurried yet deliberate in their choice of verdict. Pearl paused in her incessant knitting only long enough to scribble quickly on the slip before resuming her endless task; Kalsi stared up to the ceiling as if seeking spiritual guidance from the rough white paintwork; Danno took his time, until a sharp nod from Pitbull steeled him into action; Kaftan pushed her paper back unfolded until Pearl, impossibly aware of all her surroundings, nodded towards the offending scrap, which was hastily retrieved and doubled over. That left Alex and Bob. Each waiting for the other to complete the task first, the ten slips already completed forming an untidy gathering in the table's centre.

'Come on, Alex,' Stalin sniped. 'You got your secret ballot, now vote.' A flurry of movement next to him indicated that Bob had cast his vote. Alex wrote his own decision carefully and threw it into the jury lottery. Bob gathered the slips together slowly, then straightened each out, face down, and began to read their pronouncements.

'Guilty.' He placed it on the table face up.

'Guilty,' he read from the second and repeated the exercise.

'Guilty.' His voice was flat.

'Looking good so far,' Pitbull commented, then was hushed down by Pearl.

'Guilty,' Bob continued, and reached for the next small missive.

'Not guilty.'

'What?' Stalin whispered, then turned to Kaftan.

'Yours, I believe.'

She smiled.

'Like I said, weird things happen.'

Bob ignored the outburst.

'Guilty.' Alex could feel the atmosphere thickening. It all felt so surreal, like a strange party game, but the stakes could not be higher for Jenny Fox. That made it 5–1 for a conviction.

'Guilty,' Bob continued, the two piles side by side, one growing whilst the other stagnated.

'Guilty.' As Bob spoke, Alex noticed a small vein at the side of his right temple beating out a pulse; so, it was getting to him too.

'Not guilty.'

'That's seven to two,' Stalin said, almost to himself.

'We can count,' Princess Grace remarked acidly, 'and without moving our lips.'

'Quiet, please,' the Prof demanded, back in the classroom once more, but Bob was unmoved by the unpleasantness. He raised another slip.

'Guilty,' and placed it on the growing mound then took another. Christ, Alex thought, is it just me and Kaftan? Things were getting close now. Even Pearl had placed her knitting down on the table-top and he could hear the sound of the others' breathing through the relative quiet of the jury room. 'Guilty,' Bob said quietly.

'How many do we need for a majority verdict?' Princess Grace asked.

'Ten, I think,' Denzel whispered, and all eyes, even the Mouse's, were on the remaining slip, held tightly between Bob's fingers.

'That's nine to two guilty,' Pitbull said out of the corner of his mouth to Danno. Bob looked up from the paper and chewed momentarily on his bottom lip, his eyes eventually settling on the Mouse's with a mild glare.

'Not guilty,' he said slowly.

'You have got to be fucking joking,' Pitbull shouted.

'Recount,' Danno added.

'Bullshit,' Stalin concluded.

'The jury's votes,' Alex said.

'Hold your horses,' Bob ordered, one calming hand in the air. 'There are obviously some problems we haven't dealt with in our discussions.'

'Problems? Problems?' Stalin screamed. 'I'll give you problems: a business that won't run itself, while I'm stuck in this room with three tree-huggers, that's a problem.'

His eyes flashed from Mouse to Kaftan, then wavered around the remaining members until settling menacingly on Alex. A knock at the door caused a momentary cessation in the hostilities. An usher popped her grey head around the corner.

'Judge wants you back in court in five minutes, please,' she said pleasantly. 'He wants to give you a direction on majority verdicts.' She dipped back outside and closed the door.

'We know the votes,' Stalin said, his anger boiling low and mean. 'What's the point?'

Bob smiled grimly then stared at the Mouse for a moment too long.

'People have been known to change their minds.'

In both directions, Alex thought, reaching for his jacket and leaving the jury room with the others.

3.44 p.m., Incident Command Vehicle, Aylesbury Street Observation Point

Major Daniel Bonnington edged into the dark blue command vehicle and sat next to Superintendent Goodswen watching the four closed-circuit TV screens at the console. There was a dull but ominous buzz resonating around the metallic interior. It emanated from the computers' fans and was accompanied by the echoing hiss of the idle open radio link to the Cabinet Office.

The air was dry and hot in the vehicle and all three police officers were down to their shirtsleeves, which were by now slightly crumpled and damp. In contrast to the white Met issue shirts, Bonnington's all-black Special Air Service urban combat fatigues were perfectly pressed and bone dry despite the fact that he had just covered a swift 400-metre sprint from his own observation point at the other side of St Anthony's Square. After twenty years trekking through jungles and deserts with a 200-pound kitbag and weapons strapped to his back, the London afternoon sunshine didn't excite his sweat glands one iota. Even his felt beret with its tight leather band glued fast to his broad brow was faultlessly positioned to dress parade standard.

'What's the response from COBRA, superintendent?' he asked.

'Nothing for seven minutes. I requested authority to hand over to you but nothing as yet. The judge is going to have the jury back in for a majority verdict direction. I suppose they're waiting for the outcome on the basis that he won't do anything until the verdict so we've got some time.'

'Typical, sitting on the damn fence are they? Why don't you get on and tell them that we could have been in and out by now and put this bastard in his place. Six foot under terra firma, isn't that right, boys?' Bonnington said, whipping off his beret and winking at the other two young officers in the van.

The barrack-room humour prised a welcome but edgy chuckle from the men although their eyes never left the monitors. The four screens, which simultaneously scanned the target area outside were fed from tiny remote-controlled cameras positioned on nearby rooftops.

'We're going to get into position now, coming from the north end of Charlotte Street with vehicle one and the south end of Woodbridge Road with vehicle two.'

'Patch us in tight on four: we should be able to get a look,' Goodswen said.

'Close-up on camera four. Check,' came the response and instantaneously the main screen flicked to the bright smooth white plastered façade of the synagogue which sat incongruously on the eastern side of the old Victorian square.

The covert sweep of the area by plain-clothes officers had left the square virtually empty. They could only hope that the streets to the front of the synagogue were the blind spot they needed. The roads leading to the two schools within the first sector were blocked off with tape and policemen about three hundred metres away and no one was being allowed back in once they'd left the area. The best estimate at present was that they had cut the potential victim toll by at least thirty per cent without arousing the suspicions of the kidnappers.

'Take us in closer,' Goodswen demanded. The camera zoomed in on the activity below. A young long-haired painter and decorator, perched at the top of his aluminium ladder, still hadn't been ushered out of the area by the police and was going about his business oblivious to the drama unfolding around him. Walkman headphones clamped to his ears pumping heavy metal into his skull, he had no way of knowing that just around the corner the crowds had begun gathering in anticipation.

Several ambulances from Barts were now beginning to queue in a car park adjacent to the market and Goodswen clocked one or two mobile TV units huddling in the corner beside a community bottle bank.

'Jesus, would you look at that,' Goodswen declared in exasperation.

'I guess they don't know what's going on; just following their noses.'

'We'll have to move them: that whole area will be a wind tunnel full of glass if it blows.'

'I just hope someone at COBRA has had the sense to get a D notice – we don't want them broadcasting this live.'

The view panned back along the street for a hundred metres. 'Hold it,' said Bonnington. 'That's them.' To the left of the main door of a now-deserted butcher's shop in the corner of the square, a burgundy-coloured Ford family saloon car stood with its engine running. Inside, the shadowy figures of four people could be seen. Bonnington removed a matt black miniature radio attached with Velcro to his belt and whispered into the mouthpiece, 'Come on board, vehicle one.'

'Vehicle one receiving, sir.'

'OK, you know the drill. Move on the signal. Stand by.'

'What about the guy on the ladder?'

'Forget him, sergeant, he shouldn't notice if you're quick enough, but if he does, try and signal him to the end of the street: the police will pick him up there.'

'Roger.'

'Switch to monitor three,' Goodswen ordered. The screen flicked to a different view and another car: this time a red Vauxhall estate stationary at the junction.

'Vehicle two, come on board. Are you receiving?'

'We hear you, sir. What's occurring? The lads are a touch anxious to get moving.'

'That's what I like to hear. They'll get their chance, don't you worry, Scottie. OK, we are moving to phase one on my signal. Stand by.'

'Yes, sir. We go on your word. Roger.'

Bonnington turned to Goodswen. 'Can you patch up cameras three and four on the central screen? I'm going to move them into the synagogue main building and from there they can make their way to the annexe: we'll be ready when COBRA gives the green light.'

'Switch us to split view,' Goodswen ordered.

'OK. Let's go in. Vehicle one, move.' The Ford on the left of the screen responded like a remote-control child's toy, bowling down the street and then suddenly coming to a halt outside the synagogue's dark wood doors. The two rear and front passenger doors flew open and three black-hooded men hurled themselves against the pavement, deftly rolling and landing tight up against the doors. Within seconds they were inside the building. The radio in Bonnington's hand crackled into life once more.

'We're in, sir. All quiet.'

'Good, sergeant. I'm sending Scottie's team in. Scottie, come in. You are now free to move into target area.'

The second car suddenly screeched into view outside the doors and another three men carrying black holdalls quickly entered the synagogue.

'Patch up the rear view of the stronghold,' Bonnington demanded. 'Camera five. Full screen.' The view changed to show the courtyard behind the front walls of the synagogue.

'Everyone present and correct, sir. No problems.'

'Can you see a rear exit door?'

'Twenty metres to our right, sir.'

'OK, that should lead to the rear courtyard: the door to the caretaker's is about ten yards further down on the left-hand side. Opposite that is what looks like storage outbuildings. Move to the exit door, assemble the equipment and wait. Maintain radio silence. Do you copy?'

'We copy, sir. Over and out.'

'How do you hope to get them into the courtyard without being seen from the caretaker's apartment?' Goodswen asked.

'I don't, is the straight answer to that.'

'What do you mean?'

'Once they go through that door then that's it. There's no turning back from that point: either they go in all the way or we can all kiss goodbye to next Christmas.'

'If he has set the timer on that bomb we can kiss it goodbye anyway.'

'That's why we call it shoot-to-kill time, superintendent. From the moment they go into the yard anything that moves can consider itself dead. Once I give the order it will take less than thirty seconds to move into the stronghold and neutralise its inhabitants.'

'What about the Attorney General?'

'No guarantees in this situation, superintendent: no rules, no guarantees.'

'I guess it's all down to COBRA then.' Goodswen swallowed hard. 'God help him and those poor kids if they don't get it right. It's only six minutes to the bell.' The two men looked at each other in mutual acknowledgement that whatever they did, whichever way they looked at it, their own lives and those of their team were in someone else's hands. The moment was interrupted by one of the young officers.

'Here, take a look at this, sir.'

Goodswen and Bonnington turned their attention to the screen that had now flashed back to the street outside the synagogue. The painter and decorator was descending the ladder beating his head to the rhythm of the guitars inside, unaware that a team of trained killers only forty metres to his right were preparing for a showdown.

3.47 p.m., Cabinet Office Briefing Room

'What the hell is happening? Someone give me an estimate, please,' Haversham shouted across the room.

'The judge has taken soundings from counsel and they're ready to bring the jury back. I make it about eight minutes after that we're on borrowed time: it's anyone's guess, Prime Minister.'

'OK, that's eight minutes of time we didn't have before, so that's good, isn't it? You mean eight minutes physically to get the jury from its retiring room to the court and back again?'

'Yes, allowing a minute for the judge to give them the majority direction.'

'OK, so there's potentially more time, but at least those eight minutes allow those children to get out of the area as they normally would. Parents collecting them, school buses, that sort of thing. It wouldn't arouse suspicion with the kidnappers that way, would it? Whereas if we go in now, doesn't it mean they are going to know something is up when they start pouring out in single file?'

'The whole idea is that we hit him simultaneously with the military assault. He won't have time to react.'

'Maybe not, but why now? The situation is stable. Listen to Ray Prince, he has to be right. What the hell is this guy doing it all for if he doesn't wait for the verdict? That's the key to this entire situation, I'm sure of it.'

'We have an opportunity and we have to take it now. Every second that goes by is wasted opportunity to resolve this: the fact that the jury has come back for the majority verdict direction should not interfere with our decision. I agree it gives us more time in all probability but all the more reason to go in now – let's not wait for it to happen. We've got the area sealed off, I say go in.'

Just then an analyst crossed the room and handed a faxed sheet to Elizabeth Arlington. She scanned the document quickly. 'It's from Contingency Planning. The Liquidator is apparently the genuine article. Responsible for the bombing of the French naval frigate in dry dock last September, amongst other things. It was about to sail protecting the transporter ships laden with nuclear test missiles bound for the South Pacific. No known identity but he's either a suspected deserter from the Russian Army or someone with very close contacts because the weaponry used is all ex-Soviet issue. Looks like we'll be paying back a lot of favours if we put this one to rest satisfactorily.'

'Let me look at that?' Haversham ordered and was passed the sheet. 'This is the part that's important: his conclusion is firmly in favour of holding back. We have him covered. There's a chance to bargain his way out and he's bound to take it.'

94

Haversham had no longer finished the sentence than the panicked voice of Superintendent Goodswen barked through on the radio loudspeakers. 'COBRA, come in, COBRA, we have a major problem developing here. Civilian breaching police lines, repeat request for authority to move in.'

3.51 p.m., Incident Command Vehicle

Bonnington saw the woman first. Wearing a long cream-coloured trenchcoat and dark blue trouser suit. Pragmatic looking and, kind of determined, he could sense she was trouble. She was striding around from policeman to policeman gesticulating wildly. As the camera had zoomed in on her face he could see her mouth imploring the officers to divulge the truth. She had acted like an all-consuming magnet drawing together the other concerned parents like iron filings. Within minutes of her arrival on the scene the atmosphere at the front line had changed dramatically. Bonnington and Goodswen watched on like chemistry students witnessing a slow burn catalyst spark through the crowd. The parents began pressing the police line, now in unison demanding a response from the increasingly defensive officers. The bright yellow fluorescent tape that marked the police boundary looked no more than the flimsy symbol it really was. Goodswen was worried any disturbance could unsettle the kidnappers; they had to contain the threat. He was reaching for the radio handset to authorise a removal when suddenly she disappeared from view. He scanned the other camera views in rapid succession attempting to locate her. It took less than a minute for her to reappear behind the wheel of a silver 3 series BMW screaming down the street towards the tape. The blue line of police officers scattered apart like rabbits on a motorway as she burst through, car engine grinding out a deep, throaty growl. As it careered ever closer to the synagogue, Goodswen shouted down the link to COBRA for the second time. The car would be visible to the kidnappers by now as it braked hard into the kerb outside the infant school. They could wait no longer. The order took only a second. And so it was that at 4.01 and ten seconds they went in.

The blistering white flash that followed the shards of glass would have been enough to render Mrs Hocking unconscious where she stood in the kitchen. But as it turned out, it was the first smoke canister smashing into her face that saved her from seeing the lightning sparks under the muzzle of the automatic. Her body shuddered as she took fifteen rapid rounds to the chest and head. Before she had fallen to the ground, the second wave of black-hooded men crashed into the corridor and sprayed another cloud of bullets into the living room.

Mr Hocking, the caretaker, didn't even have time to switch channels on the new satellite TV system which had been installed on a no-strings free trial only yesterday. The line of holes, full of hot metal, started just below his left shoulder and curved only slightly to end in his right thigh. His face was paralysed in a death mask grimace; his wide-open eyes saw nothing.

It took several seconds for silence to fall and the gunsmoke to clear. When it did all six of them saw what they'd achieved.

The lemon tart that Mrs Hocking had been about to remove from the oven offered up its sweet aroma, challenging the cordite stench in the air. In her left hand she still clutched the blender, its wheels spinning intermittently as her death throes forced her fingers into contact with the switch.

The sergeant removed his mask and picked through the wreckage to find eighty-year-old Martha Goldberg unable to speak with shock. She sat in her wheelchair, head flopped slightly to one side, her whole body trembling rhythmically. A thin dribble of blood traced its way across the wrinkled flesh of her neck. At least she was alive, but two ricochet wounds to the head were serious enough to require surgery. He reached into his chest pocket and extracted the radio.

'Control, come in.'

'This is control. Status report, sergeant. Opposition first?'

'Two dead, sir, and one injured.'

'Home side?'

'All accounted for.'

'Excellent.'

'Sorry, sir, I'm just . . .'

'Are you all right, sergeant? You sound distracted.'

'You could say that, sir.'

'Well, pull yourself together. The Attorney General, how is he?'

'He's not here, sir.'

'What do you mean, man?'

'Like I say, he's not here. In fact he's never been here. No bomb, no bloody politician, no kidnappers, no nothing.'

'Sergeant?'

'We've been had, sir, and the mess isn't going to be cleared easily. These poor fuckers are civilians.'

'What the hell . . . ?'

4.03 p.m., The Jury Room

'A verdict upon which at least ten of you have agreed.' The judge's words had caused a stifled groan from the 'Hawks' of the jury who were silenced by his final pronouncement. 'But I must stress, you must still strive to reach a verdict upon which you are all agreed. That is all.'

They had then been ushered back to the claustrophobic cloisters of their retiring room. Fresh coffee and tea, cheap mineral water – flat as Alex's mood – and some digestive biscuits were produced and consumed in mutual silence. Even Uncle Bob seemed weighed down by the stalemate. He was rubbing his chin thoughtfully, sharp eyes now flat with the exhaustion of his onerous post.

'The clock's still ticking, Bob,' said Alex. 'Your clock, I mean – we're travelling around its dial.'

The old man ignored his remark. He needed to be brought out of his reverie for progress to be made.

'I still think it's a great idea, the human clock: it's working, got us all thinking,' Alex said.

'Come on, Robert,' Pearl said. 'Our generation never ducked a job, no matter how hard. How does it go? "Two world wars and a depression, and I've still got all me own teeth".' Pearl smiled warmly.

Bob looked to her, smiled, then laughed, 'You might have. I'm beginning to think I've lost mine.'

They're still sharp enough, Bob, Alex thought: still got a good bite radius and a firm grip. Bob turned to Alex.

'You sure you still want me to do the job?'

Alex couldn't understand why the question had been directed at him in particular, but it was the others who answered in the affirmative. Only Princess Grace had anything to add.

'I really don't care who the foreperson is as long as I can make my county squash match at nine.'

'This is a little more important than a squash match, don't you think?' Kalsi asked, her gaze resting reasonably on Grace.

'Of course, it's just that I have made . . .'

'Your mind up?' Kalsi interrupted. 'I thought we were all going to debate the problems we have with the case.'

'I don't believe there are any problems. She did it, they proved it, she's guilty,' Grace answered airily, whilst Stalin clapped her announcement enthusiastically.

'Way to go, girl. Got some common sense after all.'

Grace sniffed. 'One doesn't need to be common to possess sense.'

Stalin smirked. 'Maybe not, maybe not. But none of us can help our class, not even you.'

'People,' Bob interrupted. 'It's time to get back to work.'

'Does that mean I can do my fingerprint stuff now?' Danno asked hopefully. Bob nodded. 'Great. Like before I was rudely interrupted,' he grinned at Stalin, who returned the gesture, 'I was saying that her dabs were all over the murder weapon, no doubt about it. Now,' he continued and pulled a small book from underneath his bundle of jury documents, 'this is a real help. *Reader's Digest*, last year's, October, an article all about fingerprinting.' He turned his attention to their foreman. 'It must have dropped out of your pocket when you came over for dinner last week.'

'And very nice it was too. I wondered what had happened to it,' Bob replied.

'Only found it last night, had a bit of a flick through it and, well . . .'

'Bob's your uncle?' Alex suggested. 'Or your dinner guest, at least.'

'Got a problem with that, Alex?' Bob asked him.

'No, not really: just a joke.'

'I've had a couple of pints with Bob,' Pitbull whispered. 'Got a problem with that, Aaalex?' He stretched the letters of his name sarcastically.

Alex shook his head. 'It's just the judge told us not to discuss the case until we had heard all the evidence.'

'And we didn't, did we, Uncle Bob?' Pitbull replied with a wink.

'Certainly not,' the foreman answered indignantly.

'Anyway, this article,' Danno held aloft the chunky book like a forensic Bible, 'reckons it's impossible to make a mistake on fingerprints. No two people in the world have the same; not even identical twins. It's all about ridge characteristics and whorls and loops and stuff.'

He opened the book to where a corner of one page had been folded back. 'Here it is. England has the second highest standard of comparison in the world: sixteen points. I mean, that's more points than Norway get in the Eurovision Song Contest.'

'Nice one,' Pitbull said, laughing appreciatively.

'But the defendant's prints had twenty-eight points of comparison,' Danno went on, enjoying his status as forensic sleuth. 'As I said, all over the shop. She never denied they were her prints: well, she couldn't, could she? I mean, if she was asked, "Are these yours?" she couldn't, like, say, "Er, no, I bought 'em off a bloke in the pub."'

'Or "They fell off the back of a lorry",' Pitbull suggested. They both began to giggle.

'This is serious,' the Prof said sternly.

'But her defence isn't,' Pitbull replied. 'It's a laugh, and while we are on this stuff, can I save us all a little bit of time, so we can get to our squash matches or our businesses, or whatever it is we want to get to. What about the powder burns on her clothes?'

'Let's do things in order,' Bob suggested, for once meekly.

'It makes sense to deal with it together, my turn on the dial, all the science clap-trap.'

As no one else objected, Bob nodded for him to continue.

'Right, powder burns.' Pitbull reached for the large exhibit bag. 'One black Lycra suit, as modelled by the lovely Dr Jenny Fox on the evening of the dirty deed. Murder weapon fired into head of deceased, three times. Powder traces expected to be found on right sleeve, as killer is right-handed, as is the Doc. Knock me down with a Magnum, there it is: an exact match. Bang, bang, bang, guilty, guilty, guilty.'

He tossed the exhibit bag on to the table and sat back breathing heavily.

'And what I can't understand is what you people – well, three of you at least – are playing at.'

'What if she's telling the truth?' Alex asked him. Pitbull nodded.

'So you're the third, Aaaalex. I wondered; couldn't be sure. What is it, fancy her, do you? Give her a get-out-of-jail card, then the come-into-bed professional-man's eyes?'

Alex smiled coldly. 'That might be the way you operate, Pit—'

'What did you call me? Or what were you going to call me? Got a moniker, have I? You smug bastard.' He began to climb to his feet. Alex did the same.

'I was going to say, pity,' he offered lamely.

'Well, I pity you, when I get my hands on you.'

'Sit down,' Bob shouted in a voice thronging with command. Pitbull looked uneasy and Alex unclenched his fists and, eyeing Pitbull warily, returned to his seat. Pitbull growled, 'Later, Mr Architect,' and sat.

'I'll be ready,' Alex answered.

'Men,' Kalsi muttered. 'Starting wars where children suffer until women end them.' Her disgust was real and, Alex sensed, sprang from personal suffering.

'Go on, Alex,' Bob commanded.

He took a deep breath. 'We have to look at all the evidence in the case, not just what the prosecution had to say. Now,' he nodded to Pitbull, 'I have to agree with you about the powder burns: it looks really damning.'

'Cheers,' Pitbull responded, unimpressed. Alex turned to Danno.

'And with you about the fingerprints. It looks bad, really bad.' Danno patted his *Reader's Digest*. 'But maybe that's how it was meant to look. I mean, how stupid is she?' He looked around the table. 'A top research scientist who gets caught so easily, who leaves a trail of clues like a legal paperchase. It's not just inept, it's criminally stupid and, I think you will agree, when she gave her evidence she was anything but.'

Denzel raised one hand languidly in the air. Alex granted him the floor with a nod.

'She had a lot of time to think about things, Alex: a lot of time staring at the walls of a cell to come up with something.' He lounged back against the uncomfortable chair. 'So she had to think of a story that matched all the scientific jive, 'cos she's a scientist and knows you don't cross swords with lab results. So,' he shrugged, 'she comes up with "I've been set up by the bad guys" and hopes we swallow it. She got no other way out, Alex, man. Desperate woman, desperate story, end of story.'

Alex could see a number of the others nodding their agreement with Denzel's cool appraisal of the situation.

'OK, but what if, just what if, she is telling the truth? How are we going to feel in ten years' time when new evidence comes to light that she's innocent, and we have failed to consider her case properly?' Alex could see he had struck a minor chord with some of the jury. 'The Guildford Four would have been long dead if we still had capital punishment. As it was, they only lost fifteen years of their lives instead.'

'That was different, Alex,' Bob said. 'They confessed, albeit under duress, but the jury still heard the confessions, still believed them.'

'Because they were so appalled at the crime they wanted someone to answer for it. We can't afford to make the same mistake.'

'But she hasn't confessed, has she? Hours and hours of interviews, yet she held the line,' said Bob.

It was a subtle point, but Alex had expected it.

'Isn't consistency the hallmark of truth?'

They were now locked eye to eye, each calm and measured.

103

RANKIN DAVIS

'Or the sign of an accomplished liar. Just because the same absurd story is repeated endlessly doesn't change its basic nature: a lie is a lie is a lie.'

'The prosecution has to make us sure she's lying: that's the test.'

Bob nodded knowingly before replying. 'If I tell you that I am twenty-one years of age a hundred thousand times, would you believe me?' Alex shook his head. 'That is because your eyes and ears and common sense dictate your response. These wrinkles, this body, my attitudes, everything points to the contrary. It's the same with the rest of the evidence against Dr Fox.'

Alex was impressed with the foreman's powers of oratory. At the same time he noticed a slight, but perceptible change in Bob's accent. He pressed on.

'But isn't that precisely the point? Surely that is how we are meant to think, what *they* intend us to conclude?'

Bob shook his head sadly. 'Just who are *they*, Alex? The police? The government? The chemical firms? Where does it end?'

'If Jenny Fox is right about her research, then the Circle of Poison exists. If it exists then it has to be stopped; or she does. Imagine what her findings would do to the pesticide industry: just try to grasp the massive law suits against them, the crippling compensation.'

'But there is no evidence that any outside agency was involved,' Bob retorted. It was Alex's turn to shake his head.

'And if they had been, with all the resources at their disposal, do you think for one moment they would be stupid enough to leave any traces?'

'Oh, I think I follow your argument now. Sorry for being so pedestrian.' Bob's brow was furrowed with concentration. 'You're saying the reason we can be sure that this whole murder was set up by a third party is that there is absolutely no evidence of it.' He exhaled slowly and looked around the other tired faces in the room. 'Well, I don't know about everybody else, but that is a little too complex for me to grasp.'

Alex watched in dismay as each of the others nodded their

104

agreement of Bob's appraisal. Not for the first time he felt drained of energy. Above the murmurings of discontent, the annoyingly tinny electro-beat of Stalin's wristwatch brought round five p.m. and they were deadlocked.

'Let's have another vote,' Stalin suggested.

'I'm not changing mine,' Alex replied. 'Not until someone convinces me, beyond reasonable doubt, that she did it.'

'Others might change their minds,' Stalin mused, looking side-long at the Mouse.

'Not me,' Kaftan said firmly. 'I can see that girl's soul and she's no killer.'

'Give me strength,' Stalin muttered. 'I wasn't on about you.' Alex watched him continue to stare at the Mouse, who switched her gaze quickly from the table-top to Stalin's face.

'I don't care for bullies; had enough of that at the convent.' She turned to look at Alex. 'Some of us vote with our heads, some with our hearts. I've tried both, but this,' she indicated her crucifix, 'tells me the heart is best: not guilty.'

'Thank you,' Alex whispered.

A knock at the retiring room door broke the moment. Instanta-neously, their usher opened the door and walked through.

'I am instructed by His Lordship to ask if you have a unanimous verdict.'

'Afraid not,' Bob answered for them. The usher's face reflected the disappointment in the foreman's voice.

'A majority verdict?' she continued hopefully. Bob shook his head slowly. 'Oh dear, well it'll be back into court, then. Now, have you all brought your overnight bags as instructed?'

Alex glanced to the left-hand corner of the room where the small stockpile lay.

'Good. Accommodation has been arranged. His Lordship will do the formal stuff in court, if you would like to follow me.'

Alex could feel the antipathy from Stalin and the other Guilties and received a small smile from the Mouse and a knowing nod from Kaftan. But Bob – Bob drummed his fingers thoughtfully on the table-top.

Who are you, Uncle Bob? And how did you come to leave – accidentally, of course – an article on fingerprints at Danno's house? Why have you befriended so many of the jury? What is it you want?

Alex followed the others from their retiring room towards the open mouth of the court.

6.05 p.m., Cabinet Office Briefing Room

For the first time in his life, just as Edward Haversham was leaving the hastily arranged, deliberately brief and utterly dishonest press conference, it struck him square in the head. At the extreme right of the crowded room he spotted two senior journalists, commentators of high repute and recognised integrity. Both had survived many administrations, publicly judged and then outlived them while managing to ruin countless political lives along the way. Haversham recalled verbatim the words of Bill Botcheby, the elder of the two. Very early in his career Botcheby had labelled him a 'political charlatan whose much hyped passion and sensitivity was as false as the brittle hope he was offering to the new generation'.

Haversham who was usually impervious to such personal attacks nevertheless discreetly continued to monitor Botcheby's copy over the years. Upon his election to Number 10 the quote had bitten deeper than ever. Was it because the truth was in there lurking in plain sight? The words ran through his mind once more: 'With an astonishing lack of concern it seems not only the party faithful but the British electorate has entirely failed to grasp the near certain fact that a new age scientist, whose entire philosophy has been steeped in the blind pragmatism of maintaining economic growth at all costs, is by definition bereft of the skills necessary to tackle what is and always has been an art and not a science.

'When the time comes to test this very supposition I regret there will be little room for even the most lingering doubt about its accuracy. For finding himself sadly lacking in the ability to formulate an unhindered, truly original and independently created style of leadership befitting the challenge of a bright new dawn at the millennium, the new Prime Minister will be obliged to acknowledge that unlike his more illustrious predecessors there is little lead in his political pencil.'

Haversham was collecting his papers together, trying to conceal the anxious tremble in his hands when a look was quickly exchanged between the men. One simple narrowing of Botcheby's eyes said it all, a silent challenge, a pitying sort of glance devoid of any real respect, as if he didn't deserve the chance to be there at all. Myriad conflicting thoughts rushed into Haversham's brain but that look was all it took to unleash the harsh and uncompromising paranoia that inhabits the minds of those with no one else to turn to.

He left the room fighting through his anger and the waste of it all, cursing those who made this tragedy happen, those who forced him into this crisis, compounding the lies in the interests of the state. Then almost imperceptibly creeping through the shame he felt the vague beginnings of something he had sworn to himself did not exist. It wasn't the sharp but now all-too-familiar self-loathing that he experienced after every lie told in pursuit of power or every morally suspect deed sanctioned in the name of political survival. No, it was something very different developing deep inside him. A change was coming, a change he sensed, that would alter his life for ever just as the chimes of Big Ben had done all those years ago.

The force seemed to be mocking him, taunting him, even daring him to tackle the ultimate questions about himself. Am I really worthy of the title? It was useless attempting to ignore it and futile to resist but uncannily his fears at the same time seemed to be subsiding. He realised that no matter how long or deep his analysis of the paper possibilities, the answer would not be found there. It was as if he were being pulled towards a specific moment when he would meet himself as never before. It was meant that way.

A wave of sadness touched him when he thought again of the innocents, Mr and Mrs Hocking, who had died, slain by the bullets of those who were there to protect them. However painful the prospect was, an admission of responsibility for the deaths of those two people, would some day have to be made. But still there was something bigger to come and it had to do with Botcheby's words. Suddenly he hit upon it like a smart bomb locating its target. Instinct. The word bounced around repeatedly in his skull. Instinct, he repeated under his breath, sheer, naked and unadulterated. He had to take total control and follow his gut instinct. People's lives had already been sacrificed in this débâcle and, if he was to emerge from office with the stamp of greatness he so fervently desired, then now was the time to embrace his new-found inner strength however humbling the thought of eventual public accountability might be.

6.08 p.m., Prime Minister's Private Quarters, Downing Street

Haversham could think of only one place to be right now. He needed Emma. He needed to see her face and feel her presence. It seemed that his brother's fate was lingering at a busy crossroads now like a car without a driver. Knowing which way to turn the wheel was the all-important question. As he climbed the stairs to his flat, he gradually saw the plan. By the time he had reached the door he was ready to motor. The first gear to engage was Emma.

Opening the door quietly he stepped into the corridor. He was about to walk along to the study, following the sound of the television, which was still belching out the evening news, when he glimpsed her. The back of her tall, willowy frame glided past the open doorway into the tiny kitchenette to the left of the dining room. She hadn't heard him approach as he stood at the doorway watching her arrange two mugs beside the steaming kettle.

'Expecting someone?' he said softly, causing her to whip round in surprise.

'Only you,' she replied still clutching the coffee spoon, 'I knew you'd come.'

'Did you watch the press conference?'

'Do you need to ask?'

'Sorry. Silly thing to say.'

'No, it's not, just natural. Do you want to know what I think?'

'Naturally,' he stated with a grin, sitting down at the small oak table bought the day after they married and which they had taken wherever they had lived. She sat beside him, with the steaming mugs of coffee.

'You may have convinced them but I knew you were uncomfortable. What really happened out there? It's not Geoffrey, is it?'

'Geoffrey was never there in the first place. The kidnappers were using some sort of communications deflector, frustrating the signal from the telephone. Everyone downstairs was convinced it was the stronghold. Apparently some woman at the scene lost control when she was told she couldn't enter the area to collect her child from school. She drove her car straight through the police lines and was heading straight for the school gates. It all happened so quickly, COBRA decided there was no option but to go in, and gave the green light.'

'Jesus Christ, Edward. Where were you?'

'On my way to sign a D notice to get the press off our backs. The jury had come back into court for the majority direction. I thought everything was stable and we could allow the schools to empty naturally. Looks like I was wrong. It was all over in about fifty seconds.'

'No one could have predicted that, Edward. You can't blame yourself.'

'You think not,' he said. 'I can't see many others sharing that view when it comes to counting the costs. Can you?' he ended bitterly

'It's the job you wanted, Edward. No chance to go back, that's what you said when we walked through the front door,' she replied, holding his eyes with her own.

'I know, I'm sorry.'

'You should be. What about the two dead people?'

'Didn't know a thing about it. They were in the wrong place at the wrong time, that's all.'

'When are you going to identify them? Surely their families have a right to know?'

'Geoffrey's still out there somewhere, Emma, and until we find

110

him there's a news blackout. It will cause a mass panic if we admit we've lost control.'

'Sounds like you never had any control to lose in the first place. What are you going to do?'

'Pull out of the briefing room.'

'Are you sure?'

'It's unjustifiable to stay. What if something else equally unforeseeable happens? Would I do anything different?'

'I don't know. Would you?'

'I don't want to find out, Emma. There has to be another way through this.'

'How?'

'Look, the jury's out and that means we have sixteen hours until they return to court. I have to believe that Geoffrey's safe until then.'

'Why? It can only be a maniac who's holding him.'

'Maybe, but then again maybe not.'

'Come on, please. Reality bites, Edward. He's fanatical, already demonstrated a taste for extreme violence and really doesn't care who gets in his way so long as he gets what he wants. You have no way of knowing what he'll do next.'

'Just back-track there a moment.'

'What?'

'You said it just now. The fact that he wants something. That's where we've gone wrong.'

'You're losing me.'

'Don't you see, Emma? Our policy has been no deals, no bargaining, no listening. I can't change that myself and I can't expect others to circumvent it either on account of my position. But it troubles me deeply that we don't listen sometimes. What if he is right? What if there is something in what he says?'

'There can't be. Fox is guilty and the whole charade is a publicity exercise for the cause.'

'I'm surprised at you, Emma.'

'Why?'

'Because when you were at the Bar, you didn't think that way. Everyone accused of a crime deserves to be heard as an innocent, equal before the law. They should appear unburdened by inference

111

and prejudice until no doubt remains . . . Your words, Emma. Do I need to go on? It was that passion I admired most in you.'

'That was before I had spent a single day in court doing the job. I should have read less text books and listened to more cases.'

'You don't believe that.'

'I don't want to believe the alternative any more, Edward, especially not now.'

'I don't think there is a choice. If there is a possibility that Fox is genuinely innocent, I have to know and I'm going to get to the truth whatever it costs.'

'What you are saying legitimises terrorism in the process. We wouldn't stand a chance in the aftermath.'

'I'm not legitimising terrorism, Emma. I'm trying to save my brother's life.'

'Look, don't you remember that dinner with Geoffrey just after the election? You remember he talked about the Fox case? Nailed on coffin-tight. Those were his words, not mine.'

'I do remember him saying that, but I also recall he was anxious about the prospect of inheriting his predecessor's methods.'

'What did he mean by that?'

'I don't know. He said it though. That's what makes me believe I should start looking at the thing from a different angle.'

'What are you going to do?'

'I'm going to follow my instincts, Emma.'

6.21 p.m., Prime Minister's Study

The bone-shaped handle of the telephone nestled in the Prime Minister's hand as he waited for Ray Prince to shift his position to a more private location within the Central Communications Complex at Scotland Yard. Judging by the initial stutter Haversham guessed that

Prince had been very surprised to receive the call. Surprise turned to astonishment when the Premier had asked him if he could be overheard easily. A couple of seconds later he was on line again.

'I am at your service, sir,' Prince said a little uneasily.

'I hope that I haven't disturbed you in any way, superintendent.'

'Quite all right, sir. As I said, I am at your service,' he parried, still unsure of the situation.

'Good man. First of all, may I personally thank you for all that you are doing on our behalf,' Haversham opened.

'I only wish, Prime Minister, that I could have done more to prevent the tragedy. My advice will be on record,' Prince answered, then quickly went on, 'although I hope you understand that I do not seek to distance this unit from any responsibility, sir.'

'That's precisely the reason I called you instead of COBRA, I need to seek your advice on something. I'm sure the assessment given by your team was the correct one in the circumstances immediately prior to the incident. I have thought the matter through very carefully and I shall be going on record to confirm the same.'

'Thank you, sir. I'm sure that the entire team will be grateful that the work they do is recognised.'

'I'm pleased that we understand one another, superintendent. Now then, I trust you will be aware I have to insist on utter confidentiality in this matter.'

'Of course, sir.'

'I intend to start viewing this situation from an angle, which in some circles could be misconstrued as an affront to the existing policy. Some might even say that it would compromise the government's integrity as a whole.'

'I can appreciate your position, sir, and assure you of my complete loyalty. How can we help?'

'I want to know what your evaluation of the demand made by the kidnappers really is?'

'I think it's reasonably clear.'

'Is it?'

'He isn't going to stop until he gets what he wants.'

'Why?'

'Because he is an exceptionally well-motivated individual. He functions, I would guess, at a much higher level of efficiency than most individuals. The majority of his analytical strength comes from the ability to execute a plan almost instinctively.'

'Now there's something. Instinct, you say?'

'Sorry, sir?'

'It doesn't matter. So you firmly believe that he has an inflexible agenda?'

'That's affirmative, sir. He means what he says. That's why the request is so specific.'

'And that must mean, even if we wanted to begin a dialogue, he wouldn't be interested.'

'Exactly, sir. He has to follow the plan; there is no other option available to him. In fact he has deliberately closed the doors himself.'

'How do we get to the endgame then?'

'We wait.'

'For what?'

'For him to tell us when he wants it.'

'What about taking it to him?'

'Only way possible is to meet the demand on his terms.'

'So he gets to win either way.'

'Like I said at the outset, it's a no-lose situation for him.'

'There has to be some risk to him.'

'The only risks he could not have foreseen are those flukes, which could happen to anyone. Rest of the time he's plain sailing until the verdict.'

'Thank you, superintendent, I think you have just confirmed my own view.'

'If you don't mind me asking, sir, what are you going to do about it?'

'I'm going to resign, superintendent.'

'Sir?'

'Temporarily.'

'I see, sir.'

'Do you really?'

'As much as I need to.'

'Good. I'm so pleased we had this conversation. You wouldn't find it an extra burden to your duties if I called again to run one or two things past you, would you? On a sort of one-to-one basis.'

'Not at all, sir.'

'Excellent. Well I must go now. There's a statement I have to make, but it would be helpful in the meantime if you were to address your much undervalued resources to the question of court logs and transcripts of evidence.'

'In what respect, sir?'

'In respect of making sure that by whatever means I have copies lifted from the court files and on my desk within the hour.'

7.00 p.m., Cabinet Office Briefing Room

He walked slowly back to the Cabinet Office with vivid memories of his youth spilling into focus. Faces, conversations, moments of clarity were competing fiercely with moments of pain. 'Where are you now, Father? he muttered softly. Whether he wanted to shout for help or for forgiveness was unclear to him and a nagging suspicion that the distinction was unimportant now only served to heighten his confusion. Always ruthlessly confined by an unshakeable belief in his firmly logistical approach to politics, Haversham had often cruelly dismissed his father's equally impassioned faith in the notion of a higher instinct which was gifted only to the great leaders in history.

As he approached the double doors to the office an overwhelming compulsion drove him on. Unfettered now by the restraints of logic, it was time to take control. By the time his polished Oxford toecaps breezed almost noiselessly over the brass-plated threshold, he was ready to begin the search for the truth, whatever that may be. One or two of the junior staff at work stations closest to him caught at firsthand a full frontal glance of the expression no spin-doctor could ever allow the public to witness. The comfortable, evenly balanced smile and carefully manufactured statesman's look adorning every poster, photograph and party workers' flyer across the country had disintegrated. Now his whole face was alive. Every tiny nerve ending in his body was responding to the siren call. The inescapable fact that it was his brother's life that could have ended in the bloody assault on the stronghold laid uneasily across his thoughts and he knew that nothing short of complete control would suffice from now on if the worst was to be avoided. His earlier blind fury had transformed itself subliminally into positive strength. Feelings he'd never before experienced were now buzzing around, creating a sense of unbridled freedom. For a brief moment all he could hear was the unrelenting beat of his own blood being pumped around his body by a racing heart.

It wasn't just the intensity etched across the line of his eyes or the firmly set jawbone that choked the natural energy in the room. It was something else more powerful moving with him from the doorway to the centre stage like a black squall instantly swallowing up the air space of those all around until they were compelled to his presence. The main board members, now including the deputy Prime Minister, were assembled around the circular table. They rose in unison as he approached. 'Please be seated, all of you,' Haversham responded with a wave of his arm. Five people obeyed his command, but the uniformed military liaison officer stood fast to attention.

'What's the matter, general?' Haversham asked.

'I am instructed to deliver a personal message from the Chief of Staff regarding today's events, sir.'

'It's not necessary, general. I'm sure those of us who weren't present are in no position to insist on explanations or apologies.'

'I appreciate your candour, sir, but it would be considered a failure if my orders were not carried out to the letter.'

'Of course, general, I understand and in that case I'm listening.'

'On behalf of the Chief and the Squadron may I express our deepest regret following the unsuccessful mission. I can assure you that this embarrassment, sir, is something which will never be forgotten by the units concerned, and the Squadron as a whole. We remain your servants and earnestly pray that your confidence in the service returns with a speedy and successful end to this appalling affair.'

'Thank you, general. I know you will ensure that the Chief of Staff is informed that so far as I am concerned there will be a recommendation of blanket immunity for the men involved in the operation. This war is not of our making.'

'Affirmative, sir.' The general saluted briskly and sat down.

'Now I would like to make a declaration for the record. Could someone arrange a tape, please.'

Haversham marshalled his thoughts whilst a cassette recorder was placed in the centre of the table and a fresh tape inserted. It was clear this was not the time to interrupt. The others could do no more than wait in silence for him to begin. After a minute or so had elapsed, Haversham glanced at the clock, took a deep breath and pressed the record button.

'This is Edward Haversham, Prime Minister of Great Britain. I am recording this declaration in the hope that one day soon my brother will be amongst those able to listen to my reasoning. Only the passage of time will establish whether my decision now is the right course of action to be adopted. It is Monday the 21st of July just after 7.00 p.m. and the jury in the trial of Dr Jennifer Fox are presently being transported to a hotel. They will return to court tomorrow morning at 10.30 a.m. Accordingly we now enjoy the relative luxury of some extra time to rationalise the effects of this wicked and unenviable crisis. I believe an honest reflection at this point shows our early optimism of a swift conclusion to have been grossly inaccurate. Clearly our adversary is an individual of some considerable experience and determined mind and carries an unshakeable commitment to achieving his goals. This operation will continue unabated in its resolve to eliminate the risk posed to our citizens at the earliest opportunity but without the necessary intelligence we must all fear the worst.

'It will come as no surprise to any of you that following the tragic events of the last hour, waiting for us at the other end of this nightmare is sure to be a public mauling from our detractors. I do not propose to dwell upon the details now but recommend that each and every one of you at the conclusion of your duties here makes as full a record as possible of your own actions for examination by whoever is set the task of judging us.

'We must now also acknowledge that from the beginning this entire situation has proven to be nothing less than a complete

117

disaster with our efforts proving ineffectual. As you know, in addition to the continued threat to the life of the Attorney General we are now at the very least implicated in the decision-making process that has resulted in the manslaughter of two innocent citizens. We still do not have a location on the bomb and we must therefore assume, if activated, the terrorist threat is capable not only of exacting significant human suffering but also destabilising the unparalleled international reputation our country has earned as a democracy which will not tolerate violence as a means of subverting the rule of law.

'I have imparted the barest details to the press at present in the hope that a successful resolution will occur before the eyes of the world focus upon our example. It is, I'm afraid, only a question of time before they unravel the reality of the threat and current opinion from the judiciary is not favourable, were evidence to emerge later that intelligence capable of preventing injury was unreasonably withheld by us at the time.

'This all leads me to the conclusion that our first priority must remain a commitment to preventing further loss of life. If we are all agreed to that, it must mean that approaching the option of co-operation with the enemy afresh, by employing a more flexible attitude, is a live issue and worth exploring. I am not, I hasten to add, seeking to declare a unilateral policy shift but merely stating as a matter of record my personal intention to investigate the circumstances of the Fox trial with every urgency and facility of office at my disposal.

'For the sake of clarity I concede now that my continued presence in the briefing room may conceivably present a challenge to its operational function and authority. I alone accept responsibility for overruling the standard and well-documented procedure which the state had envisaged at the commencement of my tenure and my brother's appointment. This would have removed my input from the outset. I further acknowledge that my earlier interruptions were motivated and governed to some extent by the personal relationship, which binds me so closely to the matter.

'I have therefore given lengthy consideration to the principles upon which my brother and I have always stood. I am compelled to the view, despite the powerful urge and natural desire to protect

my own family, that those interests must remain subservient to the overriding supremacy of the state.

'To this end I expect some of those present will recall my initial pledge to relinquish overall operational authority to the deputy Prime Minister in the event of a challenge to my objectivity and I stand by that promise. In five minutes I will endorse the necessary documentation removing myself from that role.

'By this action I am entrusting the responsibility for my brother's life to you. It is without a shadow of doubt the most agonising dilemma I have ever encountered.

'It would be unnatural were I not to urge your continued attention to the utmost caution in discharging your duty. Before embarking upon a course of conduct which realistically leads to the certain death of my brother, I implore restraint. I have been impressed with the advice tendered by Superintendent Ray Prince at Contingency Planning and essentially the interests of the Haversham family have so far been best served by following his counsel. I do understand, however, given the volatility of this situation, there may well come a time when restraint can no longer be justified.

'Should such a situation arise, I trust that none of you will suffer any conflict by virtue of an association with the Haversham family. Rather, you should rest content in the knowledge that your decision was endorsed with our consent.'

The Prime Minister reached across the table and depressed the stop button. Then he flipped the eject button and examined the tape. Everyone watched him in absolute silence. They knew they had been privileged to witness something unique, a special humbling moment of principle and courage that separates true leaders from the rest of humanity.

As the tape was boxed and sealed Haversham stood transfixed, completely absorbed in the irony that his first instinctive step towards proving Botcheby wrong was chronicled on cheap magnetic tape instead of being carved in stone. He stood up without further comment and strode elegantly to the door focused on one thing. Who really did kill Dr Charles Easterman?

7.10 p.m., The Beaumont Hotel, Hertfordshire

Alex Parrish leaned against the mahogany door leading to the hotel's reception room. The other eleven sat or stood in similar dismay in the Victorian foyer. This was to be their home for the night. Alex viewed the dreadful velvet plush of the interior, the blistered, peeling paint of the high ceilings, the awful portraits in heavy gilt frames, all of which promised discomfort from a bygone era. To his right a huge staircase swept grandly in an arc to the first floor, to his left the tarnished promise of 'The Prince Albert Bar'.

Nobody was happy. The judge in particular had not been happy on their return to the courtroom. He had shaken his great head in stunned incomprehension at their failure to reach a majority verdict, before consigning them to this place. It was the moment when they left the Old Bailey by the back entrance that things became decidedly weird. Alex and the others were directed towards a white fourteen-seat minibus, surrounded by heavily armed police. An Alsatian sniffer dog was led from the bus, barking happily, tail sweeping side to side, as they were ushered on board to take their seats. He had found himself next to Denzel, who had foregone a seat proffered by Princess Grace, to her pursed-lipped annoyance.

The windows were mirrored, black to the outside world, transparent within; was this normal? Alex doubted it, then consoled himself that theirs was a terrorist trial where every precaution must be taken.

The ushers informed them that the journey would take about an hour, without informing them of the intended destination. Then things got stranger still. The bus progressed in a high-speed convoy, led, followed and flanked by marked police cars, sirens shrieking, lights blazing. Now this couldn't be normal, Alex had remarked to Denzel who could only shrug in puzzlement. He heard it before he saw it. A helicopter, first directly overhead, then from time to time swooping and dipping ahead, like a swift scout blazing their trail to this place.

They had been kept on board the bus for a further twenty minutes whilst a hoard of police and their trusty dogs scoured the hotel. Judging by the faces of the others, they were as alarmed as Alex. Except Bob: no, Bob seemed more interested than alarmed, taking each unsettling occurrence in his short stride.

Alex could see him now, inside the dim reception, with its ugly aspidistras and large floral pots, hobnobbing with the ushers. He touched one of them lightly on the back and shared a joke that was greeted with a warm smile; good old Bob, always knew the right thing to say at the right time.

On the wall above him Alex noticed the brass and wood holding rods for newspapers gleaming dully, but there were no newspapers in them. One of the ushers asked for silence.

'I have a list of instructions from the judge and some general information.' She looked down her half-rim spectacles at a sheet of paper. 'Nobody is to leave, or attempt to leave, the hotel before you are returned to the Old Bailey tomorrow morning for 9.30 a.m. I require from each of you a contact number for your family or relatives. They will be informed of the facts but will not be told where you are. All telephones are working on an internal system only.'

Alex raised his eyebrows: this wasn't jury sequestration, it was imprisonment. He could see the disquiet on his fellow jurors' faces.

'All newspapers have been removed; there will be none delivered in the morning. Television sets are tuned to the in-house video channel only, and hotel-room radios have been disconnected for the present. This is to ensure that your deliberations are not influenced by media coverage. The judge sends his sincere apologies, but does not wish any matter to interfere with your findings in the case. There are armed guards stationed along the perimeter of the hotel's grounds, so we know you will sleep safely.'

'This is bloody Colditz,' Stalin shouted. 'I'm not having this.' He began to walk towards the exit.

'Dave, wait,' Bob shouted after him, 'I'm sure there's a good reason for all this.'

But Stalin continued until he reached the door where two armed policemen appeared suddenly and barred his way.

'Might not be safe out there, sir, best remain inside.'

Stalin tried to barge past them, but was restrained swiftly and firmly.

'Just following orders, sir,' one of them explained, but Bob was already talking him down.

'We're stuck here, lad, nothing we can do about it, just accept it, eh?'

'My business, Bob.'

'It'll be there in the morning, won't it?'

Stalin seemed shaken. 'That's just the thing,' he whispered, 'it might not be.'

Bob nodded to the policemen, who relinquished custody of Stalin into his care.

'I think we need a drink.' Bob glared fiercely at the chief usher. 'That's if his lordship hasn't closed the bar as well.'

She shrugged. 'In moderation.'

Bob turned sharply away, leading Stalin by the arm into the bar and out of their sight. The remaining ten were separated into two groups: male and female. They were then led up the grand staircase, the women deposited on the first floor, the men on the third. They stood in line waiting for their keys, Alex at the rear. Pitbull and Danno jostled in the queue, jockeying for a position that would allow them adjoining rooms. As the impossibly large keys, each moored to a block of wood, were dispatched, they each gave their chosen contact number for restricted access to the outside world.

Alex was just behind the Prof, who was whistling monotonously, apparently happy with his legal lot. As his turn arrived, Alex could see there were three keys remaining. He smiled at Edna, the usher.

'Could you put me next to Bob?'

She cocked her head to one side suspiciously, but Alex merely held out his hand, as if his request was a thinly disguised order. She complied.

'I hope they don't drink too much in the bar.'

'I'm sure Bob will keep things right.'

He grasped the key: room 35, to his left, three doors down. He could hear Pitbull and Danno laughing as he passed 32, saw the Prof quietly close the door to 34, across the corridor from Alex, then he entered his own room for the night. Inside, a single bed with autumn-brown duvet hugged the fading regency wallpaper in an effort to enlarge the room's dimensions. A reproduction dressing-table dominated the centre wall with a bowl of shrivelled fruit that had probably been offered to Prince Albert himself. The room was clean and functional and after all, Alex reminded himself, it would only be for one night; or would it?

He hastily decamped his toiletries into the tiny en-suite bathroom and decided against a shave before dinner. He stripped down to his boxers and idly spun the dial of the shower. After several clanks and a shudder from the basin, a thin trickle of lukewarm water dripped from the 'power shower' head and echoed on the plastic flooring thinly. Alex hopped in and out, his hopes of a body-pummelling cloudburst dashed by the hotel's antiquity.

Whilst he rubbed himself dry, though this was almost unnecessary, he wondered why he had given his parents' telephone number to Edna the usher rather than Lucy's. She was his partner, had been for a whirlwind six months since they had met at a planning application for the health club soon to be in development. But the trial had given Alex time to think and speculate about the future; and he wondered if Lucy had been doing the same.

She was bright and beautiful, not unlike Jenny Fox, talented too, in so far as a specialist planning consultant had to be, but one thing she lacked was any real core of seriousness; she just wanted to have fun. That was fine by him, but not for ever, not all the time. It was as if the great gusts of early passion had been depleted to the gentler breeze of knowing regularity. Sure, his parents would call her and tell her he was fine, but she was intelligent enough to read the subtext. When this trial was put to bed, it would be time for some very serious thought about their future.

Donning fresh underwear and a blue polo shirt, loafers and some khaki chinos, he brushed his dark hair back, glanced in the smudged dresser mirror, saw he looked like a Tenerife timeshare seller and messed it up again. Grasping the huge key in his hand, Alex grabbed a jacket and wandered down the corridor towards the strains of conversation. It had been a hugely long and exhausting day but he could sense the evening was far from over. Too much had been said and done, too many hearts and minds laid almost naked by their discussions.

In the Prince Albert Bar, Bob and Stalin were drinking pints of lager at a small brass-topped table in the right-hand corner. Alex wouldn't have marked Bob down as a lager drinker, but the chameleon nature of his foreman dictated that he would drink another man's poison if only to convince himself that it wasn't. Stalin was hunched forward, rapt in Bob's words, which were muttered low but unintelligible. Pitbull and Danno were drinking the same popular tipple, talking quietly, as if the headmaster might be listening, at the bar itself, side by side, identical right feet resting on the brass foot rest in front of then. The inevitable *Four Seasons* murmured in the background from speakers, hidden behind leggy pot plants.

The barman smiled as he approached, wiping his hands on a towel.

'A large vodka and tonic, please.'

'Ice and a slice?'

Alex nodded, Pitbull glanced sideways at him.

'Ponce's drink.'

Danno snickered, Alex smiled more broadly than he felt.

'Ponces drink all kinds of things.' He dropped his eyes to Pitbull's yellow pint. 'Besides, that's all chemicals; not much of a boost at the end of a long day.'

'Good enough for us,' Pitbull replied testily. Alex's drink was placed before him on a 'with compliments' doily. Alex eyed it appreciatively, swept it up and downed it in one long draught. He smiled at the barman and nodded down to his drink, then turned to Pitbull and Danno.

'I've got no problems with what you drink, or what you think, just trying to get along and get this thing over with.'

Pitbull eyed him over his right shoulder.

'It could have been over, if you'd voted different.'

Alex smiled, already on his second drink; this time he sipped it.

'Could have been if we'd all voted different. It's not a one-way street, nothing is.'

Bob's voice cut over his shoulder.

'You heard what the judge said, no discussions in front of anyone who's not a juror.'

Alex swivelled around. Bob was staring at the barman, who furiously began to wash glasses.

'Sorry,' all three said together. Bob returned to his seat with Stalin without further conversation. Alex had to make a move on Pitbull and Danno: if they were ever going to clear their minds he must first clear the air.

'Look, lads.' He had their attention, for the moment. 'I think we got off on the wrong foot and we've been dancing to a different tune ever since. This trial is something none of us will ever forget. The judge told us we'd be excused jury service for the rest of our lives, so this is it.' He took another sip from his glass, and noticed the two do the same. 'We've all been under tremendous pressure for the last month – every day for hours on end listening to this stuff – then they expect us to go back to our lives as if nothing has changed.'

They were listening, he had struck a truth; that was universal to the twelve of them.

'But it has.'

Bob coughed loudly in his direction. Alex waved a supplicatory arm.

'Now I don't know yet if that's for good or bad, time will tell, but I think one thing it has taught me is to be more tolerant of other people and their opinions.'

'You don't say,' Pitbull scoffed.

'I didn't say I'd succeeded.'

Alex walked the two yards to where they stood. Danno swayed back slightly, his almond eyes flitting nervously, but Pitbull stood his ground and straightened his back.

'Here's my hand, and if I've offended you by my intolerance, then I apologise.'

Pitbull looked him up and down warily, as if expecting a hand-shake of peace to be followed swiftly by a head-butt of hatred. Alex stared back, face set but not unfriendly, Pitbull leaned forward and gave his hand a cursory shake.

'Handsome of you to admit it, Alex. Takes a bit of guts to do that, in front of witnesses and all.'

Alex offered his hand to Danno, who followed Pitbull's lead limply. Alex then swivelled to the barman who had given up all pretence of glass washing.

'Two pints of piss and a VAT.'

Alex kept his face straight then winked at Pitbull, who sprouted a reluctant smile which then flowered into a wide slash of amuse-ment.

'You're a boy, Alex, yes you are: pints of piss, hah. Still, like to see you try it at my local.'

'I wouldn't,' Alex replied. 'End up on the wrong end of a ventilator, and rightly so.'

Pitbull nodded appreciatively. Alex had given him the one thing he needed to make it through the brawling morass that was his life: respect.

During the next half-hour the other jurors made their appearances as Alex listened to Pitbull and Danno argue the merits of their respective football teams. Stalin appeared calmed by Bob's words and was seeing off another pint. The piped music had devolved to a syrupy compilation of late-twentieth-century love songs and Barry Manilow was crooning about 'Mandy'. Their ushers stood sentinel at the bar's entrance.

Pearl had for once forsaken her woolly paraphernalia and sipped a small sherry sitting solidly between Denzel and Princess Grace, like a moral buffer zone. Grace had changed for dinner. Alex guessed it was her favourite 'little black number' and showed off long shapely legs to her advantage and Denzel's fascination. Kalsi sipped mineral water from a tall glass as Mouse nibbled on salted peanuts from a stainless steel bowl. The Prof sat on his own with a pot of tea, thumbing through a battered paperback on black holes. Kaftan requested and eventually received a glass of peppermint tea that steamed away as she practised deep breathing exercises.

Alex checked his watch; eight o'clock and all was not well, at least not with him. The number of votes for a not-guilty verdict was too slim for any real comfort. He remembered his older brother James's court martial, five years before. He'd joined the Regiment straight from university, and was a Captain with a fast track to Staff College. Then the rape allegation was made in Germany. The whole family had gone over there for the trial. A civilian QC had been briefed at crippling cost. James denied his guilt throughout. Alex knew his brother, he knew it was a lie. But there were political pressures from the German government, too many squaddies assaulting too many local women; an example had to be made. That example was Captain James Parrish. One of the tribunal was clearly unhappy with the quality of the weeping woman's evidence, but he was over-ruled, or shouted down, it didn't matter which; the result was the same: five years in the 'glass-house' and a Dishonourable Discharge. James denied it to the end. Even his suicide note screamed his innocence. Alex wasn't going to allow the weight of numbers to determine Jenny Fox's fate. He returned his attention to the jury. Kaftan seemed resolute, but was too flaky for complete reliability whilst Mouse's timidity might see her backed into a pressure chamber of uncertainty. Edna the usher broke his chain of thought.

'Ladies and gentlemen, dinner is served. Please follow me through to the dining room.'

They all followed meekly behind. Alex carried his drink and smiled wryly as Denzel held the door open for Grace to sway languidly through. The dining room was oak clad, warm and comfortable. A huge stone fireplace with a growling fire consumed one wall, above it numerous coats of arms in dark crimsons and eggshell blues peppered the mantel. The floor was highly polished and dominated by a vast Persian rug, on top of which a magnificent mahogany table was set with cheap cutlery and petrol station wine glasses.

They each took their preferred seats. Alex positioned himself next to the Prof and the retired teacher appeared distractedly pleased with the half-promise of friendship. Bob sat himself between Kaftan and Mouse, skilfully separating the two with a glib excuse that a rheumatic neck wouldn't be helped by the chilling draught from the window. Pitbull and Danno, almost joined at the hip, plumped themselves on Alex's right, Denzel and Grace, equally Siamese, next to them. Stalin and Kaftan ensured they were as far away from each other as possible. Pearl tucked herself next to Stalin whose face was reddened by the swift effect of alcohol and stress.

Bob coughed.

'Now, those who want to can say grace with me, but it's not compulsory.'

Alex watched them one by one lower their heads in simple obedience, unwilling to be branded heathen by indifference, except Kalsi who stared ahead. Alex felt his own head drop as the half-forgotten words stumbled from his mouth, like intoning the Lord's Prayer at a christening, the words invoking an older, more innocent time.

Dinner was, as he had anticipated, a fairly dismal occurrence. Brown Windsor soup warmed the stomach but dulled the tastebuds. Kalsi, a vegetarian, chewed thoughtfully on a bread roll. Chicken à la King was poor royalty, Pitbull asking which king, Henry the Eighth? Kalsi toyed with an omelette. Any attempts to discuss the trial were immediately scotched by a watchful Bob, but Alex could see he was deep in hushed conversation with Mouse, who chewed and nodded politely.

The trouble started with Stalin. Alex noted that the wine, one bottle between three, was disappearing more rapidly when it was passed to him. He reached forward to replenish his empty glass.

'Got to keep a clear head,' Pearl said, her soft hand reaching forward to cover its rim. But Stalin's mind was elsewhere, his face blank but high in colour, he continued to pour, the wine drenching Pearl's hand and sleeve of her blouse.

'Leave it out,' Pitbull shouted across the table. Pearl withdrew her hand quickly and dabbed at it with a pink napkin.

'Accidents will happen,' she muttered kindly.

'He's pissed,' Pitbull continued. Stalin looked around the table. Failing to comprehend, he shook his head from side to side.

'I'm sorry. I'm so . . .'

'It's all right,' Pearl soothed, 'really it is. No harm done.'

'It's just . . .' Stalin said, attempting to explain.

'We're all very tired,' Bob said, and a number of other voices murmured their agreement, even Princess Grace, dropping her head in sincere shame for him. Stalin was on the edge. His outburst on

129

their arrival at the hotel explained the source of his worry and even Uncle Bob's advice had failed to eradicate his concern. Sensing their embarrassment, Stalin's face hardened into a scowl.

'Don't pity me, don't you dare pity me,' he demanded, tears of frustration in his beady eyes. 'Hate me, fear me, but not that.'

Bob walked around the table and put an arm around Stalin's shoulders.

'Come on, Dave, don't know about you, but this food's giving me heartburn. Let's have a pint in the bar and head off to bed. What about it?'

But Stalin was not for giving up so easily.

'We don't need to be here, could be at home sorting things out, getting my business straight. But you bleeding hearts,' he turned to Mouse, Kaftan and Alex in turn, 'are driving me up the bleeding wall. What is it? She's one of us, one of the caring middle class. If *she* could murder someone, what does it say about the rest of us? How far could we go if pushed?'

'Dave!' Bob warned, but Alex could tell that the warning was half-hearted.

'You think,' Stalin shouted, 'that just because you've shagged your way through degrees and private education that you have a monopoly on intelligence. I've spat out people like you in my business; no meat to you, no body, no heart.'

Alex hesitated momentarily, but knew he had to speak out. Mouse was dangerously close to tears and Kaftan had begun to hum a breathy mantra.

'You're right, Dave.'

'What?' Stalin replied, bewildered. Alex laid his hands flat on the table and stared steadily at the angry juror.

'We're afraid to look in the mirror, the view might be too much for us to handle. But I've stared long and hard during this trial, at Jenny Fox and myself. Wondered what I would have done in her situation.'

Bob raised a finger accusingly at him.

'Alex, the judge said . . .'

'I know what he said, but it's ludicrous to put us in this pressure cooker and expect us to ignore the reason we've all been ripped from our families and homes and,' he looked to Stalin, 'our businesses.'

'I'm warning you,' Bob threatened.

'Bob,' Alex began, 'you're doing a great job as foreman and you have everyone's respect, but we all deserve respect; we all have a view and a vote. Now, if you think I'm out of order then tell the judge about it tomorrow, but this is all too important to be hidebound by stupid rules.'

Bob measured the faces of the others before nodding unhappily. Alex took up the thread again.

'The answer to my question, "Could I have done it?" is yes, probably, or at least I think I could, but I am me, Alex Parrish, struggling architect, middle-class liberal. I am not a healer, a dedicated physician, consumed by a need to save lives. So, Dave,' he addressed Stalin, 'the reason I voted for a not-guilty verdict is because I believe the worst of myself and the best of Jenny Fox.'

'You're ignoring the evidence,' Bob spat angrily.

'We've still got six more questions to go, including mine,' Alex replied. 'All I'm asking is that we keep our minds open until then.'

Bob tapped Stalin gently on the shoulder. He climbed to his feet, lost in thought and alcohol. They were leaving the room when Bob whispered something over his shoulder.

'What was that?' Alex asked the Prof, who pushed his thick glasses back up his nose and replied.

'He said that his would be the last question before the verdict.'

The others began to file away from the dining room until Alex was left alone, wondering what it was that Bob was saving until the twelfth hour.

8.28 p.m., Prime Minister's Private Quarters

T he Havershams were sitting side by side at the dining-room table. Ray Prince had been good to his word. Bundles of papers carrying the central criminal court seal were neatly stacked in piles opposite them. A wooden cheeseboard with the half-eaten remains of a full Stilton, some creamy chunks of Brie and a selection tin of biscuits sat between them. They were about to start searching through the documents in an effort to isolate a starting point.

'Edward, you have asked the same question in about ten different ways now and you keep getting the same answer from me. I mean, which part of "I don't know" is it you have difficulty with?'

'But there has to be an answer – you accept that surely?'

'Maybe I do, but all the same it doesn't necessarily mean that we would be able to find it without speaking to the person himself. There could be any number of reasons why this man believes in Jenny Fox's innocence.'

'OK, let's go back to basics.'

'It's an eco thing,' she sighed. 'What more is there?'

'On the face of it I agree. So let's focus on exactly what it was that the doctor was saying in her defence.'

'She talked about her research and Dr Easterman's own studies.'

'The emphasis being on incompatibility of results between them.'

'So?'

'So we have to find out exactly what it was that they were actually examining.'

'Don't you know?'

'No, I'm afraid I don't, Emma. All I know is she was a radical opposed wholeheartedly to all environmentally unsound issues. That's the party line, you know how it is.'

'I know,' she said with more than a hint of resignation.

'You have to remember that the only information I have seen is a fifteen-line memo in a routine press brief on the first day of the trial. Geoffrey and I haven't talked about it whilst the case has been going on. You know what he's like about that sort of thing. So why don't you tell me what you know?'

'Well, all I have gathered from the press is that she's painting herself like some sort of Mother Theresa character, the patron saint of children.'

'Not a very charitable attitude to Dr Fox. You surprise me.'

'I don't know why it should surprise you. It's the height of hypocrisy, creating a smoke screen to hide her true character.'

'But nevertheless it does appear that she was specifically interested in the incidence of leukaemia around chemical plants in Britain. Right?'

'Yes. But she was involved in all sorts of other things, I'm sure. I saw an interview with one of her friends in the newspaper talking all about their exploits.'

'What? So she's been to a few hunt saboteur meets?'

'Amongst other things. Who knows how deep she was into it? She's been spotted at road protests, Greenpeace rallies, all sorts.'

'Emma, you have to understand that the network of underground radicals is still relatively small and it is not unusual to see them floating around from demo to demo protesting about wildly different things. They give each other support even if they don't truly understand or perhaps even truly believe the issues concerned.'

'Where does that take us?'

'It means we cannot be sure that the kidnappers know any more than we do about the death of Charles Easterman. They only know that Jenny Fox is one of their own and that, as far as they are concerned, she couldn't kill anybody.'

'Hence the demand for the real killer to be exposed.'

'Exactly. That's why we have to focus upon a specific issue and then dredge back to find another motive for the murder. If we assume that they are right.'

'But the issue is specific, isn't it?'

'In what way?'

'Jenny Fox maintained that she was approached by Easterman to discuss something connected with her studies on soil samples. Those samples were collected by her and analysed by her alone.'

'What does she say about them?'

'She claims her results proved that they contained carcinogenic qualities.'

'And Easterman was the person who had pilloried her in the academic press up until that point?'

'That's my understanding. Yes.'

'But the samples themselves as gathered by Fox had never been examined physically by Easterman?'

'You've got the point.'

'So he couldn't empirically disprove her evidence?'

'No. The only reason and justification she put forward was that he had to discount her findings.'

'Why?'

'Because he was the official government scientist who examines specimens in connection with the importation of the chemicals allegedly responsible for the results she had obtained.'

'So why hadn't Easterman ever offered to examine the samples she produced himself?'

'Same reason I suppose that no one accepts her innocence.'

'What do you mean?'

'He had no reason to doubt his own findings, had he? Just like the prosecution case against her. The evidence is there, so why bother to look any deeper?'

'But surely she would have given him the opportunity of examination?'

'She probably did at some stage but because she is renowned as a radical she was afforded little credibility by any of the establishment scientists. For a start I suspect they would be highly sceptical regarding the source of the samples; she could have got them from anywhere, and lied about the location.'

'So there was no way of verification?'

'Not unless they had all gone together to a prearranged destination and gathered independent samples, analysed them separately and then compared results.'

'Why didn't she go to some other body then?'

'I guess no one is interested enough.'

'Right. What we need to find is whether or not there is anything in the testimony of the witnesses that could verify her story that she had been invited by Easterman to visit him.'

'There won't be anything.'

'How can you be sure?'

'Because the defence would have found it by now.'

'OK. So we have to assume that they will have attempted every avenue of support for Jenny Fox's version of events but were unsuccessful. What about Easterman's notes, personal diary, that sort of thing? Wouldn't they give any clues as to what he was thinking when he invited her to talk with him?'

'I suppose so.'

'So where would we find those amongst this little lot?'

'I don't know.'

'Why not?'

'Because I'm not a lawyer any more, Edward. A lot of things change in twenty years, you know.'

'Come off it, Emma. It's like riding a bike: you never forget how to do it.'

'Yes, but the trouble is you came along and I didn't get the chance to ride without stabilisers in the court very often, now did I?'

'No regrets though.'

'I'll tell you the answer to that when we get out of this place. Maybe I'll write a book about it one day.'

'Kiss and tell.'

'More like kiss and hell,' she smirked.

'You don't mean that?'

'You have to admit Edward, there are easier ways to make a living and bring up your family than deciding you want to be Prime Minister.'

'But none quite as exciting.'

'Or dangerous,' she said flatly

They looked at one another, both well aware that Geoffrey had just found out precisely how dangerous a life in the public eye can be. Edward was first to drop his gaze, anxious to avoid dwelling upon Geoffrey's predicament whilst there was work to be done which could mean an end to his brother's suffering. Emma rose to clear the cheeseboard and make more coffee, leaving him to reflect a while.

There was a little over thirteen hours to go before the jury would return to Court and although his confidence was high, the monumental task facing him was beginning to seem even bigger with each minute hand sweep of the Rolex Oyster on his wrist. He was only too conscious of the fact that by opening up avenues that had previously been unexplored, he was perhaps placing his entire government under a cloud of unwelcome suspicion in its infancy. Any perceived weakness on his behalf now would simply amplify the possibility of a challenge to his leadership, especially in view of his temporarily disenfranchised status as Prime Minister without portfolio. Emma returned with a cafetière and sat beside him, fixing her reading spectacles in place. He shook his misgivings away with some difficulty and turned his attention to the papers.

'Come on, let's give it a shot. There must be something in this forest,' he said as she plunged the silver pole back into the flask of fresh coffee.

'The only documentation relating to Easterman in the court bundle will be the papers generated by the original investigation and they should be on the exhibits schedule.'

'Lets start with that, then.'

9.10 p.m., Prime Minister's Jaguar
Travelling West to Mayfair

Edward Haversham was still speed-reading with a voracious appetite as he and Emma headed towards his brother's home. Emma was hurriedly scribbling down notes as she talked on the mobile telephone. The air was clearing after the daily downpour and the dark London night seemed to be closing in much earlier than usual. The flashing blue strobe lights of two police motorcycle escorts danced around the Jag's plush interior as the bikes expertly weaved a path ahead of the car. The police lights competed for attention with the fizzy orange sodium street lamps as the vehicles sped along Whitehall past the Abbey and on to Abingdon Street. The intermittent flashes were proving to be an annoying distraction for Haversham as he scanned the words on the pages.

His new-found confidence to follow the rhythm of his basic instinct told him the way ahead. Since deciding that the only way through this was to adopt the proposition that the Liquidator was correct in his assertions, his mood had darkened. Getting up to speed with the issues from the other side of the tracks was no easy trip. He had to try to understand what it was like to harbour a genuinely held belief in Dr Fox's innocence. Still working on the assumption that Ray Prince's prediction of a standoff until the verdict was correct, he had now a little over thirteen hours to find the truth.

Even a personal telephone call to the Lord Chief Justice had failed to placate the growing feeling that he was chasing the impossible. After fifteen minutes of briefing, Haversham had grasped the basic outline but was no further forward in his quest. No one in the legal fraternity, it seemed, shared the view expressed by the Liquidator. The case against Fox was watertight and the consensus was Geoffrey had done the business.

Since they had decided to start trawling through the documents secured by Ray Prince, nothing seemed to be getting clearer. Over the previous ninety minutes he had devoured a thousand pages of transcript evidence from the trial of Regina v. Dr Jennifer Fox. Occasionally he probed Emma for further information on the significance of particular portions of the evidence but as he blasted through the fifth bundle he had found nothing to support an alternative view. Then, just as he had begun to lose heart, Emma had discovered a small but nevertheless unusual anomaly from the court record. They had expected to find at least some reference to Easterman's personal notes in the exhibits schedule, thinking that such notes would be essential to proving that Fox was telling the truth when she stated that he had invited her to a meeting. The strange thing was that there didn't appear to be any reference to them at all in the papers. Surely it was inconceivable that a person like Easterman wouldn't have kept a journal of some description where they could check upon his movements? During the course of the trial, Fox's defence counsel had certainly asked the witnesses from the laboratory about their own knowledge of such a meeting but each one had replied in the negative. This served only to strengthen the case against Fox, and Geoffrey Haversham had made full use of it during his closing speech to the jury, as had the judge.

Only one witness had testified to Easterman having seemed a little anxious in the hours before his death and that was his secretary at the lab. She confirmed during cross-examination that she was responsible for compiling his daily schedule along with the other chief scientists but definitely there was no mention that day of a meeting at 8.00 p.m. with anyone, let alone Jenny Fox. She was adamant that she would have made no mistakes and produced a printout of the amalgamated schedule for the lab that day as proof. Pushed agonisingly hard on the issue by the defence she couldn't put her finger on exactly why she felt the doctor was displaying signs of anxiety and on reflection regretted any misleading inference she had caused by mentioning it. After all, she'd said, I don't suppose it was that unusual given the highly pressured nature of his work. The cross-examination ground to a halt when tearfully she clammed up, stating by the time she had left work that day at 5.30 p.m. he was his usual self again.

What Emma had pointed to was the fact that the printout she produced seemed to be the only piece of tangible evidence to have emanated from the lab. There was absolutely nothing else listed in the schedule of exhibits. Emma had then traced back through the court log to discover that when the case was in its preliminary stages an application was made to the Court by the prosecution to withhold certain documentary evidence from the defence upon the grounds of Public Interest Immunity. There was no record relating to this application, which had been conducted legitimately in the absence of the defence, and the schedule of unused material simply gave a reference number to the documents in question. The only place they could think of that might provide further clues was Geoffrey Haversham's townhouse.

As the convoy rounded the junction at the Mall and moved into Constitution Hill Haversham glanced up at his wife who was busy punching yet another number into her mobile telephone. He reached over the grey leather seat and gently stroked her thigh.

'No reply,' she said closing the flip down mouthpiece in frustration after a few seconds.

'Who are you trying to catch?'

'James Brannigan.'

'That's the one who acted as Geoffrey's noting junior, isn't it?'

'The self and same.'

'He's just there to scribble down the evidence though.'

'And keeping the court bundles organised amongst other things.'

'Is there something I'm missing here? Why do you think we ought to speak with him?'

'According to the court log the application for Public Interest Immunity was made on the third of February this year.'

'So what?'

'In case you have forgotten, darling, I seem to recall that you were in opposition at that time.'

'Christ, yes. I see what you mean.'

'I'm so glad.'

'All right, all right. So I'm getting a little slow in my old age, you've made your point.'

He smiled. 'That means there is no way Geoffrey could possibly have conducted the application, he hadn't even been appointed then.'

'David Rowlands was the Attorney General at the time. He retired after the election, didn't he?'

'That's right. To somewhere in Southern Ireland, I think.'

'Junior counsel was Chris Baker, and he's presently prosecuting some sex scandal in the British armed forces base in Gibraltar.'

'Yes, he's doing a court martial there, I read somewhere. So Brannigan is the only one left?'

'He's been the noting junior throughout the case and the only one who could possibly have any record of what was said at that application.'

'Apart from Geoffrey, of course. I hate to say it but it's inconceivable to think that Geoffrey wasn't aware of it. He must have come across it when he was preparing for trial.'

'What's more, Edward, I just hope we're not on the way to solving that little riddle he set you.'

'What are you talking about?'

'You said as much earlier, didn't you?'

'Go on.'

'Remember you mentioned what he said at dinner shortly after the election . . .' Emma paused looking directly into her husband's eyes.

'. . . He told me he didn't agree with the methods of his predecessor.' Haversham finished the sentence for her.

Suddenly he felt a cold shiver run through his body. If he did find something on his brother's computer, which proved important, then what would he do with it when he found it?

141

9.19 p.m., Grosvenor Crescent Mews

Everything down to the smell in the house reminded Haversham of his brother as he walked slowly down the corridor, followed by Emma. The armed police escort waited outside and the two of them were soon alone facing the laptop which still hummed softly. Next to it lay an open copy of the *All England Law Reports*, the pages separated by the gold Mont Blanc Edward recognised as the one he had given to his brother on the day of his appointment. The red leather briefcase he so cherished stood alongside the chair leg with its lid open to expose a yellow legal pad covered in tiny handwritten notes with the heading, 'Extradition treaty', lying on top of some blue files. Emma watched as Haversham delicately retrieved the pen and placed it almost reverently inside the case. She came up beside him and gently placed her hands on his shoulders. 'He'll be back for it, don't worry.'

'I hope so, Emma, I really do.'

He closed the case and turned to the computer, which was still displaying the flying-through-space screensaver with stars rocketing towards them at lightning pace.

'Come on, let's get down to it.'

'OK, let me drive.' Emma sat at the console

'Where do we start?'

'I should think he'll have a major file, which gives an overview of the case. I'm going to open the root directory in his word processing program to find that first.'

'How do you know all this stuff? I mean, I've seen you beavering away with Tom and Nicholas's computer but I thought you were just helping them with homework in the holidays.'

'You should try listening to the children occasionally, Edward.

It's amazing what you can pick up from them,' Emma answered, referring to their teenage sons. 'I could of course be using the computer at home to write a novel. Hasn't that occurred to you?'

'You're not, surely?'

'What's the matter?' she protested whilst flipping through file names on the computer display.

'Well, nothing, I suppose, just a little surprised.' He paused looking over her shoulder at the names flying past. 'It's not full of sex and politics, is it?' he asked suspiciously. 'How does the song go? Anything Edwina does, I can do better.' She pouted. 'You never know, we might be needing the money some day.' Then before he had a chance to respond she saw it. 'Look, there it is: R v. Fox with a lot of associated sub-directories listed.'

'Good. Hurry and open it up.'

She clicked the mouse button and the screen immediately filled with Geoffrey's notes on the case. The only trouble was they didn't seem to make much sense. Numbers, dates, names and accompanying passages of apparently unrelated information whizzed past. She tried to click on to the associated files but was denied access. Ten minutes later and they were still getting nowhere.

'It's just typical of Geoffrey,' Emma sighed

'What do you mean?'

'I don't know; sort of possessive with his working notes, I mean. He was always extremely careful to ensure his papers were pretty much incomprehensible to anyone else when he was in private practice. It used to infuriate his colleagues in chambers.'

'Probably a hang-up from school. He was the type of kid who covers his exam papers with his whole arm even when the desks are three yards apart, but I never had him down as producing incomprehensible answers,' Haversham said, puzzled.

'He'll obviously know what they mean and how they link up with one another and he'll carry a lot of information in his head. But come on now, surely you must have seen notes he's made before. He uses these curious little abbreviations. Look at them, they're full of mnemonics, acronyms, back-to-front filing systems, all that.'

'Now you come to mention it, I think I do remember him explaining it to me one night. Doesn't it have something to do with some

self-help guru who he met in the States one time? He came back full
of it. How to maximise your hidden potential, that sort of thing?'

'That's it; he went to New York on the pretence of attending
lectures given by the American Bar association, but basically it
was a tax-free holiday.'

'Now that is typical of Geoffrey but it doesn't help us. We
could spend for ever trying to decipher this lot. I mean just look
at that mess.'

'That's why I thought of the noting junior. He may be able
to help with these codes. It's fairly likely Geoffrey would have
swapped disks frequently with Brannigan to review the daily state
of play during the trial and to get into them he must have had the
codes, do you see?'

'Yes, but is that Geoffrey's style?'

'It's been twenty years since I was his pupil, but I bet he hasn't
changed his methods one jot.'

'OK. Give him another try.'

Emma reached over to the telephone on the desk and dialled
Brannigan's number. This time the connection was barely made
before a soft Irish accent drifted into the earpiece with just a hint
of a well-oiled slur.

'Brannigan speaking.'

'Hello, Mr Brannigan. My name is Emma Haversham. I hope you
will forgive me for calling you at this late hour but my husband and
I need some assistance.'

'Emma Haversham? Now I don't believe I've ever had the pleashure.
Sho you tell me how you got my number and I'll think about
absholution for your sins,' he chortled playfully, lazy pronunciation
confirming where he'd spent the earlier part of the evening.

'No, we haven't met but I believe you are well acquainted with
my brother-in-law, the Attorney General, and I was kindly given
your home number by the Head of your chambers, Sir Peter,'
replied Emma slowly. There was a distinct spluttering from the
other end of the line.

'Did, did I hear you say Emma Haversham?'

'That's correct.'

'And would that by any chance be the Haversham as in the
Havershams of Downing Street?'

'Now we're getting somewhere, Mr Brannigan.'

'Oh Jesus, Joseph, Mary mother of God, I do most earnestly apologise, madam, for my overly familiar manner. No offence, but I'm not used to receiving telephone calls from, well . . .'

'No need. I'm just glad that I've caught you at last,' Emma interrupted quickly. 'Now listen carefully, please. As I said, my husband and I require your assistance.'

'Your husband! That would be the Prime Minister . . . hic.'

'Very observant, Mr Brannigan! We need to know whether you will be able to decipher any of the Attorney General's notes or give us a clue as to the whereabouts of some documentation which I believe formed part of an application for Public Interest Immunity in the case of Dr Fox.'

'I think I'd better just pour myself a drink if you don't mind, madam,' he slurred. 'I'm not quite . . .'

'Look, Mr Brannigan, I don't wish to sound sharp or interfere with your social life but it is rather important.'

'Oh for sure, for sure.'

'Well?'

'Well, what . . . ?'

'Can you help us?'

'Oh, yes, I see what you mean, notes, yesh the notes.'

'What about them?'

'No, I'm afraid I can't help you there.'

'Why not?' Emma said, exasperated

'Because they don't make sense to anyone.'

'But you are the noting junior on the Fox case.'

'That I am but I still can't help.'

'I don't understand, Mr Brannigan. Would it help if we sent a car for you to come and see our difficulties for yourself?'

'All I do is take a handwritten note of the evidence in court. The Attorney General is in the habit of extracting what he considers to be important from them. After that I don't see them again nor, might I add, do I want to.'

'I beg your pardon?'

'I didn't want to be kept on the case from the start.'

'What on earth do you mean, Mr Brannigan?'

145

'She is innocent, madam, as sure as day follows night she is innocent.'

'How can you possibly know that, young man? Are you quite sure that you have your drinking under control?'

'No, I'm not certain that I have, but it won't change anything. Jenny Fox is innocent, but there's nothing anyone can do to help her now.'

'I think you'd better sober up before the morning.'

'I hope I don't, because that way I won't have to look in her pitiful eyes any more. She'll be convicted when the jury returns and I'll be on my way home.'

Emma turned her face towards Haversham with a look of complete shock. She could hear a loud commotion on the other end of the line, a baby crying and a woman's voice hollering to Brannigan in the background.

'Mr Brannigan, you must tell me what it is you know.'

'Me, I know nothing, madam, but I can feel it. I have to go now. I'm sorry.'

'Mr Brannigan please wait . . .'

'I can't. Goodbye, Mrs Haversham.'

'Please don't be stupid as well as drunk. We could have you picked up within minutes. This is very important,' Emma implored. There was a long pause at the other end. 'Mr Brannigan, are you still there . . . ?'

'Find the judge's notebook for the immunity hearing, Mrs Haversham, and you won't need to decipher any notes.'

'The judge's notebook! But . . .'

'Goodbye, Mrs Haversham. I'm taking my family back home.'

9.23 p.m., Maida Vale, In Motion

Geoffrey Haversham woke to the crushing pain of his snapped fingers and shook his head to drive away the chemically induced haziness. The van was in motion. Haversham could feel the thrum of the transmission through his back. A face loomed into view, the one in charge, who had ruined his fingers so effortlessly. A hard face, gaunt and sallow, heavily lined, with deeply recessed eyes that seemed to drink in the available light. Haversham tried to sit up but the bulk of the explosive waistcoat prevented him.

'Be still,' the man commanded. Haversham slumped back, surprised at his immediate response to the man's voice. He breathed deeply, and modulated his voice to a deep timbre.

'Tell me your name.'

'Names are unnecessary; only the truth matters.'

Haversham nodded. 'You call kidnap and torture the truth?'

'They are the means to the truth, Mr Haversham.'

'Geoffrey,' the Attorney General suggested.

His captor smiled wryly. 'The Stockholm syndrome, I believe.'

'Don't know what you mean,' Haversham lied.

'Politicians,' his captor sighed. 'The nature of the beast crosses many cultures and languages.'

Haversham shrugged his shoulders but remained silent.

147

'Aristotle defined politics as "the art of living together", but this is quite wrong: it is the art of lying together.'

'Perhaps in your country,' Haversham countered. His captor's face seemed to darken as he replied.

'I have no country.'

Haversham desperately wanted to sit up. He was severely disadvantaged, trussed and floundering: less human, easier to kill.

'Help me sit up, please.'

The man raised one eyebrow in sardonic amusement. 'You are tenacious, that much I will give you.'

He reached forward, took two handfuls of the waistcoat and lifted Haversham like a rag doll to a sitting position. He smiled bleakly. 'There, and I will still kill you without a moment's hesitation. Are you thirsty?'

Haversham nodded, surprised by the thoughtfulness of the request. A deep guttural male voice, heavy with Soviet inflection, shouted from the driver's cabin.

'There is heavy traffic ahead, what must I do, Pavel?'

Haversham expected his kidnapper to be angry; instead, he grinned.

'The answer to your earlier question.' Then he shouted back, 'Keep listening to the police band; avoid the congestion. Our guest is now awake. No more names, Serge.' Pavel laughed.

Haversham shook his head and muttered, 'Probably not his real name.'

'Probably not,' Pavel replied, handing Haversham a plastic cup half-filled with water, which he attempted to grasp with his mangled hand. Pavel stared into the Attorney General's eyes.

'I apologise. I had forgotten.'

'I haven't,' Haversham replied bitterly, then mentally rebuked himself: this was not the way to build up trust. He added, 'Am I a dead man, Pavel?'

'Nobody wants to die, but die we must,' Pavel replied, allowing Haversham to take gentle sips from the cup.

'Will you really kill me?'

'I am a soldier – I must do my duty.'

'And who do you fight for?' Haversham asked, hoping that any paymaster could be outbidded.

148

'The Earth.'

Haversham swallowed the last draught of water with a gulp. Pavel crushed the cup in his hand and dropped it into a small waste bin, secured to the floor.

'And what do you fight for, Mr Haversham? Fame? Wealth? Power?'

'Justice,' he whispered. Pavel took a seat opposite him and folded his legs into the lotus position with apparent ease.

'And yet you prosecuted Jenny Fox: that is not just.'

'It was the right thing to do. Why does she bother you so much?'

Pavel placed both hands flat on his knees.

'We must all look after our own. She is also a soldier – no, more a field surgeon – in the fight.'

His lawyer's training superseded Haversham's sense of survival.

'I know the evidence in the case like I know my own body.'

Pavel's eyes dropped to Haversham's mangled hand.

'But you do not know Jenny Fox.'

Haversham's ears twitched, his cross-examination was beginning to pay dividends.

'And you do, I suppose?'

Pavel's eyes flashed angrily. 'You are not in the Old Bailey now, Mr Prosecutor. This is my courtroom, and you have been found guilty.'

'Of what?' Haversham demanded.

'The charges will be decided at a later date.'

Haversham snorted. 'Typical. At least Miss Fox knew the accusations against her: she at least has a jury to decide her guilt.'

'Or innocence,' Pavel added. The lawyer was tempted to comment 'highly unlikely' but his self-preservation had reasserted itself.

'Or innocence,' the Attorney General whispered, 'but at least the jury has a choice.'

'Not with the case you have presented, Mr Prosecutor.'

Haversham slumped back. 'Are you always so perverse, Pavel?'

His captor smiled knowingly. 'It is in the Georgian temperament; I have no choice.'

They sat quietly, each unblinkingly staring into the other's eyes as the bogus ambulance continued its swaying journey through the darkening London streets. From above, Haversham heard a deep grumble of thunder and seconds later a burst of rain danced noisily on the vehicle's roof. Pavel reached into his left breast pocket and removed a packet of Sobrane cigarettes complete with black holders. He removed the holder, tore off the filter then reinserted the cigarette.

'You?' he asked, offering it to Haversham.

'Bad for one's health,' he answered wryly. Pavel laughed.

'So is being the Attorney General.' Despite the graveness of his position, Haversham forced a smile. Pavel lit up his Sobrane with a crude brass Zippo and inhaled languidly. The rain was now beating insistently on the roof in one long extended drum roll. Haversham could hear the swish of the ambulance's tyres as they cut through the deluge of water. Pavel's senses, finely tuned, felt the beginning of a slide as the vehicle banked into a corner. He heard a scream of 'Shit' from Serge the driver as it began to snake along the road.

Pavel snapped from his yoga position in an instant and leapt towards Haversham. He threw him roughly down to the space between the ambulance beds, then wedged himself on top. The lawyer screamed as his fingers were twisted underneath his body. The van was now travelling sideways, across the road. Impact was inevitable: a split second later it came. Serge screamed once more, then was silent. The left side of the van crumpled in towards them. Pavel dragged Haversham one foot away with all his strength. The van bounced off a wall, then crunched to a halt. The impact had set the siren and lights flaring and blaring.

Haversham looked up. Pavel was laid unconscious across him. Blood was seeping from a gash where his head had collided with the bed's restraint bar. Haversham summoned all his strength and pushed. Pavel was not that heavy, but his ordeal and the waistcoat hampered him. He took a deep breath and pushed once more. This time he managed to budge him. Pavel moaned. Haversham struggled sideways as Pavel's inert body slumped into the void he had created. Next he struggled to his knees, then painfully stretched one leg and hurled himself up. He staggered sideways once more and bounced off the bed rail with his hip: Christ that hurt.

He had to get away. He reached forward for the door handle, his back to Pavel and scrabbled for a hand-hold. Just then the emergency lights flicked on and startled him: he swivelled around. Pavel had a gun in his right hand; his left wiped away the blood from his wound.

'Leaving us so soon?' he muttered climbing to his feet. Haversham stopped dead. The man was insane enough to shoot, to kill him there and then. Pavel shouted, 'Serge! Lydia!'

A woman's voice answered, hollow and raspy. 'He's dead, I'm coming around.'

Haversham could hear the sirens; the police couldn't be far away. If he could just stall them . . . Pavel pushed past him and kicked open the ambulance door with a well-practised delivery.

'Now, Mr Prosecutor, we have to leave. If you struggle I will kill the first person I see, man, woman or child. It will be your fault.' Pavel jumped down.

Outside, the scene was utter chaos. The ambulance had left a trail of destruction in its wake. Several cars had piled up in front and behind. Car headlights, turned at impossible angles bathed the carnage in an eerie light. The rain continued to rip down. Haversham could hear the panicked screams of the injured and the dying. Each was tending to his own, the peace of Maida Vale shattered by Serge's loss of control.

Pavel gathered a coat around Haversham's shoulders to hide the Semtex waistcoat. Lydia limped round and took his arm. Pavel took the other. Haversham wanted to scream and shout but could not doubt that his captors would not hesitate to carry out their threat.

'Injured man,' Pavel shouted, 'let me through.' But the growing crowd was too riveted by the horrific occurrence to pay real attention to those lucky enough to walk away from the catastrophe. Haversham was bundled away down a side street, his vision swimming with the incessant rain. A tube sign caught his attention through the haze: St John's Wood. He had friends there, but they might as well have been in Kathmandu for all the help they could give him.

'Keep walking, Mr Prosecutor,' Pavel ordered from the corner of his mouth. 'Try to give anyone a sign and you sign their death warrant.'

Haversham walked, and wondered if he was walking to his death.

10.15 p.m., The Residents' Lounge, The Beaumont Hotel

'W ho developed X-rays and was the first winner of a Nobel Prize for Physics?' Alex, smiling, asked the Prof, holding the oblong Trivial Pursuit card in his hand. Pearl and Kaftan had three cheeses each, Alex two, but the Prof was struggling for his first triangle.

'Right up your street, this.' But the Prof was running data through his head, dragging the lake of his memory. After the outburst in the dining room, all the jury, except Bob and Stalin, had found their way to the residents' lounge. Battered chess boards, solitaire, a couple of decks of cards and the big green square of the TP game had been laid out in anticipation of their arrival.

Pitbull and Danno played a couple of hands of pontoon, before securing a run of *Independence Day* on the hotel video system, and left via the bar for a room to watch the patriotic 'shoot 'em up'. Denzel and Grace had hovered for a while before retiring, obviously and separately, for the night. Kalsi, fittingly, played solitaire, whilst the Mouse silently watched her concentrated endeavour.

'Come on,' Alex droned nasally, a pale imitation of Jeremy Paxman. The Prof smiled.

'Wilhelm Roentgen,' he pronounced grandly.

'Is the correct answer. Give the man a cheese,' Alex responded.

'Things are hotting up.' He winked at Pearl, who nodded knowingly.

'They certainly are, Alex, dear, and things will get a lot warmer before this is all over.' She sipped demurely from a china cup, as the Prof rolled again and moved his marker around the board to an Entertainment oblong. Alex read the question.

'Which page three girl once said, "I've always been a lot maturer than what I am"?' The Prof didn't even blink.

'Samantha Fox.'

Alex grinned. 'Bit of a fan?'

The Prof blushed slightly. 'Oh, some of the younger teachers used to leave copies of the *Sun* in the staff room.'

'Of course they did,' Pearl cooed sweetly, a definite sparkle in her wise eyes.

Kaftan laughed. 'Just a body, like anyone else's.'

Not quite, Alex thought, then continued his dialogue with Pearl.

'And how do you see the "game" progressing?'

She paused, the cup hovering inches away from her mouth.

'I think there are two very dedicated players in the field, each with different objectives and techniques.'

The Prof rolled once more, on to Geography, then excused himself for five minutes. Kaftan took the opportunity to visit the ladies' room.

'These players, do you think they are evenly matched?'

'One is young and impetuous, a lot to learn, the other's older and wiser, a lot to teach, but there won't be any lessons in this game.'

Alex nodded thoughtfully, and took a long pull on his nightcap of Remy Martin.

'How should the young one play it?'

'Cannily, craftily, like the older one would. My old man's a dab hand at chess, because he thinks ahead, plans, then puts his pieces where he wants them until . . .' She moved her cup over the top of Alex's brandy glass.

'A guilty verdict,' Alex whispered. Pearl tutted.

'I thought we were talking about Trivial Pursuit.' Her expression was slightly disapproving, but her eyes shone with amusement. Alex heard a voice behind him.

'Well there's one to bed.' It was Bob, busy and vigorous, walking

towards them. He pulled an over-stuffed armchair to the table.
'Aptly named game, young Alex?' The Prof and Kaftan entered
the lounge together; bickering about the relative merits of astrology
and astronomy. Alex looked across to Bob.

'What game do you prefer?'

'Lots of them, depends on the circumstances. This game,' he
gestured to the table, 'is fair enough, but you either know the answer
or you don't: no logic involved, you see, just knowledge; no skill,
just facts.'

The Prof and Kaftan had quietened, Pearl, hands joined across her
waist, listened intently.

'I'm losing this one badly,' Alex replied. Bob glanced down at the
table-top then back into Alex's eyes.

'I think you're learning as you go.'

'Let's play something else, Bob, any suggestions?'

'Well, I noticed they've got a snooker table here: you ever
played, Alex?'

'Time to time, not for a while. There was a three-quarter table at
university.'

'This one's full, big-time, fancy it?'

'You bet.'

'I never bet, even when I know the outcome.'

'It wasn't a question.'

'It wasn't an answer.'

Alex excused himself from the trivia game to the grumbles of the
Prof and the equanimity of Kaftan. Pearl nodded knowingly as they
departed.

Bob led the way from the lounge, down a slim corridor to a heavy
oak door marked 'Games Room' in scrolled writing on a brass plate.
Alex noticed one of the screws was missing. As they entered, Bob
reached to his left in the darkness and confidently pressed a light
switch that barely illuminated the gloomy interior. The table looked
huge and overwhelmed the room's dimensions. To its sides, Alex
could just make out the thin wooden benches for players to perch
upon and the large scoreboard with brass fittings affixed to the far
wall. Over the table a large bucket light hung menacingly from the
ceiling. Bob flicked another switch and the light flared up, where the
balls were already paraded in multi-coloured readiness. In silence

155

they both removed their jackets and selected a cue each. Alex had gazed down the length of several, checking for bends in the wood that would send a shot away from the true. Bob had chosen his without hesitation.

'Do you reckon they have the balls set up all the time then, Bob?'

The foreman shrugged and removed a coin from the pocket of his waistcoat which he flipped into the air and slapped down, covered, on the back of his hand.

'Heads,' Alex whispered. Bob raised his covering hand and nodded.

'Tails. You break.' He repocketed the coin quickly. Alex would have loved to have seen it. Bob smiled sharkily, as if he knew what Alex was thinking. Alex chalked his cue then positioned the white ball carefully on the D.

'No rush, Alex, a man must always know where he's starting from in order to finish properly.'

Alex struck the white sweetly. It contacted the triangle of reds with an angel's kiss, pushing one out to the side cushion, before returning obediently to within four inches of its starting point. Bob thumped the butt end of his cue appreciatively on the slatted wooden flooring.

'You *have* played before.'

'Played what?' Alex tempted him, but Bob was already lining up his shot and wasn't to be drawn. He snicked the loose red with the cue ball, sending it back into the pack and returning the white back up the table and behind the brown; Alex thumped his own cue appreciatively. 'Master stroke. Do you spend much time doing this?'

Bob perched on the rough bench and rechalked his cue end. 'Never exactly this, no, but a game is a game is a game; just takes a little thought, a little skill and . . .'

'A lot of luck?'

'If luck is the art of labouring under correct knowledge, then yes, it's about covering all the angles.'

'And you're very good at that, aren't you, Bob?'

'Take your shot.' Alex played off two cushions then the white rested gently against the pack.

'You're not giving me much to stick away, young Alex,' Bob muttered, searching for a safe haven for the white. Alex wanted to pull Bob out into the open, force him beyond subtext into truth.

'You've done all right so far, Bob.'

He nodded appreciatively. 'It's early yet, too early to really know the outcome, don't you think?'

'Beyond doubt, or should that be "beyond reasonable doubt"?'

Bob played a fine cut that rolled a red against another, where the shudder sent a red from the pack trundling into the corner pocket. The white settled nicely on the far side of the blue. With his cue, Alex racked up the first point on the scoreboard, the brass slide squeaking from lack of oil and use. Bob swiftly dispatched the blue; Alex added another five points to the total.

'Funny that expression, "beyond reasonable doubt",' Bob mused as he rechalked. 'Trips off the tongue for the judge and the lawyers, but I wonder what it really means? You're an educated bloke, Alex – university, a professional – what does it mean to you?' Bob kissed another red into the corner pocket, almost absentmindedly.

'So that I'm sure.'

'How sure can we really be of anything, Alex? Even ourselves. I mean, forgive the wanderings of an old man.'

'Only in the body, not the head,' Alex offered.

'Too kind, I'm sure. But who are we really? All these other people on the jury, do we know anything about them apart from the fact we've been thrown together by chance?' Bob attempted another cut on the blue, but it bobbled at the pocket's jaw.

'You seem to know everybody pretty well, Bob.'

'I like to take an interest.'

Alex went for a three-quarter shot which buried a red with a rewarding clunk, but he lost position; the white rolling, then stopping snug against the table's side.

'Got to think ahead, Alex, work it out: it's not just now that matters, it's what it leads to.'

'You're the second person tonight who's said that.'

Bob looked puzzled for a moment until a mental tumbler clicked and he smiled cannily. 'She's a fine, clever woman that one, a looker too, her old man's lucky. You won't find her struggling with what "reasonable doubt" might mean.'

'Not yet,' Alex replied, attempting a long pot on the brown into the corner pocket. This also bobbled, but then its momentum carried it on and in. 'Definitions might not change, but a point of view can.'

Bob mulled this over for a moment. 'And what does it take to make Alex Parrish change his point of view?'

'Heart and head together.'

'I always follow the head myself,' Bob replied.

'You see this shot?' Alex indicated a red which would have to be clipped at an impossible angle to hit the pocket. Bob nodded. 'Well my head tells me it can't be done, but my heart says "go for it", so what do I do?' Bob shrugged non-committally, but the overhead lamp caught his gaze of intense interest. 'Well, I tell my head that nothing is impossible and . . .' He slammed the white forward where it sent the red in question screaming sideways into the corner pocket. 'See, it's both head, heart and reason.'

Bob chalked up his new score. 'You took an enormous risk, very dangerous, the way the reds have spread: had you missed, then the game would have been over.'

'But I didn't and it isn't,' Alex said, walking right up to Bob and gazing into his alert eyes. 'It's far from over, we both know that.' Bob stared unflinchingly back. His eyes seemed deeper, denser, more powerful and knowing than any Alex had ever encountered. He almost shuddered. Bob spoke coldly.

'Always know the stakes, Mr Parrish.'

'I thought you never bet.'

'I'm a player not a punter; there's a difference between winnings and the prize.'

'What is the prize?'

'That, you have to work out for yourself.' Bob moved away to a seat. 'All this talk is putting me off my game.'

'Sorry,' Alex replied, unashamed by his insincerity. They played on in total silence, except when a fine shot or snooker was played with accuracy or stunning guile, then butts were brought noisily to the floor in grudging admiration. Alex had played well in the past, but never to this level of expertise. He felt he was playing for a greater prize than mere victory in this game; it sounded silly, but he felt as if he were playing for Jenny Fox's life.

The game swung from one to the other, then back again. Alex

potted dangerously whilst Bob played the waiting game, always leaving a difficult but enticing shot. Bob racked up points by wily snookers, Alex with red and colour combinations. It was a black-ball game. With seven points on the table, Bob led by six. They both needed it for victory. It nestled against the balk cushion, the white almost on the black's spot at the opposing end. Alex's polo shirt clung damply on his back. He was pleased to see that even the wrinkled forehead of the adroitly cool Bob was perspiring gently.

It was Alex's shot, having sunk the pink to close the gap. Alex was more nervous than he had ever been. Examinations of every description faded into insignificance against the apprehension of the next few minutes. He looked at his opponent: what would you do now, Bob? How would you play this thing out? Alex remembered what Pearl had said about their different approaches; at that moment he decided to change his *modus operandi*. Alex stared down his cue. The black seemed impossibly far away, the ball telescoping away from him across miles of green baize. It had to be exact. The position of both balls was vital if it was to come off. He took a deep breath then, just as he was about to bring the cue forward for impact, began to exhale slowly. He struck it smoothly. The white trundled forward, slowly eating the gap. It struck the black gently. The black rebounded from the end cushion at an angle, as did the white, but the collision had robbed it of some of its momentum. The black wandered towards the middle pocket, the white at an angle that split the degrees between the corner pocket and the black.

'Shit,' Alex whispered. Bob looked confident until he viewed the shot from behind his own cue. It wasn't the black that was the problem, that was an easy shot. It was where the white ball went after. Alex knew Bob would have to play the shot with backspin to avoid the white being swallowed by the corner pocket's hungry jaws. Backspin was not his most proficient shot, but the temptation to take the chance was overwhelming. Bob tried to relax. He rolled his shoulders in an attempt to unravel the knots of tension.

'Just a game, Bob,' Alex whispered. Bob glared in response. He went for it. Alex heard the strike, heard the plop of the black as it in turn was struck, then the thud of its acceptance by the netting of the pocket. But two pairs of eyes were riveted on the white. It was slow, impossibly slow, yet it continued to move off one cushion back towards the corner pocket. Alex couldn't breathe as it continued its inexorable progress. Bob's eyes were narrowed as it appeared to almost come to a halt, before a loose piece of chalk on the baize gave it a kick. It rattled quietly against the jaws before it paused, as if gasping for air, then, defying gravity no longer, dropped into the pocket.

'Foul, seven points. I'll re-spot,' Alex offered, but Bob appeared shattered by the whole experience.

'No, it's your game, Alex. I won't say it was fair and square, but you drew me in, played me at my own game, played to my weakness.'

Their handshake was firm, with no suggestion of a re-match, at least not in the snooker room. There was another battlefield where they knew they would soon meet.

10.32 p.m., Prime Minister's Jaguar

Emma Haversham sat in silence as her husband waited for the telephone at Counter Terrorism and Contingency Planning to be answered. They had left Geoffrey Haversham's mews home and were heading back to Downing Street with the files from his computer loaded on to seven floppy disks.

'Superintendent Prince, it's . . .'

'It's quite all right, sir, I recognise your voice. I assume you got the transcripts.'

'We did, thank you, but we need some more information.'

'I'll do my best to help.'

'OK. I want you to get someone down to the records department at the Bailey now and liberate the judge's notebook for the period the third of February.'

'It shouldn't be a problem, we already have someone down there watching the court building and surrounding area.'

'Good. When you have it, can you fax a copy straight away to my private line at Downing Street. You can get the number from Donald Taylor.'

'Affirmative, sir.'

'I'll call you to confirm once it comes through.'

'Why the third of February?'

'There was a preliminary application to Court that day in the Fox case and we need to see the substance of it.'

'Anything we can help with?'

'I'm not sure yet. The noting junior on the case said something about it which we can't ignore.'

'Do you have any idea what sort of application it was?'

'Yes. It involved the withholding of certain documentation on the grounds of public interest but that's all we know.'

'The defence were not aware of it, then?'

'That's right. It must have been made on an ex-parte basis with only the judge and the prosecution present at the hearing.'

'We should have it, sir, by the time you arrive back. Good luck.'

'What's happening at your end?'

'We think it's likely that the stronghold used by the kidnappers was a fake ambulance. They were mobile all the time; no wonder we couldn't locate him.'

'How do you know all this?'

'We have had some information from COBRA.'

'Spit it out, superintendent.'

'The information was regarding a serious RTA in Maida Vale.'

'What!'

'Traffic reported the incident at around nine thirty. The area is still being searched for any sign of your brother but nothing as yet. The ambulance was written off with heavy front end damage and the driver was killed outright.'

'Christ almighty!'

'Look, there's no reason to believe at present that your brother has been injured.'

'Did nobody witness it?'

'Officers are still taking statements but there's no sign of them at all, so if he's managed to get away from the scene he must be on foot, and if he's managed to do that then he can't be in bad shape.'

'What else do you have?'

'There is some bloodstaining in the back of the ambulance which is being tested for a match to the Attorney General but we don't have the results just yet.'

'The tide is turning against them, superintendent. I only hope this character doesn't start behaving like King Canute. Keep me posted if you hear anything else.'

'That's affirmative, sir.'

10.36 p.m., The Sewers, Central London

Pavel knew the authorities would be searching for them by now. Once the police and emergency services had cleared the debris and accounted for the dead, the conundrum of the ambulance would be posed: 'Where did it come from and where are the crew?' The intelligence services would have little difficulty in putting the pieces together. He held the British in high regard. Like his hostage, they were passionless and hidebound by protocol, but once decided they would stop at nothing to achieve the desired result. They would have descriptions by now. Two men, one bleeding from the head, the other strapped into a bulky waistcoat; one woman, slim, dark hair, limping badly.

Pavel turned to his right. Lydia grimaced as she placed one painful foot in front of the other. A good soldier, Pavel thought. Serge too was a good man on the ground; soon he would be six feet underneath it. They had undergone many operations together, one too many as it had transpired, but there was no time to mourn now.

Haversham was looking tired, but Pavel reminded himself that the lawyer had been through an ordeal few could cope with. They walked the sewers of London, having no other choice. Pavel had wrestled the top from a manhole cover at the back of St John's Wood

162

tube station, then Lydia, Haversham and he had lowered themselves into its murky depths. They had been walking for just over an hour. Pavel had to steer them three miles to where the back-up van was locked from sight in a rented garage. He used his compass to keep them in the right direction and prayed that their descent had not been witnessed.

The storm had passed but the rainwater continued to flood their shoes as they walked. The three squelched tiredly, Pavel's torch illuminating the way only dimly. It was just enough to keep the rats at bay. He could hear their fractious squeaking echo in between their wet footfalls. Haversham was breathing hard; his own head throbbed, but that discomfort was minor compared to the weariness of the rest of his aching body. He was careful with the wound, to which Lydia had skilfully applied a field dressing, mindful that rat's urine could cause Weil's disease if it came into contact with a cut. One of his comrades had fallen to that disgusting illness, it was no way for a man with dignity to die. Pavel knew one thing for certain: when his time came he would be remembered for his dignity not for his disgrace.

Haversham spoke.

'I need to rest.'

'We all do,' Pavel replied. 'That does not mean that we can.'

Before them the tunnel split into three forks. Pavel checked his compass, and steered Haversham to the west; Lydia's breathing was becoming raspier with a defined rattle at the end of her exhalation.

'It's not just your leg, is it?'

'I will survive,' she whispered, forcing her injured leg forward once more.

'We rest,' Pavel declared. Haversham slumped back against the concave brick wall; Lydia glared at her leader.

'I need to rest, Lydia,' he explained unconvincingly.

'Five minutes and no longer,' she demanded and checked her wristwatch. Pavel nodded grimly, then bent down to rest his buttocks on the back of his heels.

'She's badly hurt, Pavel,' Haversham gasped. 'You've lost one friend, why risk another?'

'Silence, Mr Prosecutor,' Pavel demanded. 'You lawyers: so much wind and piss, no substance. The same in my country.'

Haversham forced some fetid air through his straining lungs. 'I thought you had no country.'

Pavel looked up through the gloom and switched his torch on to Haversham's pale face.

'You listen well, perhaps too well: it could be fatal.'

Haversham forced a pencil-thin smile.

'No, a route march through a rat-infested sewer, that's fatal – as is a major car crash and being shot in the neck with a dart – but picking you up on inconsistencies in your sales pitch is not.'

Pavel nodded.

'You are right, Mr Prosecutor, luck seems to be on your side. Let us hope your brother is sharing the same fortune.'

Haversham looked around the sewer and pointed to the floor, where human excrement and condoms sailed past.

'This is hardly what I would call winning the lottery.'

'You are luckier than Jenny Fox,' Pavel spat, 'she will spend the rest of her life in conditions like this if I fail.'

'You may have failed already: what if the jury have already returned a verdict?'

Pavel looked sly and removed a telephone pager from his pocket.

'Then I would know, and you would be dead.'

Haversham took another gulp of stale air.

'Enough talk,' Lydia wheezed. 'We have far to go.'

Pavel rose abruptly and whispered, 'The woods are lovely, dark and deep, and I have promises to keep and miles to go before I sleep.'

'Robert Frost,' the Attorney General said, recognising the poem from his school days. 'And tell me, Pavel, does the world end in "Fire or Ice"?'

Pavel began to walk.

'Just in pain, Mr Prosecutor, just in pain.'

10.43 p.m., The Albert Bar, The Beaumont Hotel

The Prof sat alone, the bar now deserted, the muzak the overdue victim of a mercy killing. The barman looked pointedly at his watch as Alex ordered a large cognac and shuffled over to join his fellow jury member. The Prof was scribbling notes in a loose-leaf binder distractedly, but took a second out to nod Alex to an adjacent chair.

As he sat, taking a slug from the bulbous glass, he could feel the tension throbbing across his shoulders and neck. It was as if he had run a half-marathon rather than pushed a few balls around the green baize. It had been more than a game of snooker, more than a battle of wills, more like a war. Like two opposing generals on the eve of bloodshed, marking out the rules of engagment, they had each laid down their ideological markers for the following day; Alex exhaled slowly.

'Tired?' the Prof asked.

Alex shrugged. 'Long day. You?'

'Never sleep much since my wife passed on.'

Alex nodded solemnly, feeling equal measures of sympathy for the Prof's loss and embarrassment for the unsolicited intimacy.

'It was a long time ago,' the Prof muttered. 'But my work is my comfort now, that and my grandchildren.'

'See much of them?'

165

'Difficult. They live in Australia, Adelaide.' He scribbled as he talked, without raising his eyes from the binder. 'But you know, British Telecom, "It's good to talk".'

'Good to talk about most things,' Alex replied. 'Like today: healthy debate, different points of view. Funny how we all approach things so differently.'

The Prof nodded, then looked up over his thick-lensed glasses.

'None of us walked into this trial newly born. We all bring with us different histories and experience. For my part I'm a scientist, facts are my god and logic my religion.'

'Any room for mercy?'

'Of course, but only if the facts prove that it is deserving, indiscriminate mercy is merely weakness; it devalues its own coinage.'

'Shouldn't it come first?'

'It all depends on the initial situation. Precious little mercy was shown to Easterman or the security guard; *ergo*, Jennifer Fox should in all fairness be placed in the same position until she proves otherwise.'

Alex took another swig of the smoothly burning liquid.

'Guilty until proved innocent?' he asked evenly.

'That isn't quite what I said.' The Prof's voice had developed an edge.

'Isn't it? In an experiment you might anticipate results but until they physically exist you keep an open mind, just in case. Yet in this trial isn't it too easy to accept without questioning?'

'Clearly not for you, but I am more than satisfied that the scientific evidence in the case is overwhelming. These experts we have heard are the top men in their fields and the defence have chosen not to challenge their findings.'

'Isn't that what we are meant to conclude?'

The Prof shook his head.

'You're going to tell me about the man on the grassy knoll next. No, Alex, that's not the way it works, at least not for me. If you are looking for another convert to your crusade then your judgement is wanting.'

'What would it take to change your mind?'

'More than you can offer, Alex. The evidence is closed. The

experiment is over, all the results are in, you know my conclusion.'

Alex pressed on.

'But what if I could prove that there can be a different conclusion based on the same facts?'

The Prof pushed himself up from the chair and assembled his notes.

'Can you?' He watched intently and waited in vain for a reply. 'I'll bid you good night, Alex.'

'Would you listen if I could?'

'We were told, ordered, not to discuss the case and however unrealistic that may be, we must obey. Besides, you'll have your say tomorrow.'

Alex was left alone. He hadn't meant it to go that way; Bob wouldn't have allowed it to. No, he would have steered a more canny course through the conversation until he reached his intended port of call. He had to think like Bob, anticipate and execute like he did. Instead he had insulted a decent, lonely man. Alex finished his drink and returned his glass to the scowling barman.

'I'll settle my bill now,' he said, reaching inside his pocket for his wallet; but it was gone. 'Must have dropped it,' he muttered, 'sorry.' He left to return to the snooker room.

The corridor was silent as he approached, then just as his hand reached for the door handle he heard a gasp from inside, followed by very heavy breathing. Christ, it could be Bob in the throes of a heart attack or some kind of fit. Alex threw open the door quickly, the room was in darkness. He reached for the light switch, shouted 'Bob, Bob, are you OK?' and flicked it on. His eyes swept the room, then fixed on the top of the snooker table where two figures were frozen in a sexual tableau. Her little black number was wrenched up high on her thighs, his buttocks had stopped thrusting and glistened with sweat. It was Grace and Denzel. Her eyes were screwed shut in horror, his whites, impossibly bright in the half-gloom, bored into Alex's.

'Sorry, I . . .' Alex began, then hastily switched off the light, pulled the door to and began to walk away.

'Alex!' Denzel shouted after him. He turned; Denzel was hanging out of the door, zipping up his fly.

'Come back, man.'

Alex continued to walk.

'None of my business,' he replied over his shoulder.

'Please, hey, it's not as if it's a crime.'

'Exactly.'

'Not for me, for the lady.'

Alex stopped. He had seen enough of Grace during the preceding months to anticipate that her life would crumble without her spotless reputation, and being discovered with her dress around her hips in the grip of adultery might not be the key to looking the world right in the eye.

'OK. I was just looking for my wallet.'

'Whatever,' Denzel replied, his eyes flitting behind Alex to ensure that there were no other witnesses to the scene. 'Just come back in. If this lady ain't got her class, she ain't got jack.'

He turned and knocked on the open door, whispered 'room service' and re-entered, Alex following behind. Grace was lighting a cigarette. Her hand shaking slightly, her hair mussed and damp, she stood against the table with her eyes fixed on the baize.

'It isn't how it looks.'

Alex shrugged, any reply inadequate.

'I mean, it is but it isn't. You don't know the pressures.'

'Like I said, not my business. If you two want to get it on, then that's your affair.'

Grace glared at him.

'Sorry, wrong choice of word.' He moved to the back of the room where his jacket had lain, and there on the floor was his wallet. He stooped to retrieve it, showed it to them with a flourish and smiled.

'Look, I'm not going to say anything, sorry to interrupt. But I'm an open-minded man: people have their reasons for all kinds of behaviour.'

'You promise you won't say anything?' Grace asked, her voice a little-girl whisper.

What would Bob do in this situation? Alex wondered – probably use it to his own advantage, milk it like a prize Friesian. He was torn. It would be dishonest to use their predicament to further his own ends, but to balance the problem they were both in the 'guilty'

168

camp and Jenny Fox was in desperate need of friends, however reluctant.

'Well, from what I could see, you weren't discussing the case.'

Denzel laughed, but a harsh look from Grace stifled his amusement.

'But I'll trade with you. If you each answer me one question, then I never walked in here.'

'You can't buy my vote, man,' Denzel warned. Grace did not appear so sure.

'I'm not trying to, and I swear that it will not touch directly on the trial.'

Denzel glanced across at Grace and waited for her to consider the offer. She was quick to nod her agreement. Denzel pushed out his bottom lip and raised his eyebrows, awaiting the question.

'Have either of you had anything to do with Uncle Bob outside of the case?'

'Strange question, Alex,' Denzel said.

'Humour me.'

'Ladies first,' Denzel suggested.

'I don't feel much like a lady,' Grace whispered, drawing heavily on her cigarette and exhaling slowly like the anti-heroine of a film noir. 'The answer is yes.'

'Curious mix,' Alex replied.

'Is that us, or Bob and me?' Grace responded icily.

'How?' Alex wanted details.

'A couple of weeks ago, when we . . .' She indicated Denzel with a languid flap of her slim wrist. 'Anyway, it was during a lunchtime adjournment: I'd been having some problems at home, considering my options, not for the first time, when Bob asked me if things were OK. He was very kind, understanding, you know?'

Alex knew only too well.

'The circle I move in is not renowned for its ability to keep secrets: you just have to think something and five minutes later there's a bulletin on the squash club noticeboard with chapter and verse. Bob listened very patiently, non-judgementally: it's as if he has this ability to draw the truth out of one.'

169

'What did he say?' Alex asked, feeling the awakenings of sympathy for the brittle woman and her life in the shallow end of society.

'That you can't legislate for the human heart. He said it was more than a fleshy pump for circulating blood around the body and infinitely more complex than an illustration on a Valentine's card.'

'Very profound,' Alex remarked, once more impressed by Bob's numerous abilities; now, it transpired he was an agony uncle. 'I bet he gave you an example of that.'

Grace's eyes widened.

'How did you . . . ?'

'Lucky guess,' Alex replied, his brain clicking into the rhythm of Bob's. 'Let me have another shot in the dark.' Grace nodded for him to continue. 'He talked about Jenny Fox, said that she cared so much about her work with the leukaemia victims that she lost control and snapped.'

Grace's eyebrows were knotted suspiciously.

'Alex, were you listening?'

'No, just playing the averages. So his rules about not discussing the case were ignored?'

'He said he felt bad about that, but we were all just human, particularly Jenny Fox and that the judge would take that into account when he sentenced her.'

Alex shook his head.

'There's only one sentence for murder and that's life imprisonment. He had you convicting her weeks ago, before we even finished with the evidence. Is that fair?'

Grace shook her head.

'It just sounded so reasonable at the time.'

'And how do things look now?' Alex asked, staring hard at the centre of the table, where a clear oval imprint lay against the nap of the baize. Grace blushed.

'Clearer.'

'Steady, Alex,' Denzel said, his voice low, menacing. Alex forged on regardless; at last he was getting somewhere.

'Look, Bob wasn't buying your vote, he was charming it out of you. Did he say or do anything that made you suspicious?'

'One question, Alex, that was the deal,' Denzel replied for her.

'I can answer for myself. You're my lover, not my mouthpiece.'

Denzel raised his hands in the air, palms upwards.

'There was one thing. It probably isn't important, but he knew my husband's name. He said Giles and I had a lot of talking to do, but the thing is, I can't remember ever telling him anything about my husband; there was no reason to.'

Alex smiled, he had experienced a similar situation. He turned to Denzel.

'Well?'

'It's private.' Denzel's chin was firmly set.

'You agreed.'

Denzel folded his arms, looked to Grace, who was staring back at him hard, willing him not to welsh.

'OK. Like before, no further than this room. I got a brother, a bit wild you know, runs with some naughty boys, but he's impressed by a little bit of flash, some wheels and ready cash. Not a bad boy, just . . .'

'Misguided?' Alex suggested.

'Anyway, first week of the trial, gets busted for possession of six tabs of E on a suss stop. This puts him in breach of probation for the same thing; he's going away, man, no doubts. I get the call to go to the station, midnight. I'm tired, he needs someone, I go. Anyway, I'm walking up to the desk, when Bob comes out from behind the door. He's shaking hands with some uniformed brass, then he sees me, puts the "man" on hold and gets the story from me. Then it was just like magic: twenty minutes later, my little brother is released without charge. I owe him.'

'What did your brother say about the offence?'

'That he was set up, the stuff was planted by a drugs squad officer.'

'Did you believe him?'

Denzel pursed his lips. 'He's no liar. He may be guilty of many things, but he's always honest with me.'

'Did you find out what Bob was doing there?'

'Tried to, but hey, I was grateful, wasn't going to push too

171

far. I tried to thank him, he said it was nothing; asked him if there was anything I could do for him, he said no, then maybe. Said I shouldn't be suspicious of all police, that the ones in the trial were different, to be respected. If Bob the man respects them, then that's my road.' Alex wondered how many other members of the jury had crossed the remarkable Bob's path during the trial.

'Don't you think it's a stunning coincidence that a man you have never met before in your life suddenly turns up at a police station and arranges your brother's release?'

Denzel pushed his hands into his trouser pockets.

'Like I said, grateful, but what are you getting at, Alex?'

'Tomorrow, OK? All I ask from you is that you do what you promised to do at the start of all this and keep an open mind.'

'I won't be blackmailed,' Grace said.

'And I'm not a blackmailer,' Alex replied angrily. 'I thought that was obvious. If I was, I'd be threatening to call your husband as soon as this thing is over, but I'm not.'

'What exactly are you doing, Alex?' Denzel asked, intrigued.

'Giving Jenny Fox what she deserves, a fair trial.'

'She's already had that,' Grace replied.

'Oh no, she's had a trial all right, but the more I hear the more I'm convinced it's anything but fair.' Alex walked towards the door, then turned. 'If by the time we've gone round the clock, you're still convinced of her guilt, then so be it, but if you have any doubt at all, you vote with me?'

'And if we don't agree?' Grace asked.

'Then nothing, no threat, no ultimatum, just an appeal to your sense of fairness.'

'OK by me,' Denzel replied. Alex looked towards Grace, who nodded her agreement.

'Then I'll say good night. One thing.' They both looked towards him. 'There's one question you might want to ask yourselves: who stands to gain from Jenny Fox's conviction?'

Alex pulled the door closed gently behind him. It was time for bed, if not to sleep at least to think, to plot and plan, to scheme and conquer, just like Bob. Who are you, Robert Orde? Who are you really?

11.15 p.m., Prime Minister's Private Quarters, 10 Downing Street

Emma Haversham waited patiently for her husband to retrieve another page from the fax machine, which had been busy spilling data since they had arrived back from Geoffrey's house. The contents of the judge's notebook proved that there had indeed been an application to withhold evidence upon the ground of public interest immunity made well before Geoffrey Haversham inherited the case, after the general election in April. Eventually they held fifteen flimsy sheets detailing the hearing on 3 February before Mr Justice Broomfield.

'Broomfield isn't the trial judge though, is he?'

'No, but it doesn't matter; any judge can hear preliminary applications. It's desirable but not essential, that the trial judge should adjudicate, especially when such applications are made without the defence being allowed to participate.'

'So it's possible that the court hearing the trial knows nothing about these documents?'

'I'd say that it's highly probable.'

'Unless the trial judge has looked right the way through the court record.'

'That's right, but why would he do that unless someone had drawn particular attention to it? Remember, the defence have no idea that this application was ever made and the Crown have got what they want so the trial goes ahead with whatever evidence is contained in the main bundles.'

'In effect, Broomfield was being asked to assess the materiality of these documents without really knowing what Fox's defence was. Is that what you're saying here?'

'He may have been given some rough idea but without the defence being present to balance the argument does it matter?'

'But how could he possibly perform that function with any degree of fairness?'

'He doesn't have to, you should know that. The only basis for a successful application against disclosure is for the Crown to satisfy him that it would be in some way injurious to the public interest or the affairs of state to release the information.'

'And no questions asked?'

''Fraid so, that's the criterion and it's as wide as the Thames estuary when you think about it.'

'So whatever is contained in the list he has deemed to be privileged?'

'Until such time as it becomes of historical interest only, yes.'

'What we really need is to see the physical documents themselves.'

'Yes, but let's go through it step by step first,' Emma suggested. 'That way we may be able to isolate something in particular. This lot is hiding a mound of paper.'

'Right. Whose name is on the application?' the Prime Minister asked.

'Rowlands, the ex-Attorney General.'

'Was he the one who appeared in front of the judge?'

'Along with Brannigan and Baker.'

'So basically a decision was made to extract some of the documents gathered from the initial police investigation and claim privilege over them.'

'Yes.'

'Right. What's the first entry in the notebook?'

'It's a précis of Rowlands' submissions and a record of the formal ex-parte notice.'

'Go on.'

'Rowlands was saying that basically the Laboratory was a government institution and any documentation generated by its day to day functioning was therefore subject to privilege and ultimately immunity since it is in fact owned by the government department responsible for its administration and running costs.'

'The Department of Trade and Industry.'

174

'That's right.'

'So the Minister of State must have overall responsibility?'

'Yes. There's a reference here to an affidavit sworn in support of the application by Julian Walsh the Secretary of State at the time. The judge has then gone on to list all the separate documents that come under the umbrella.'

'What are they?'

'First thing on the list is an entire library of records relating to all the chemical samples submitted for examination by commercial manufacturers in order to gain export licences.'

'There must be thousands of them.'

'At least twenty a day since the lab's inception in 1988.'

'What else?'

'Second heading is Dr Easterman's private journals.'

'Anything listed underneath?'

'No, it's just a blanket title, there could be anything in that lot from his working notes to personal itinerary.'

'Go on to the next.'

'There's a huge section dealing with what looks like the analytical tables held by the DTI in relation to the largest manufacturers of chemicals in the country.'

'Pass that one over.'

Emma handed the sheet over and Haversham studied it for a few moments. 'Just a second. Just a second now,' he exclaimed. 'What do you make of this?'

'What is it?'

He handed the page back.

'There's a long list of statements that have been shown to the judge concerning a company called Biotron Limited. It doesn't detail what was in them but why would they be withheld from the defence? I'll get on to Ray Prince immediately. Where will this lot be stored?'

'At the Director of Public Prosecutions' Offices, I should imagine.'

Haversham turned to Emma. 'Get on to Donald Taylor. Tell him to organise a skeleton staff to work through the night and put the DTI on alert. I want to speak with their minister in due course.'

2.00 a.m., Uncle Bob's Room, The Beaumont Hotel

Robert Orde lay on a life-support machine with little chance of recovery, his brain in a vegetative state since the blood clot had starved his craving organs of their needs. That was the real Robert Orde, widower from the East End, watchmaker, no children. The man who had assumed his identity sat on his bed pondering the next move.

He had searched for the right candidate for months until this shallow breathing husk had come to his attention. It was necessary if not vital to the operation. Having selected his persona, the next problem was ensuring that the ailing pensioner was chosen from the electoral roll for jury service. With the hackers and crackers at his call it was no more than a cursor away to ensure that for the week of Jenny Fox's trial Robert Orde would be present.

It was a simple matter to gain entry to Robert Orde's sparse flat awaiting the slap on the hall floor of the brown buff envelope marked 'Lord Chancellor's Department'. The pool had narrowed from the voters of Greater London to a panel of fifty – four jurors and two spares – this was where human intervention threatened his planning. A clerk of the court could very easily select everybody but Robert Orde from the regularly shuffled jury cards and this was why he had spent the month preceding the trial getting to know the clerk. What an amazing coincidence that Bob should be in the deck of jurors.

But the clerk knew of his fascination with the law, his loneliness, his willingness to do his public duty. Many of the other potential jurors had manufactured excuses to avoid a month-long trial, but not 'Bob'. The clerk had a twinkle in his eye as the name 'Robert Orde' was read to the court and he, satisfied with a hard job done well, took his place with the other eleven.

Thereafter it was merely a question of ingratiating himself with the other jurors. That, compared to engineering his appearance on the jury, was very easy meat. The same hackers researched the other eleven and by the end of the first week of the trial 'Bob' knew everything about them except their favoured position for sex and even that information was obtainable if it mattered. Then began the subtle process of subversion.

His employers believed in overkill. He had argued, without success, that the evidence in the case was of such magnitude that the jury would come to the correct conclusion without interference; after all, that was how he had planned it. But they felt unable to take the risk. He now knew that they were right: Alex Parrish, Alexander James Parrish, architect and bachelor, keen sports and business man, now septic thorn in his side, an unwanted intrusion to be removed. The question was how?

He stretched, painfully aware that his medically ordained exercise routine had been a necessary sacrifice to remain in character, and tapped a finger on his knee. Parrish *had* to be removed; his influence with the jury was growing not diminishing. The paymasters would not be willing to meet their end of the contract if Fox was acquitted; neither could they afford a re-trial, the chances of threading one of their own inside again were slim.

He leaned down and under his bed, reached into a holdall and removed a plastic-wrapped package. Inside it was a tiny high-powered mobile phone. This was an emergency-only contingency, to be used once and once only, without providing any log of cross-referencing numbers for interested parties. It was registered under a bogus name and paid for six months in advance.

He paused, following his own orders. Is it necessary? Yes. But is it vital? The answer, after a moment's hesitation, the same. Will this place me in future difficulty? Possibly, he replied to himself, but if it works it will remove the problem. With that he keyed in a number, listened as the beeps sped the information through the night sky, heard the pulse of the ring at the far end, then a voice.

'*Times* newspaper, night editor, what can I do for you?'

Bob raised his tone of voice and his accent before replying.

'It's what I can do for you. How would you like the inside track on the jury's deliberations in the Jenny Fox trial?'

Alex's Room, The Beaumont

The hammering on his door dragged him quickly from a listless sleep. He glanced towards his watch on the table: it was 2.30 a.m.

'What is it?' he shouted. 'What's going on?' as he wrapped a towel around his waist and wrenched the door open. It was Bob dressed in striped pyjamas; he looked worried.

'What's the problem, Bob?'

'It's Dave Conran,' Bob whispered. 'I heard noises, groaning. I knocked on his door; couldn't get any answer. I'm worried, Alex. He's under a lot of stress, probably had too much to drink. I gave him a couple of sleeping tablets; wish I hadn't now.' Alex could see that Bob's chest was rising and falling rapidly. He placed a comforting hand on the foreman's shoulder.

'Look, you stay here, I'll try and wake him. If I can't we'll get the ushers: they'll get the night porter to open the door.'

Bob nodded miserably as Alex crossed the corridor swiftly. He rapped firmly on Stalin's door.

'Dave, Dave Conran, it's me, Alex Parrish. Bob was worried about you.'

He turned to give Bob an encouraging smile, but the foreman had disappeared inside Alex's room. Alex tried again, reaching forward to knock more firmly when the door was wrenched open. Stalin's face was crimson with beer and fury.

'What the fuck are you playing at, Parrish?' he stuck a finger into Alex's chest. 'Is this the next tack to change my mind, sleep deprivation?'

'Like I said, Bob was worried about you,' Alex replied uncertainly. He spun around. There behind him stood their foreman.

'Alex is right, Dave, I thought I heard something from your room, tried to wake you. I was worried, sorry.'

Stalin's face slackened as he rubbed it.

'No harm done, Uncle Bob, nice to know someone cares,' he said, glaring at Alex.

'Cheers,' Alex replied as he searched Bob's face for any sign that this was some kind of engineered set-up. The old man just appeared relieved that Stalin was alive.

'You've recovered quickly,' Alex muttered on the way back to his room.

'I'm sorry, truly I am.'

Alex kept walking, then, on an impulse, turned his head quickly back to Bob, who was smiling triumphantly, but once caught slid his features back to a caring frown.

'I'm sure,' Alex muttered, closing the door to the bedroom behind him. He was suspicious. Stalin had come to the door like a half-castrated bull. It had taken just one firm knock to wake him. So, why had Bob woken him? There were others – Pitbull and Danno, even the Prof – who would feature higher up the level of preference than he, yet it was his door that Uncle Bob had come knocking at.

It was his smile that had said it all, when Alex's quick spin had caught him with his well-prepared guard down. It said, 'I've won, young Alex, you don't know it yet, but I have.' But won what? And how? If there was nothing wrong with Stalin, apart from any redeeming features, that is, then Bob's arrival was a ruse. If it was a ruse, it had a purpose and obviously required only a few seconds to carry that purpose through. Bob either had to be searching for something, but there was too little time for that, or leaving something for someone else to find.

Alex began to hunt through his room. His holdall provided no more surprises than stale socks and underwear, the bed and mattress nothing but fluff and a couple of ancient unpleasant stains. He thrust his arm down the side of the armchair but only discovered an old ten-pence piece and a safety pin. His trawl through the bathroom was equally fruitless. He forced himself to think like Bob. Where would the doughty foreman hide something? After a couple of seconds, Alex thought he had the answer; in plain sight.

Alex screwed his eyes closed and tried to visualise the room as it was before he had switched off the bedside lamp. He reopened them and went through a mental inventory, trouser press, kettle, cup

180

and saucer, vase of flowers, Gideon bible, television set, remote control. He paused; remote control. The small piece of black plastic lay inoffensively on top of the set. He hadn't used it – with the ban on television he had no reason to – yet he was sure that its control buttons were facing upwards when he had checked into the room; now they were hidden. Alex moved towards it. Outside he heard the shriek of sirens. He pulled back the curtain to look out on the grounds where three marked police cars were drawing to a savage gravel-crunching halt and somehow he knew that their arrival was linked directly to Bob.

Alex reached down to the remote and flicked it on to its back; the cheap plastic control box had been miraculously transmuted into a state-of-the-art mobile telephone – with trouble stamped all over it. It had obviously been planted by Bob, for whatever reason Alex could only guess. He had to act quickly, but what could he do? If he hid the phone, it would be found. If he accused Bob of planting it, he would never be believed. No, he had to use it to his own advantage. Alex quickly pulled some boxer shorts on and sprang for his door. He padded down the corridor to Stalin's room.

He was working on the assumption that Stalin would not have bothered to relock his door after Alex had disturbed him. He didn't have much time. He grasped the handle and turned it; he was right. He held his breath and swung the door open gently, Stalin's snoring told him the rest. Alex gingerly stepped over to the television set and felt around for the remote control. He found it with his foot, the television flared into life; he repeated the operation immediately, it turned itself back off. Stalin didn't budge. Alex reached down, picked up the remote and carefully wiped the mobile free of fingerprints. He could hear shouting from the stairway. He dropped it next to the set and padded back to the corridor.

He could hear boots thundering up the stairs as he sprinted across the hall into his own room, and barely had time to switch off his light and scamper back into bed before a series of savage knocks echoed on all the landing's doors. Alex placed a towel around him and answered the door. A stern looking policeman informed him that the judge had given orders to search all their rooms. They were to dress and assemble on the landing. Alex attempted to appear bemused by the entire proceedings and to an extent was helped by the fact that he was genuinely puzzled.

Outside, Pitbull, Danno, the Prof and Uncle Bob stood shrugging their incomprehension as their rooms were systematically searched. Stalin appeared too, grumbling about needing a good night's sleep. Five puzzled minutes later a triumphant PC emerged from Stalin's room clutching a small mobile phone. Alex turned to watch Uncle Bob, who appeared confused for a moment, but only a moment, before turning to Alex and nodding just once; whatever was meant to happen to Alex would now happen to Stalin, one of the 'guilties'.

Stalin was marched away without explanation, but Bob sought one from Edna the usher. She explained that each of them would have a guard for the night, that they were not to discuss anything until their return to court. The men peeled away, until only Bob, Alex and their minders were left on the landing. Alex glared across the divide but Bob just smiled. Alex nodded grimly and mouthed the words 'see you in court'. Bob shook his head, still in character, decent and honest.

Alex breathed a massive sigh of relief when he collapsed into bed. He felt bad about Stalin: bad, but not distraught. The man was the worst kind of boor, but whatever shit was coming his way wasn't deserved. But Alex had no option. Bob wanted him off the jury. He had tried and failed. For reasons known only to himself Uncle Bob desperately wanted to see Jenny Fox convicted and Alex wasn't going to allow that to happen. He had seen the face of the enemy and it had wrinkles and a benevolent frown, but the morals of a monkey house and the soul of a tiger shark.

2.36 a.m., Prime Minister's Study, 10 Downing Street

The Prime Minister walked over from the drinks cabinet with a tumbler of malt swilling around effortlessly in a clear crystal glass. He glanced at Emma who had fallen asleep in the armchair. He bent down to remove her reading glasses gently, which were threatening to topple off the bridge of her nose. If she was uncomfortable she was too tired to notice. One leg was tucked beneath her, the other dangled inches over the heap of papers on the floor. Haversham resumed pacing the room, still trying to work through the ever-growing conundrum posed by the documents being relayed from the DPP's office. As he reached his desk beside the window the telephone next to him purred softly.

'Haversham.'

'Superintendent Prince, sir.'

'What have you got for me, superintendent?'

'There's something definitely going off here, sir.'

'What's the matter?'

'My team has been through the entire investigation storage room and, well, I don't know exactly how to say this but . . .'

'Spit it out, man.'

'It seems that a large number of the documents from the list are missing.'

183

'What! How come?'

'According to the sergeant in charge who checked the register, there's an entry logged in for the fifth of May listing a whole boatload of it which has been shipped out.'

'How the hell has that been allowed to happen?'

'I don't know, sir. I couldn't take it much further with the sergeant. I mean he has no recollection of the physical removal, there's stuff going in and out of the property store all the time. All it requires is the release form.'

'Whose signature is on that?'

'Looks like the Force solicitor. Bernard Palton.'

'Any explanation?'

'A note next to the entry indicates that there was a formal request made under the Police Property Act to have them returned to the owners.'

'How is that possible?'

'We get applications all the time concerning property held by us which ultimately may not be used during the eventual trial. Once the CPS lawyers have made a decision we really have no say in the matter.'

'But those documents were part of a criminal investigation.'

'I know, but there's no power to hold them after privilege has been declared.'

'So who made the application?'

'A firm of commercial lawyers called Malaig and Co.'

'A big outfit on the Broadgate development in the city. I've come across them before. Their main business is acting on behalf of large industrial clients.'

'It looks like they've come in heavy handed here, probably threatening all sorts of injunctions against us.'

'Which documents in particular were released?'

'All the papers submitted to the laboratory relating to a company called Biotron Limited.'

'There's that name again. Easterman was monitoring them.'

'That's right, the interesting thing is that if you cross-reference the name with the entries contained in Easterman's working notes I think you'll find that it occurs with increasing frequency as you approach the thirteenth of October, the night he was murdered.'

'Hold on a minute.' Haversham grabbed Easterman's journals from the pile of papers closest to him. They were covered in mathematical formulae and columns of numbers, which made no sense at all to him, but one thing was absolutely clear. Prince was right: there seemed to be a distinct urgency implicit in the pages, revealing that Dr Easterman had been deeply interested in the samples being submitted by the Company in the weeks leading up to his death. Entries for other companies didn't occupy half as much space.

'I see what you mean, superintendent,' Haversham said, 'but do we have any way of deciphering the numbers?'

'Only way would be to call in one of his colleagues to go through them.'

'OK, do it. I want to know exactly what he was working on. I want a breakdown of the results he's obtained and I want a comparison with anything which Jenny Fox was saying.'

'What about the company concerned? Shall we make some enquiries?'

'No, we can run a company search from this end.'

'And the lawyers? What about them? We could raid their offices'.

'Not yet. I want to see what comes out before we go blasting in there.'

'OK, sir. Anything else?'

'Not for the present, superintendent. Give me an update in an hour.'

'Affirmative, sir.'

Haversham depressed the cradle and dialled Donald Taylor downstairs in the private office. He rubbed his tired eyes and touched the conference facility button whilst he waited for his secretary to answer. Although he hadn't slept for the last twenty-one hours, and despite burning through gallons of high-octane concentration he could still feel a reservoir of untouched energy ready to be drained. Instinct, he repeated to himself under his breath. Follow your instinct.

There were just too many things that didn't add up. Too many loose ends and half-explained theories. So many in fact that he was beginning to feel a grating uncertainty, a premonition that opening up the trail further was sure to backfire eventually. He now had incontrovertible proof that the previous government minister for state, Julian Walsh at the Department of Trade and Industry, had been party to this seemingly obvious process of burying information. Proof that a supposedly independent prosecution team were compliant with the wishes of the political executive and a firm of heavy commercial lawyers were putting their weight behind it also. The question was why? The one thing Haversham did know from experience was that wherever politicians gathered with businessmen under the flag of common purpose the usual agenda was profit and greed. Some people, usually those most closely involved, would label it differently but not him. He couldn't give up now; he knew he had to go on. Whatever the cost. Geoffrey's life depended on it.

The deep voice of Donald Taylor cut through his thoughts as the phone was answered.

'Yes, sir.'

'Donald, I want you to run a company search on an outfit called Biotron Limited.'

'Any particular emphasis?'

'No, I want the lot. I want the articles, the memorandum of association, accounts, clients, personnel, everything we can lay our hands on. You know what I'm talking about.'

'I get the picture.'

'And instruct central office to find me someone on the inside at Malaig and Co.'

'The city lawyers?'

'Yes, we must have at least one supporter on the letterhead.'

'What do you need from them?'

'I want to know who runs the account for Biotron.'

'Anything else?'

'Yes, get on to the DTI and locate the junior minister responsible for the chemical testing agencies. I want to speak to him.'

'As good as done, sir.'

'What's the word from the party, Donald?'

'Lot of disquiet from the Left, sir; whips have been doing their best but a lot of them want to know what's going on; the press are hard at it for comments, seems they know more than some of our lot.'

'Christ, I knew it! Talk to the BBC and reinforce that D notice. Tell the whips to close the drawbridge; no one talks to the press. Do I make myself clear?'

'Perfectly, sir, but the whisperings are that things are wobbly at the top end and a great many of the juniors are being pressurised by the back benchers to demand a statement.'

'Well, they'll have to wait, won't they? The less they know the better at this stage.'

The line went dead as Emma stirred in her chair. Arms stretched wide and face breaking into a yawn, she suddenly jumped up in a flurry, extracting her trapped foot and grinding it into the floor. 'Sorry, cramp,' she explained as Haversham looked on in bewilderment. The telephone purred again like an insistent cat. He grabbed the handset.

'Sir, I've got Vincent Thornton from the DTI on the line.'

'Thanks, Donald. Put him through,' Haversham said. Two seconds later one very nervous-sounding junior minister was on the loudspeak facility.

'Good evening, Thornton, I trust you realise we have a situation going on?'

'I do, sir; the phone hasn't stopped. Is there something I should know?'

'Only that I am still in control of it.'

'I see, sir, but the press say you've relinquished your leadership. I said it was nonsense of course, but they're all at it now, and what with your brother not showing at court for the Fox trial . . .'

'Thornton, did you hear me?'

'Yes, sir. Sorry, sir.'

'There is no crisis, just a situation which is being delicately worked out. It's correct to say that certain operational duties have changed hands but I stress it is only a temporary measure designed to protect any allegation of conflict, but I am still in control of the party.'

'Thank you, sir, I understand.' He still sounded a little unsure.

'Good. Now focus with me, I need to know the procedures for the testing of chemical samples,' Haversham said hoping his gentle tone would help the young politician relax.

As Thornton began to explain, Haversham realised that none

of his younger colleagues would have any experience of a party crisis after all those years in opposition. Then it was easy to accommodate inhouse squabbling and speculation under the cover of relative obscurity. But now everybody would be watching them closely. Just as Bill Botcheby had predicted in his newspaper articles, one day the time would come when the public would have to judge. Well, it might just have to be soon, he thought.

3.56 a.m., Prime Minister's Study, 10 Downing Street

Haversham was seated at the desk with his back towards the door when Donald Taylor walked in with a copy of the company search into Biotron. Emma excused herself, nodding at Taylor as she left the room to make yet another coffee. Haversham who had long since given up on coffee in favour of malt saw Taylor's reflection in the window against the pitch-black garden outside. He swivelled round, accepted the folder and turned to the summary page in the front.

'Thanks, Donald. Have central office found anyone for me yet at Malaig's?'

'Still working on it, sir. They have some idea that the ex-chairman of the South Kensington constituency is a partner there. We are still attempting to locate him.'

'Good. Keep on to it. I want to know who runs that account. What are the gossip columnists saying now?'

'Still shying away from the press I should think, the BBC haven't heard from the kidnappers since that first contact, but they are desperate to run the story in the morning news. The director general is saying the corporation's lawyers are telling him to move against the D notice, this is just too big. Chances are if we don't give them a by-line they'll go to court in the morning and challenge the validity of your action.'

'Let them try.'

Emma entered the room again with a steaming mug of coffee.

'Yes, sir.'

'All right, that's enough. Go to it! I'm relying on you, Donald, to keep this thing tight.'

'I'm trying, sir, but it's not easy.'

'What is?' Haversham said pointedly and turned away to examine the company search as Emma moved towards the desk, peering over his shoulder.

'OK, what have we got?' he said, turning to the text. 'Biotron Limited established 1981 as a research lab by a group of biochemists previously working on the same research programme at Cambridge University. The parent company is Chemitech Corporation of the United States.'

'That's a bit cosy, isn't it?' said Emma glibly as she turned back to the computer where she had been sifting through Geoffrey Haversham's case notes when Taylor arrived.

'Yes, but nothing particularly unusual about it. Once the government grants dry up and projects lose their impetus, scientists often find themselves with no alternative but to hitch up with overseas industry just to keep body and soul together. Bit like entertainers, the show must go on syndrome, and it doesn't matter where the money comes from.'

'Panto or Caesar's Palace then?'

'Something like that, Emma,' said Haversham, reading on.

'I suppose it stands to reason that if a few of them have similar interests then banding together makes sense but still it disturbs me to think they sell out to non-British interests.'

'Listen to this though,' Haversham said.

'Go on.'

'Chemitech is one of the five largest industrial conglomerates in the world. It has interests from chemical manufacturing to food processing spread across the globe.'

'Why Biotron?'

'The original team was investigating something known as bio-concentration.'

'Which is?'

189

'To do with the levels of hydrocarbons stored in animal fat apparently.'

'So why would an industrial the size of Chemitech develop an interest in that?'

'I don't know. Their original funding came from the health service budget and they were attempting to find ways to prevent accidental over-consumption of hydrocarbons by humans. The funding suddenly stopped during spending cuts and Chemitech stepped in with a partnership proposition.'

'Companies the size of Chemitech don't have partnerships, Edward, they have slaves. What was the small print?'

'It says Biotron was set up to further the research into compound pesticides which are mainly manufactured from hydrocarbons.'

'So the pay-off for money was product. Typical!'

'That's right, their brief was to carry on research and run a tandem programme with a view to developing a range of new additives for general use. Shortly after it was established, the company was capitalised with a heavy investment and within two years it was in full-scale manufacture with its first product – an insecticide known as TX33.'

'What's that?'

'Apparently a new development in chlorinated hydrocarbons which is their best selling range for export and domestic markets.'

'Who do they export to?'

'Just about everyone, by the looks of it. They are turning over millions.'

'OK, so where does that take us?'

'We know that they have to meet the minimum international safety standards in the manufacturing process; perhaps that's where the Jenny Fox connection comes in.'

'How?'

'She was taking soil samples from around chemical plants in the UK.'

'And?'

'According to this search Biotron have eight large plants spread all over England and a further two in Scotland.'

'So you're saying it's likely that the Biotron plants would have come under her scrutiny and maybe the results were a little too hard to swallow?'

'Exactly. It would provide an explanation, wouldn't it? If Jenny Fox was right and there was any link between the leukaemia clusters and Biotron's manufacturing processes then there's no way they would want any of the subsequent scandal being pushed on to the centre stage.'

'But why the connection to Easterman?'

'I don't know precisely just yet, but he was definitely watching them closely for whatever reason. I'm waiting for Ray Prince to call back. We may find something in Easterman's notes when they are deciphered.'

Haversham continued to look through the folder absorbing the information it contained when at last Ray Prince came on the line, his voice brimming with enthusiasm.

'We had Leonard Weir from the lab check through Easterman's notes and some interesting comments have come back. First of all, it seems Easterman hasn't always had an interest in Biotron samples.'

'Is that right?'

'Yes, he wasn't even the designated senior analyst for their sector.'

'So what was he then?'

'He looked after a completely different set of companies, but since August last year he started taking an interest.'

'About three months before his death.'

'That's right.'

'Why so suddenly then?'

'No one knows, but some people suspected that he was trying to disprove Jenny Fox's theories once and for all, kind of an academic obsession.'

'OK, so how do his journals break down?'

'That's the strangest part about it,' said the superintendent excitedly. 'All the calculations concern the same product.'

'Which is?'

'TX33.'

'Don't tell me, Biotron's best-selling pesticide.'

'How did you know that?'

'Just something I picked up from the company search. Go on, please.'

'Weir has analysed the calculations as far as he can but reckons they are incomplete.'

'How?'

'The basic test procedures have been carried out in relation to the criteria as set out in the lab rules of engagement but he says these calculations show that Easterman was on a totally different track, the closer he got to the end.'

'And has he identified anything that might give us an idea as to where Easterman was going with this?'

'No, is the short answer?'

'Why not?'

'Believe it or not, he has tried chasing the serial numbers from the batch of samples under testing and he is adamant that they do not match any submitted to the lab.'

'So what he's saying is that Easterman was analysing something totally different?'

'All he's saying is the samples have not come through the ordinary channels and he doesn't know where they are now.'

'But they are definitely Biotron samples?'

'He thinks so because of the method of testing for basic levels of illegal chemical residues.'

'Is there some sort of standard screening?'

'Yes. Every sample is broken down and screened for the presence of DDT, BHC, lindane, aldrin and chlordane.'

'Presumably all those are constitutents which are banned under the code of practice?'

'You got it.'

'But you say Easterman had gone beyond those tests?'

'According to Weir he was way beyond them.'

'That's the question we have to answer. What prompted Easterman other than Jenny Fox's assertions to look so deeply into the issue?'

'Chances are that Easterman had some data at home. Do you think it would be a good idea to pay a visit to his house? He left a widow but I'm sure she wouldn't object to a request for access to his papers.'

'Get on to it. Anything else?'

'The only other thing Weir could suggest was to contact the inspector responsible for collecting Biotron samples.'

'Who?'

'A guy called Dempster. Adrian Dempster.'

'And did you?'

'Well, I tried.'

'What do you mean, tried?'

'First of all we ran a check through government departments and his name doesn't appear anywhere on the civil service payroll.'

'Maybe he doesn't work there any more.'

'It's worse than that.'

'What?'

'According to the coroner's report he committed suicide three weeks before Easterman was murdered.'

6.55 a.m., A Garage, Railway Arch, Camden Lock

The journey had been hard on all of them. Pavel checked on Lydia, who was thrashing in her sleep on the rough camp bed in the corner. Once she cried out, 'Serge': he had stroked her hair then until she had slipped back into a healing limbo. Her breathing was ragged. Pavel had no doubt that she had sustained chest injuries; how bad they were, only time would tell.

The Attorney flicked open his eyes as Pavel shuffled across to the back-up van. His face was grey and dark bags hung low to the top of his cheekbones. He was shivering. Pavel placed another blanket around the lawyer's shoulders. Haversham seemed about to thank him, then bit back his gratitude. Pavel did not blame him: Haversham had not chosen this course, but he had to endure it.

The telephone pager had informed Pavel that the jury had been sent out to a hotel for the night; more time for Haversham's brother to discover the truth. Pavel rechecked the computer equipment; it would soon be time to resume contact. They had been lucky so far, apart from the crash, that is, but its aftermath had allowed their escape. They had emerged from the sewer system half a mile from the garage but the darkness had cloaked them from view as the rest of the journey was wearily undertaken.

Haversham coughed.

'Drink? Food?' Pavel offered.

'Not much point: you're going to kill me anyway,' Haversham replied bitterly.

'Maybe, maybe not.'

'Nonsense,' Haversham said, raising his knees up to his chin. 'I've seen your face, I know your name. Release me and a global man-hunt will follow.'

Pavel nodded and lit a black Sobrane.

'You are also perverse, Geoffrey.'

Haversham shrugged, but it was the first time his captor had used his Christian name.

'It's the Northerner in me: you can take the man out of the North, but you can't take the North out of the man.'

'Your brother, is he the same?'

'Pretty much; maybe more so.'

'Then that is good for you.'

Haversham shook his head.

'I doubt it. Standing orders, Pavel. No co-operation with terrorists, eco or otherwise.'

'But he is tenacious, no? And he is your brother.'

Haversham risked a bleak smile. 'First he is the Prime Minister, secondly he is my brother.'

'A hard man?'

'Yes, I suppose, but a good man.'

'And you, Geoffrey Haversham, are you a good man?'

It was a direct question rarely asked in politics or the law, and if asked, the question would rarely be answered.

'Ask my enemies,' Haversham answered flatly. 'Ask the drug cartels and the terrorist bombers – they want me dead; I must be doing something right.'

'Or wrong,' Pavel said, exhaling a thick plume of smoke. 'And does Jenny Fox think you are a good man?'

'Which criminal would?' Haversham answered as the haze of cigarette smoke cleared from Pavel's face.

'Some criminals mask their crimes with other crimes, they hide behind the weaknesses of others; they are my enemies.'

'And me, Pavel, am I your enemy?'

Pavel stretched his back. His abdomen shrieked in response, but he was used to the deep pain now.

'You are a soldier, you do your duty. It brings us into conflict: we each do what we must.'

'I had to prosecute her,' Haversham explained as if to a first-year law student.

'Precisely,' Pavel replied. 'You were used as much as Jenny.' Haversham could hear the tenderness in his voice when he mentioned her name.

'Did you love her?' he asked, attempting to make some small sense of the situation.

'We shared what we could: there is little time for love in this world.'

Lydia coughed herself awake. Her eyes focused, then she grimaced.

'I had a dream.'

'Serge?' Pavel said.

'You knew?'

Pavel turned back to Haversham.

'I must ask you to be quiet, Mr Prosecutor, there is still much to be done. Let us see how your brother has fared.'

Haversham now sat slumped by the chipped wall. Lydia busied herself inside the van. Pavel sat before the bank of computers and attempted to make contact once more.

7.00 a.m., COBRA Unit

Chance felt he was once again no more than a distant relative of sleep. Fresh coffee had his synapses snapping madly, though his adrenal gland continued to work overtime. He had to keep calm, or at least give that impression to the rest of his team. Dawn's early light probed tentatively through the blinds. Another day: no, he reminded himself, *the* day, the day of reckoning. They would have a result one

197

way or the other; what that result would be was down to the caprice of an eco-terrorist and a jury, strange animals both.

The discovery of the ambulance at the Maida Vale incident had helped to piece things together. It explained how the AG had been taken and also how they had escaped detection for so long; who would stop an ambulance? It could be a question of life or death: Haversham's death in this case, and many others besides. The dead driver was identified as Serge Vitally, a known associate of Boniak: the Liquidator.

'They are making contact, sir.'

Chance breathed a qualified sigh of relief. What state was the AG in? Was he still alive?

There was something vital that his captor needed to know to ensure Haversham's continued health. A family secret, hidden from the population: it might give Chance an edge. He turned his attention to the computer screen.

'Same format as last time?'

'Not quite; but the effect's the same,' one of the team replied. He watched as an e-mail message flipped on to the screen.

'Who really killed Charles Easterman?'

Chance typed in his response. 'Is the Attorney General still alive?'

A few seconds later a reply appeared.

'He will not be if you do not answer the question.'

'Establish video link,' Chance instructed.

'You are in no position to demand anything,' Pavel responded.

'Prove that Haversham is still alive.'

Pavel dragged the Attorney General over to the computer.

'Give me a codename, something to prove you're not dead.'

'Ask them how Frazer is?'

Pavel shook his head.

'Your dog's name is insufficient for my purposes.'

Haversham dug deep.

'Tell them that Regina v. Fitzpatrick is the extradition case for the Puma drug cartel.'

Pavel keyed the information in. Brian Chance immediately tele-phoned the PM on a protected line. Haversham confirmed that the Attorney General had been working on that project before his disappearance. Chance returned to the crisis on the computer line.

'Establish video link: I want to see him.'

Pavel ground his teeth together, but in the circumstances he too would have demanded visual verification. He positioned the video camera before Haversham, who scowled and said, 'Please don't ask me to smile for the birdie.'

Pavel returned to his consul and set the technology into execute mode.

Chance winced as the greying features of Geoffrey Haversham filled the monitor's screen. He checked the real-time read-out to ensure that this footage had not been filmed previously, and once satisfied he reopened the dialogue.

'He is ill. Let me speak to him.'

A disembodied voice dashed across the air waves: Pavel. 'Negative, Commander.'

Haversham opened his mouth to speak. Chance watched as a pair of feminine hands quickly applied a gag.

'You don't understand,' Chance continued. 'He is ill, medically ill – or will be very soon.'

Pavel listened carefully to the man's voice: it sounded desperate, and sincere. But he knew he could not stay on the line for too long.

'Explain, quickly!'

As Pavel watched Haversham, his eyes began to roll about, the whites showing alarmingly, and he started shaking violently.

'Diabetic; hypoglycaemia. He needs insulin or he will die.'

'Is this a trick?' Pavel bellowed.

Chance attempted to remain calm.

'No trick. If he dies you have nothing to bargain with. Give him up, now. For fuck's sake, look at him, man.'

Pavel watched in quiet horror as Geoffrey Haversham slumped to one side and was still.

7.01 a.m., Twickenham, London

R
ay Prince had been waiting for the past ten minutes in the unmarked police car outside number 15 Derwentside Avenue, the home of Dr Charles Easterman, deceased. The large poplar trees at the front shielded the single-storey house from his view. He'd arrived at 6.51 a.m. but decency had prevented him from ringing the doorbell before seven. Now as he walked up to the door through the neatly manicured shrubbery hugging either side of the pathway he could see the house more clearly and noticed that the curtains had been drawn in anticipation of his visit. Sure enough as he marched the last few steps the door opened and a robust lady stood at the threshold, her arms folded in a faintly menacing pose. Nothing however could have given a more misleading impression. As Ray Prince reached the doorway he could already smell the breakfast cooking. 'Superintendent, come in, come in,' she offered cheerfully in a loud voice, with an outstretched hand.

'Thank you, Mrs Easterman, I'm sorry it had to be so early but I wasn't overstating my predicament when I said the situation was urgent.'

'That's quite all right, superintendent. I realise the demands placed on the services. I used to be in the Army myself.'

'Is that right? I didn't know. I see you haven't lost the habit of waking up early.'

'Five thirty every morning; it was the same when Charles was

201

alive,' she said rather proudly. As they walked into the hallway Prince could see Easterman's study off to the left. Mrs Easterman noted his interest.

'Well, I was going to suggest that you have some breakfast but I can see your immediate focus doesn't coincide.' She nodded to the study. 'Go on then, get going. I'll bring you a bacon sandwich and a brew.'

'Thanks,' replied Prince, a little embarrassed that he had been so transparent. He walked into the study and familiarised himself with the computer on the desk. A few moments later, Mrs Easterman joined him at the console with her promised sandwich. Prince gratefully accepted the food and clicked on another file.

'What exactly is it you're looking for, superintendent?'

'I don't know if you would be able to help, Mrs Easterman?'

'I did a lot of Charles's routine typing for him, you know.'

'All right. I'm looking for any reference to a company called Biotron. I assume you know that one of your late husband's principal responsibilities was testing their products?'

'Let me find them for you.' Mrs Easterman slid the keyboard over to her side and altered the viewing angle of the screen slightly. Within seconds the screen was displaying volumes of similar calculations to those Prince had seen in Easterman's working journals.

'Do you know what he was working on in the weeks before he died, Mrs Easterman?' Prince asked, hoping for a break.

'I'm afraid I don't really, apart from the fact that he was obsessed with that Fox girl. Couldn't do anything but think about ways of proving her wrong. Stubborn wasn't the word for Charles; when he set to something he wouldn't stop until he was satisfied.'

'We are trying to work out why he developed such an intense interest in Biotron though. He was working on unauthorised samples; we don't know how he obtained them, but they certainly didn't come through the normal channels from government inspectors. We also know from some of the published articles that Jenny Fox had carried out soil analysis from Kent. It seems safe to assume that she wouldn't be able to publicly accuse, by name at any rate, one specific company, but by inference we strongly believe that she had targeted Biotron. They have a plant near Ashford in Kent and . . .'

'Ashford, did you say?' she interrupted.

'Yes. Why?'

'My oh my, the crafty little devil,' she snorted.

'I'm sorry, Mrs Easterman?' Prince said, puzzled.

'Charles.'

'Dr Easterman, what about him?'

'Two weeks before he died it was our anniversary and you'll never guess where he suggested that we spend the night?'

'Ashford, by any chance?' Prince smiled.

'No, of course not. Why ever should we wish to spend the night in Ashford?'

'I don't know, Mrs Easterman. I thought you were about to say something connected with my enquiry.' Prince was beginning to wonder about this woman's sanity.

'We spent the night at St Mary's Bay along the coast from Hythe where we were married,' she said, a watery glaze forming over her eyes.

'I see. I hope it brought back many pleasant memories.' It was all Prince could think of to say. Here he was trying to conduct an investigation with a great hulk of a woman hell bent on talking the day away with tales of her lost love. It wasn't the fact that Prince was unsympathetic to her need to grieve, there were just too many urgent issues at stake to waste time in this way. The long silence which followed was beginning to make him regret ever having suggested the visit in the first place when she surprised him again.

'You don't see, do you, superintendent?'

'Don't see what, Mrs Easterman?'

'The connection.'

'What connection?'

'Ashford and St Mary's.'

'Mrs Easterman, I haven't the faintest idea what you are talking about,' he said, exasperated.

'Take the M20 out of London until you get to Ashford. Then first left off the Sevington roundabout at junction 10 and follow the A2070 till it meets the A259. After that, just keep on going until you hit the marshes,' she said in a soft, sing-song voice. Prince was truly worried now that she had lost it.

'Oh yes, I see now,' he said gently, searching for an exit line.

'You clearly do not, superintendent. It was the directions he asked me to work out from the road map. But you couldn't know

that Charles decided we should stop off on our way to St Mary's
Bay and have lunch in Ashford.'

'What a coincidence,' he said, bordering upon blatant patronisation.

'No coincidence, superintendent,' she replied smugly.

'Please just tell me, Mrs Easterman.'

'Just like I say, Charles was most insistent that we should take
lunch there. He chose a little bistro just around the corner from the
freight depot for the Channel Tunnel. I remember commenting at
the time on the rather urban view from the window.'

'The freight depot?' said Prince beginning to feel a touch more
optimistic.

'He said he had to collect something from there for work. I didn't
question him at the time even when he came back with the box. I
saw him put it in the boot of the car.'

'A box?'

'Yes, superintendent, a box. Do you have some difficulty with
your hearing?' she said, slightly rattled as Prince stared at her in
astonishment. Why on earth hadn't this woman been questioned
before?

'I'm sorry, please do go on,' he urged.

'You see, I thought no more about it.'

'Why?'

'Well, because he was always a secret one, Charles was. That
night in the bedroom of the hotel he gave me our anniversary
present. A French carriage clock, there it is on the mantelpiece.
Do you like it?' She pointed to an antique timepiece decorated with
elaborate curves and gold leaf paint.

'Very elegant.'

'I just assumed that the box he picked up at Ashford contained the
clock and that he had pretended it was something to do with work so
as not to spoil the surprise.'

'So?'

'The other day when I was clearing out the room he used as a lab
I came across the box,' she exclaimed in delight.

'Mrs Easterman, I'm not following you. You came across the box
with the clock in it. Is that what you're saying?'

'No, I came across the box with the samples in.'

'The what?'

'The samples that you're probably looking for.'

'Are you sure?'

'Quite sure, because the box that the clock came in is in the dresser.'

'Right,' he said, unconvinced that his earlier optimism was justified.

'I thought it was just the right size for photographs. My own mother used to have a pictures box where she used to keep all those black and whites of the family. Did yours?' Mrs Easterman didn't pause long enough for the answer. 'Anyway, I digress, superintendent. The point is Charles must have had two boxes, you see, always the secretive one.'

'Where is the box with the samples in now?' Prince could barely contain himself.

'Under the stairs. Would you like me to get it?'

7.32 a.m., in Motion, Camden Town

Haversham's face was waxed grey. His breathing was increasingly shallow, his pulse faint and staccato. Pavel attempted to slap him into wakefulness, but even the stinging blows failed to register on the lawyer's consciousness. Lydia drove the back-up vehicle through the early morning traffic carefully, her eyes flicking from side to side, desperately searching for a chemist or health centre. Pavel shouted, 'He's getting worse, keep looking.'

Since Haversham's collapse, the activity had been frenzied. Pavel had to move him, had to spirit them all away from the last contact point. The authorities would be pursuing every technological avenue to trace them. Worse still, the Attorney General would soon lapse into a coma if his hypoglycaemia continued unchecked. They had left the lock-up, with eyes alert for the suspicious and the curious;

he hoped they had succeeded, but at the moment he felt unsure about everything. It had seemed so right at the time, the plan fermented in his brain; every eventuality thought through with painstaking care; his greatest task, perhaps his last. Then, his military training had subsumed the problems into mere facts, no more than puzzle solving. They had watched Haversham for weeks. He was clearly a creature of habit. The lack of security was an amazing oversight. His unaccompanied walks with his Labrador were political madness. All had gone well, as Pavel had expected, until the ambulance crashed. There was always the unknown factor, 'F for Fuck-up', in every operation, but he should have known about Haversham's medical condition. He turned back to his hostage, and shook his head in disbelief. Why hadn't Haversham told Pavel himself? The man appeared more perverse at every turn. He had gambled with his own life to slow them down, more madness. Pavel felt his stomach lurch, his nerve endings sending a familiar message to his brain, 'the pain is back, kill the pain', and Pavel followed their command. He reached into his top pocket and, retrieving the painkillers, hungrily gulped two down.

Lydia shouted, 'We have driven past a small chemist's shop. I will park around the corner. Me or you?'

'Me,' he answered without hesitation. He felt the van sway to the left and stop.

'Describe,' he ordered, clipped and minimalist, in best battlefield tone.

'One hundred metres on your left. Closed sign. Flat above, curtains drawn. Alleyway before shop, road behind.'

'Civilians?'

'Road sweeper, two hundred metres beyond; one jogger, moving away; both male.' Pavel opened the door carefully, then jumped out, smiling happily. Furtiveness engendered suspicion, confidence killed it. He sauntered nonchalantly to the front of the van.

'Five minutes. Drive on if I do not return; you know the contingency plan.'

Lydia nodded, her breathing still heavily laboured, 'Come back, Pavel,' she said, without looking at her leader. Pavel wanted to run to the chemist's shop, tear down the door, and raid the medicine cabinet. But logic warned him that the security services would be scanning the police airwaves for just such a raid as this; they knew of his captive's condition and how it could be remedied.

Instead, he walked casually, to the front of the shop window and noted, to his relief, that there was no sign of life. He retraced his steps to the point where the alleyway broke away from the main road at a right angle, and followed its lead. It turned sharply once more and gave access to the rear of the premises. A six-foot wall and a locked gate, marked 'Herds, Chemists, Deliveries' identified his target. Pavel sucked in a mouthful of air and sprang upward, grasping the top of the wall firmly. He swung his body to the side, up and over, swivelled and dropped down silently into the rear yard. It was tidy and well kept. He listened for the sound of barking at the chemist's back door, but could hear only his own breathing. He removed his Russian army knife, selected a fine pick and wheedled it inside the lock, which responded with a satisfying click. He turned the door handle delicately and pushed it open. He was in. He found himself inside a storeroom, half-filled with medical supplies with an interconnecting door to the main shop area. Once more he pushed this door open – easy, too easy; easy enough to persuade him to drop his guard. The locked medicine cabinet was to his left. He used the same blade to persuade it to open. Just as he opened the metal door, an alarm began to sound.

'Shit', he muttered, but his mission was only half accomplished. He listened intently for the tell-tale sign of movement from the flat above, as he ransacked the cabinet's interior. So many labels, so many drugs, then his eyes spied and his hand grasped several vials of insulin and four syringes with needles. He retraced his route, pulled the dead bolt aside on the walled door to the alley and sprinted back towards the main road, but pulled up just before he reached it. Pavel could hear the alarm shrieking through the early morning air. He began to walk slowly towards the van. Lydia had the engine gunned and running. It was at that moment that a young, uniformed, police officer rounded the corner at a gentle lope, speaking into a hand-held transmitter. He clocked the van and Pavel's approach in an instant.

'Stop there,' he shouted, closing the distance between them as Pavel continued towards the van and escape.

'I said stop there,' the young man commanded, withdrawing his police baton. Pavel had his hands full with the raided medical supplies; attempting to juggle them into one hand, he dropped two vials and a syringe on to the grimy street. But Lydia had also reacted. Leaving the engine running, she leapt out of the van and began to attack the policeman. She was good, not as good as Pavel or the deadly, but now deceased Serge, but her fighting skills were no match for his flashing baton.

'Go, Pavel, go,' she shouted as a blow struck her on the forearm with a telltale crunch. Another policeman was arriving on foot and withdrawing a can of CS gas. Pavel had no choice, he jumped into the driver's cab, turned to see Lydia bludgeoned on the head, and shouting, 'I will come for you,' he crunched the gears, released the clutch and sped away from the scene. In his rear-view mirror Pavel watched as the CS was administered to Lydia's face. She collapsed to the floor, tearing at her eyes, and was struck once more for good measure. 'Just me and you now, Mr Prosecutor,' he whispered. 'Let me make you well before you die.'

10.30 a.m., Court Two, The Old Bailey

It was called 'in camera' and it meant in secret. Alex and the other ten remaining jury members shifted uncomfortably in their seats. Stalin sat in Jenny Fox's place in the dock. The prosecution and defence teams were moodily present, disappointed by the lack of verdict and disquieted by the turn of events. But Alex could discern a jitteriness about them, a hushed nervousness that seemed more acute than the case merited. A decision had to be made: would Stalin be allowed to remain on the jury?

At breakfast, the jurors had been posted at eleven individual tables, each with their police minder, each warned away from any conversation. Stalin had been whisked to court in a police car, their remaining number, already hushed by the disconcerting chain of events, sworn to utter silence by a senior police officer and driven in their minibus back to the courtroom.

Stalin had been given legal representation to defend the allegation which Bob had engineered for Alex and Alex listened carefully as the QC for the Crown outlined the events.

'My lord,' he began. 'As per your direction Mr Conran has been kept separate from the other jury members since this matter came to light.'

The judge nodded gravely, his fingers interleaved, thumbs together at the apex.

'In the early hours of the morning a call was received by one Mr Tish, night editor of *The Times*. The male caller claimed to be a member of the jury in the case of the Crown against Jennifer Fox. The caller offered the inside story of the jury's deliberations and promised early notification of the verdict. The editor asked for verification from the caller and was given the name and address of the jury's hotel. He asked the caller to name his amount, which was £10,000, and Mr Tish requested time to seek permission for the sum. The caller promised to contact him later. Disquieted by this and other events' – at this, he nodded to the judge, who flicked his eyes towards the jury in a silent warning to the barrister – 'he immediately contacted the police. Your lordship was alerted and ordered an immediate search of the jury's accommodation.'

'Yes,' the judge responded, 'and might I furnish the other eleven members of the jury with a sincere apology for disturbing their rest, but I feel now, as I did then, that this action was necessary. Go on.'

'A thorough search of Mr Conran's room led to the discovery of a miniature mobile phone. By utilising certain telephonic procedures it can be proved beyond any doubt that the call to *The Times* was made from this unit.'

Alex peered along the jury bench to where Bob sat, brow knotted in surprise and dismay at Stalin's actions; he even had the nerve to shake his head from side to side. Grace barely managed to suppress a smile, whilst the others stared ahead or into their laps. The prosecutor continued.

'Mr Conran denies that the phone belongs to him, or that he made the call.'

The judge pushed out his bottom lip petulantly.

'Does he?' he muttered. 'My own view is that if proved, this is a serious contempt of my court, but that will be decided after the trial is concluded. The real question is whether Mr Conran can continue as a member of the jury. My opinion is that he cannot.'

Stalin jumped to his feet.

'What about innocent until proved guilty?' he bellowed.

Certainly changed *your* tune, Alex thought, then reminded himself that Stalin was innocent. The judge raised one threatening finger at Stalin.

'Silence, Conran.' Stalin shook his head in bewilderment then slumped, broken, to his seat.

The judge looked back to the prosecutor and the defence barrister.

'I am discharging Mr Conran from returning a verdict in this case. Do you object?' Both shook their heads.

'This raises the problem of contamination of the remaining jurors and whether they should also be discharged from the trial.'

He turned to Alex and the others.

'I am going to ask you individually two questions: one, whether any of you were aware of what Mr Conran was allegedly involved in; and two, whether what has happened today will prevent you from reaching a true verdict. Now, the gentleman on the far left.' He was referring to Bob. 'Please be good enough to stand.'

Bob did so, proud and straight-backed and, like the other ten to follow, he answered the judge's questions in the negative. The judge smiled, obviously relieved that, at least for the moment, he had avoided the delay and vast expense of a retrial. He turned once more to the barristers.

'Gentlemen, that satisfies my own doubts.' He stared menacingly at them. 'Do either of you disagree?'

Identical 'No, my lord's' were returned at speed as each sat down quickly. From day one of the trial, the judge had a firm grip on his court and was not willing to relinquish that hold so late in the proceedings.

'Mr Foreman.'

Bob stood once more.

'Have the jury reached a verdict upon which at least ten of you are agreed?'

Bob coughed lightly to clear his throat then turned to stare at Alex before replying.

'I'm afraid not, my lord.'

'Then you must retire once more until you do.'

He nodded to Edna, the usher, who began to shepherd them back to their retiring room.

She closed the door behind her as she left. The room was silent; even the hum of the air-conditioning was absent. Sheepishly they took their places, all eyes moving to and from one o'clock where

Stalin had sat the day before. Bob sighed and looked around all their faces, one by one. Pitbull shook his head.

'Who'd have thought it? I thought Dave was a good bloke.'

'They haven't proved he did it,' Alex said, turning to look into Bob's hard eyes. 'Isn't that right, Mr Foreman? He might be innocent; he might have been set up.'

Bob shook his head sadly.

'Are you back on that again, Alex? More conspiracies? The answer is no, he couldn't have been set up.'

'Why not?' Pitbull asked, genuinely puzzled.

'Because,' Bob answered gravely, 'that would mean that it was one of us who set him up.'

Bob's stark point hushed the room into silence once more. It was Bob who spoke first.

'Look, we can't start to mistrust each other. I will tell you something in confidence. It was told to me in confidence by Dave, but needs must; too much at stake.'

Go for it, Bob, Alex thought, try and bring this round to your advantage.

'His mobile phone business is about to go under, badly; he was desperate last night, had too much to drink. Stupid thing to do, but . . .'

Alex was impressed, Bob had turned betrayal into a virtue and in so doing was steering the jury away from the defence in Jenny Fox's case; that *she* had been set up. Neat, Bob, really neat. The others appeared satisfied with Bob's reading of the situation.

'Told him he had some bad karma coming,' Kaftan whispered.

'Please don't start that nonsense again,' the Prof pleaded.

'Poor, angry man,' said the Mouse.

'What will happen to him?'

'Get locked up,' Denzel replied, speaking aloud what they all believed. Once more, Alex felt dreadful about Stalin's situation, but what could he do? Jenny Fox's best interests would be served by his remaining on the jury, attempting to block Bob's every effort to put her away. After this was all over, he would put things right, but until then Bob was too lethal a weapon to remain unchecked.

'Where do we go from here?' Alex asked.

'We do as the judge commanded: reach a verdict.'

'Easier said than done,' Pitbull commented. Danno, as ever, nodded his agreement.

'We have to try,' Pearl soothed, as she rubbed her hands together, attempting to massage some feeling into them. 'Is anyone else cold?'

Alex then knew why the room had been so quiet: the air-conditioning must have gone down. 'Arthritis. I know I shouldn't knit so much. Same in the hotel last night; the heating in my room wasn't working. I don't like to complain.'

'I would have sorted it out for you,' Pitbull said with a surprising degree of fondness. Pearl beamed a smile at him.

'You get used to it. Just a body wearing out, but it did set me thinking.' She turned to look at their foreman. 'Robert, I believe it's my turn to ask a question about the case.'

He nodded for her to continue.

'Well, we had a lot of talk yesterday about fingerprints, about Jenny Fox's fingerprints and that horrible gun. I was trying to warm my hands around a nice cup of tea in my room last night and it set me to thinking about the murder. The night he was killed was a cold bright October night, cold enough to wear gloves.'

'She won't have arthritis,' the Prof remarked and not unkindly.

'True,' Pearl replied, 'but she wasn't going to see Easterman to practise her knitting technique; she went there to murder him. Everybody knows about fingerprints, my grandkids know about them. Are we really to believe that Jenny Fox didn't?'

'An oversight?' Bob suggested reasonably.

'You know, Robert, that crossed my mind too,' she replied. Bob nodded his encouragement, the wrinkles around his eyes seeming to crease slightly with pleasure. 'Then I dismissed that thought completely.'

'What?' Bob muttered.

'It's rubbish, complete cobblers, as my old man would say, and pardon my French, but cobblers it is.'

'Why on earth do you say that?' Bob replied, clearly surprised by the unforeseen change of Pearl's attitude.

'Because the two dead boys she was found with were both wearing gloves.'

Alex nodded his head in admiration, silently thanking Pearl for her fearless common sense. 'It makes no sense at all. Her hands must have stood out, well like . . .'

'Sore thumbs?' Alex said, smiling at Pearl. She nodded back at him.

'Exactly. They must have checked their weapons before they stormed the building. She would have felt the cold of the gun barrel, the snap of the cold air, the two boys would have seen that she wasn't wearing gloves, would have done something about it.'

'Hold on one minute,' Bob demanded, one hand raised in the air, his voice harsh.

'Steady on, Bob,' Pitbull growled. 'A little respect for the lady, if you don't mind.'

Bob risked a confused smile.

'Sorry, sorry, I'm tired, not like me, not like me at all.'

'Really?' Alex muttered, low enough to carry only as far as the flustered foreman, whose ears reddened at Alex's comment.

'What I meant to say was, let's think about what we are really saying here, please, everyone.' He looked to Pearl. 'If I follow your point, and forgive me if I'm confused . . .'

Nice try, Bob, Alex thought, let's see you try and win some sympathy back after that display of rudeness to Pearl.

'Are you really saying that you are sure that she was set up? Because that's the only possible conclusion to draw from your point.'

Pearl seemed to hesitate; his argument had thrown her off her stride. Alex intervened.

'With respect, Bob, that's not the test. From what the judge told us we have to be sure that she *wasn't* set up; that's what the burden of proof means. She doesn't have to convince us that she was.'

'Exactly. Thank you, Alex,' Pearl said gratefully. Bob nodded and spoke to Alex out of the corner of his mouth.

'I thought you were an architect not an advocate.'

'I'm still right,' Alex replied. 'Look, if you don't accept it, let's go back into court and ask the judge to direct us again on the law.'

It was Bob's turn to hesitate. Alex decided to press his momentary advantage.

'Let's have another ballot.' He nodded eagerly and noticed several others including Pearl agree with him.

'Are you the foreman now, Alex?' Bob asked coldly. It was his turn to appear flustered, bewildered that he had caused any offence.

'Just a suggestion; didn't mean anything by it.'

'Really?' Bob replied icily.

'But if you're afraid . . .'

'I'm not.'

'Excellent. Let's do it then.'

Alex handed out eleven slips of paper. The others watched him and Bob warily, as if suspecting that an agenda was no longer hidden. The papers were once more pushed in towards Bob. He inspected each silently. They waited. Alex was nervous. He caught Pearl's eye, which sparkled; he blew her a mental kiss.

'This isn't getting us anywhere,' Bob said angrily.

'What's the vote?' Alex demanded.

'We're hung,' he replied.

'How hung?'

'Seven guilty, four not guilty – hung.'

'We're making progress.'

'You might view it that way.'

'It means some of us have doubts.'

'Not me,' said the Prof.

'Aren't we just wasting our time?' Bob asked, his hands out flat on the table. 'Let's just tell the judge we can't possibly agree and get ourselves discharged; Jenny Fox can be someone else's headache.'

'I don't agree,' said Kalsi. 'I swore an oath to do this job properly and until the judge tells me otherwise, I intend to do it.' She was stern-faced and appeared unmovable.

Princess Grace spoke. 'Let's get on with it: my question next.'

Alex wondered how his discovery of the adulterous ice queen in the snooker room would affect her attitude. She glanced at Denzel's handsome face before speaking again.

'I don't like blackmail.'

11.10 a.m., Prime Minister's Study

Edward Haversham was waiting for the call. He sat nervously watching the television news from the BBC. The director general had defied the D-notice in spirit if not in letter. Haversham sat amazed as the picture showed a fresh faced commentator standing only yards down the street at the black railings usually mauled by tourists. He was inviting the viewer to engage in yet more fanciful speculation as to what was going on inside 10 Downing Street. Haversham grabbed the remote and switched sides but the commercial channels were following suit and the issue was now dominating the political landscape. Top item was the sudden cancellation of all his appointments for the day ahead. CNN carried a live interview with the Shadow Cabinet spokesperson making full political capital out of the situation. The obsequious anchorman was cajoling his guest into ever-greater hyperbole. 'It seems,' he was saying, 'that the days of open government have been dispatched back to the dark ages with this outright refusal to speak to the press and by inference, therefore, the public. Is that fair, would you say?' The guest laid into the opportunity with a soundbite befitting any good cabaret act. 'I would say eminently accurate with the additional and even bleaker prospect in view that this new administration seems to be devoid of any characters of sufficient strength to pull it back from that rather murky brink.' An exasperated Haversham was about to shout at the television set when the telephone pulled him away from the screen.

'Sir, it's Superintendent Prince.'

'Go ahead.'

'Good news, sir. Weir's results have come through.'

'Excellent. What's the verdict?'

'Something very odd about them according to the man.'

'In what way?'

'He has identified them as being as close to TX33 as you can get, but he is not prepared to commit himself to saying they definitely come from Biotron.'

'Why not?'

'Because he says he can't be sure of the source in the absence of any corporate markings on the canisters.'

'Damn it. But what's in them that's so important?'

'He reckons that there's no way in its present form that it could be legal to produce this stuff. Basically it's lethal.'

'Go on.'

'He has isolated over fifteen different constituent chemicals, which are banned from manufacture by the developed world.'

'Jesus Christ!'

'I know. It's sheer poison.'

'Is he prepared to stand by his analysis?'

'I think so. The technical low-down is that he discovered a group of hexachlorocyclohexane molecules combined with a chemical called dieldrin. The effects of that are they produce a carcinogen more powerful than DBCP which is the worst known so far.'

'So the question is, how do we prove that they came from Biotron in the first place? Isn't that the way ahead?'

'That's the difficult part.'

'OK. Take me through the notes you found on Easterman's computer.'

'Right.'

'From the beginning, superintendent.'

'OK. He doesn't give any real background as to why he became interested in Biotron specifically, only that he was approached by Adrian Dempster some time in August of last year.'

'And he knew Dempster from his employment as the government inspector assigned to collate samples of chemicals produced by Biotron?'

'That's right.'

'But there is no other connection between them that we know about?'

'Correct.'

'So does he give any information as to why he was approached by Dempster and what it was that he specifically said?'

'No, the only thing he records in his notes is the fact that he was sufficiently concerned about the things Dempster had said to make a telephone call to the top brass at the Department of Trade and Industry. To question them.'

'And what was the upshot of that conversation?'

'We don't know much from the DTI. No one seems to recall ever having had such a conversation with Easterman.'

'What, no one at all?'

'One person thinks he may have been sounded out.'

'What does that mean?'

'That he recalls Easterman asking about Dempster's mental wellbeing.'

'Really, sounds rather odd. Didn't he think so?'

'Only in so far as Dempster was under a lot of pressure at the time and therefore a number of queries had been raised by people who knew him.'

'Why?'

'Apparently his employers at the DTI were concerned about him since the death of his father in July.'

'Had he been acting any differently?'

'He took the news of his father's ill health badly. It was all very sudden. Within a couple of days the man was dead and after the funeral they say Dempster was very withdrawn.'

'Understandable but not exactly unique, is it?'

'I wouldn't have said so personally, no.'

'So Easterman was presumably told all this?'

'Seems so.'

'And it did the trick?'

'Yes, because when you compare his journals from the lab itself you can see that in August he conducted a couple of spot checks personally on Biotron samples coming in for analysis, but after that nothing for a while. He must have thought that whatever Dempster had told him was down to his emotional state.'

'OK, so what happens after that?'

'Everything is quiet for a while.'

'What happens to Dempster in the meantime?'

'He is given compassionate leave from the Civil Service and disappears for a while.'

'Who took over the handling of Biotron samples?'

'A newly appointed inspector called Cross. Peter Cross.'

'Has he been spoken to?'

'Yes. He knows nothing about the situation. According to him he expected to be taken off the job when Dempster returned to work.'

'But?'

'Dempster committed suicide on the twenty-fourth of September and Cross has held the post ever since.'

'But Easterman's journals show an increased frequency of sampling of Biotron products in late September and early October, in the time leading up to his death. What created that new-found urgency? Do we have anything to go on?'

'Not really. The only thing is, it's possible Dempster could have contacted him again before he topped himself.'

'Possible, yes. But is it likely?'

'I don't know. He might have felt offended that no one was listening to him if he wanted to shop Biotron for dispatching a couple of dodgy samples. He was in a state, you have to remember that.'

'No, it has to be bigger than that. I'm sure of it.'

'You mean, why did Easterman go to the trouble of setting out to get his hands on some unauthorised samples of TX33?'

'Exactly. On the face of it we have a well-respected scientist posing as a spot check inspector and barging into the Ashford freight depot to liberate samples of a chemical which proves to be carcinogenic.'

'And then, before he can publish his findings, he's killed.'

'But by who?'

'Jenny Fox looks as likely as anyone still.'

'But the motive is shifting, isn't it?'

'How? I don't think it will stand up.'

'Why not?'

'Surely it's too much of a leap of common sense to say that an organisation the size of Biotron would be bothered that a couple of below par samples had been found out. I mean, wouldn't they just take it on the chin and blame the manufacturing process? They could be dealt with in the magistrate's court, fined a couple of thousand pounds and slapped on the corporate wrist.'

'But what if it goes deeper than that? Dempster is the key to this, I'm sure of it. We need to know what he said to make Easterman so excited.'

'Any ideas?'

'Only one. In the transcript of evidence, Easterman's secretary at the lab said he was acting a little strange the day he died.'

'But she retracted that as a false impression, didn't she?'

'Not before she was asked what prompted it in the first place.'

'Which was?'

'The fact he was anxious that she managed to catch the post that evening. Something he was never normally concerned about.'

'But the explanation from the Crown was that he was concerned about getting a batch of paperwork off in time, nothing unusual there.'

'Maybe, but let's check the post book for that night, shall we?'

11.45 a.m., The Jury Room

B ob smiled indulgently at Princess Grace, then went about deconstructing her new-found fairness of mind.

'So what you are saying is, just because a rival player at your squash club slipped another member's purse into your locker, that Jenny Fox could have been set up?'

Grace's eyes slipped to Alex's; she was floundering badly, her misconstructed metaphor listing to starboard under Bob's calm waves of logic.

'I was just thinking about it,' she replied defensively, too defensively. Bob pressed ahead, fully aware that, overnight, Grace's stance had altered beyond recognition.

'But this is a little more complex than sneaking a stolen article into an aluminium locker. We have four dead bodies to consider, guns, ammunition, ski-masks, planning, eco-terrorism.'

Grace was looking more unsure of her ground as Bob's list grew.

'A cause, a brutal execution, a well-documented hatred of Easterman.'

Alex had to stop this. Bob's reasonable common sense was a deadly virus to Jenny Fox's future health.

'You sound like the Attorney General, Bob. Did you ever consider the law as a career?'

Bob half-raised one eyebrow in controlled annoyance.

'Not with my background, Alex. You?'

It was clever. Bob was emphasising the class demarcation lines and promoting Alex as a petty snob.

'I wouldn't trade places with a brief for a lottery win. Do you know that after doctors, barristers have the highest rates of depression, alcoholism and divorce in the country?'

Most of the jury shrugged away the statistic; it was difficult to feel any sympathy for a profession that appeared to be no more than gun for hire in a horse-hair wig, but Alex's interruption had allowed Grace to pull her unravelling mind back together.

'It's just a question of degree, Bob, the principle remains the same.'

Bob's eyes flashed angrily, from Grace to Alex and back again.

'And what do you know about principles?' Bob whispered, his voice low and mean.

Grace's face flushed.

'I never, I don't know what . . .' she spluttered. Denzel watched the exchange intently, half opened his mouth, then closed it firmly. Alex shook his head.

'A bit personal, don't you think, Bob?' Their foreman remained silent. Grace's eyes were brimming with tears.

'I know a lot about principles,' she said quietly, her chin quivering with each word. 'Oh, you all think I'm such a petty person, the rude pushy woman in the bank queue, that I know more about Chanel than the Channel Tunnel, but I have feelings.'

'Obviously,' Bob spat, glancing between Grace and Denzel. 'Does your husband know about them?' Keep going, Bob, Alex mentally urged, you're shooting your own case right in the foot.

'Robert!' Pearl warned. 'I'm surprised at you.'

Bob's eyes flicked with reptilian speed to her, focused intently then softened remarkably.

'I'm sorry, you're right. Don't know what came over me.' He turned his gaze to the weeping figure of the Princess. 'Helena, how can you possibly forgive me?'

She shook her head sadly. 'What you said about me is the truth, but you don't have any right to speak it. You are judging me, condemning me without knowing all the facts and that is *not* fair.'

Alex saw his opportunity.

'You and Jenny Fox both.' Princess Grace looked up at him and smiled as if subject to epiphany.

'Different, very, very different,' Bob said quietly.

'Same difference,' Alex countered.

'There is no such thing, Alex,' the Prof stated. 'It's a logical impossibility.'

'Perhaps,' Alex replied. 'But we all know it's true, we say it every day: same difference this, same difference that. It might not make much sense to the head but the heart knows it's true.'

'You're ignoring the evidence,' the Prof replied.

'Exactly,' Bob added. 'You're trying to cloud our judgement again, Alex, and *that* is not fair.'

'It's not about fairness,' Alex answered, 'it's about justice.'

'They are the same thing, Alex,' Bob replied.

'No: they are supposed to be, but they are not.'

'Rubbish,' Bob spat.

'No, it's not. Justice is about doing the right thing no matter how hard that is. I do not believe that Jenny Fox is guilty but that is hardly fair to the memory of Charles Easterman.'

'I agree,' said Princess Grace.

'But Easterman is not on trial, Jenny Fox is: she is our principal concern.'

'And what about his widow?' Bob asked. 'Doesn't she have any rights? I mean, what do we say to her? "Sorry, we were a little bit unsure so we decided to ignore all the evidence and acquit her. No hard feelings."'

'Right on, Bob,' Pitbull added.

'I never said it would be easy,' Alex replied. 'None of us wanted this job. It's a dirty one but, as they say, someone has got to do it, and that someone is us.'

'Vote time?' Pitbull asked, staring hard at Princess Grace. 'Or would that be a waste of time?'

Bob pursed his lips angrily.

'I say when we have a vote. All right?'

'OK, Bob, no offence, man,' Pitbull replied. 'Just trying to get this stuff finished.'

'He's right, Robert,' Pearl remarked.

'I agree,' the Prof added. 'We need to know where we are.'

'Hung is where we are,' Bob answered nastily.

'We need to know how hung,' Denzel said, his voice flat and calm.

'Does that go for the rest of you?' Bob asked testily. A series of nods gave him the undesired answer. 'Very well. Alex, you seem to be in the position of self-appointed paper monitor. Do the honours.'

Alex tore the paper into eleven uneven pieces once more and distributed them around the table. All eyes were firmly rooted on Princess Grace who, aware of their joint attention, blushed once more before committing her decision to paper. The slips were collected by Bob, who shuffled through them carefully, before slamming them down on the table-top.

'This is fucking crazy. What is wrong with you people?' he shouted.

'Pack it in, Bob,' Denzel warned, one long finger pointing straight at their elderly foreman's face. 'Just tell us what the count is; we all want to go home, man.'

Bob appeared totally calm but his hard eyes wandered around the table, aware that his outburst was totally out of character and might cost him dear.

'The vote is five guilty, six not guilty,' he whispered menacingly. Princess Grace swivelled her attention to Denzel, who winked, then looked away.

'I didn't change my vote, did you?' Pitbull asked Danno.

'Nah, she's guilty all right, just some people won't see it that way, berks,' his friend replied.

'No one's entitled to know who voted what way,' Denzel growled. Pitbull widened his eyes, Alex could almost hear him thinking.

'I get it now,' Pitbull continued, 'you're voting with your shag. It's a fuck vote.'

Denzel's face hardened to granite.

'When we finish this: me and you, one to one, no complaints or crying to the police, white meat.'

'That's racist talk,' Kalsi said.

'He's the racist,' Denzel replied, pointing into Pitbull's face. 'I grew up with white bigots like him, my best friend was stabbed by bigots like him; white trash, worst kind.'

'Let's do it now,' Pitbull demanded, rising from his seat. 'Fuck the trial.'

'Stop it, stop it, all of you,' the Mouse screamed, tears tearing down her face. 'This is so horrible, so . . . nasty . . . wrong.' Her hysterical outburst stopped Pitbull in his tracks.

'Look what you've done,' he said to Denzel. 'That'll be another smack in the mouth.'

'Sit down,' Pearl demanded, 'or you'll get another smack from me.'

Pitbull smiled warily and retreated back to his seat to an approving nod from Danno. Bob measured the situation with a steady gaze.

'We have to tell the judge that we are impossibly divided; get him to discharge us.'

'No!' Alex shouted. 'There are four of us with questions still to be answered, including you, Bob. I want my say and I refuse to go back into court until I have had it.' Alex folded his arms and sat back.

'I knew you would be trouble,' Bob whispered. Alex shrugged.

'I'm with Alex,' Kalsi said flatly.

'Me too,' Denzel added.

Bob nodded angrily. 'You want to be foreman, Alex, go ahead.'

'I don't.'

'Really?'

'Yes, really, but I want my say. What are you afraid of, anyway?'

Bob's eyes burrowed and probed into Alex's. 'I am not the one who should be afraid, Parrish,' he whispered and Alex believed him, he believed him more than he had ever believed anything in his life.

'My question,' Denzel said to break the chilling moment.

'Bob, just how did you fix it so that my brother walked from his drugs charge?'

12.42 p.m., Pavel's Bolthole

An attic flat with a panoramic view of the surrounding rooftops. Only one way in and one way out. One lift now disabled. One staircase, booby-trapped and their last stop. Haversham's colour had returned to something approaching normal. Pavel had driven to an underground car park to administer the insulin and to abandon the back-up van. The police officers who had attacked Lydia would have ensured that its registration number was circulated to control within seconds of his departure. He had stolen a substitute vehicle to convey them to this place. He glanced around the spartan flat. Haversham was still sleeping on the single bed and a rough table shouldered a laptop computer and modem. Pavel had hoped, when he'd rented the accommodation some months before, that he would never see it again. He cursed himself. 'Stop complaining, Pavel, you are where you are, get on with it.' His telephone pager and a web page on the Internet confirmed the jury were still out. His contact with Downing Street all but sealed Haversham's fate; they would not deal with terrorists. They had even attempted to bargain with Lydia's life, but Pavel knew her, and also knew that by now she would be dead. Just then, Haversham shuffled and opened his eyes. There was a moment of bewilderment before comprehension returned. He sighed and sat up. 'Thought it might be all over by now,' he whispered, almost disappointed.

'Were you so ready to die?'

'As you said, we all die.' He looked around. 'Nice place.'

'Thank you, but we do not entertain much,' Pavel replied acidly.

Haversham nodded. 'The girl?'

'On an errand.'

Haversham's scepticism was plain. 'Lets hope she's not too long, quite getting to like her. Anyway, what next? I assume by the fact that I am still captive and alive that the jury has not returned.'

Pavel continued to scan the rooftops. 'You assume correctly,' he replied.

Haversham looked puzzled. 'Strange that, would have bet the next election that they would have convicted her by now.'

Pavel smiled. 'You are letting your professional pride interfere with your continued existence.'

'Perhaps, but I expect you to kill me in any event, still can't help wondering what went wrong with the jury.'

It was his captor's turn to appear confused. 'Many men would have begged for their lives by now.'

Haversham shrugged, seemingly embarrassed by Pavel's oblique compliment. 'What about your life? Don't mean to be critical but I really can't see you walking away from all this,' Haversham said, genuinely curious about the terrorist's perceived future.

'Perhaps I do not intend to.'

Haversham considered his reply carefully before responding, 'Then I am right to be a little crestfallen about my chances of survival.'

Pavel yawned then lit a cigarette.

'Do I bore you?' Haversham asked angrily, suddenly furious that this stranger could find talk of his imminent death so tiresome.

Pavel appeared surprised by his response. 'I am sorry. I am tired, not uncaring.'

'Fine,' Haversham said sharply then folded his arms across his chest and the bulky waistcoat. 'Pavel?'

The terrorist nodded for him to continue.

'I know this waistcoat may well be the height of fashion in your circles, but is there any prospect of taking the damn thing off?'

'No. Lydia also has a remote unit, and if I fall she will press the button.'

Haversham glanced towards the door,

'Hasn't got lost, has she?'

Pavel exhaled.

227

'Just pray that Jenny Fox is not lost.'

The Attorney General took a deep breath. 'Look, you're going to kill me etcetera, etcetera, but I wouldn't mind knowing just a teeny bit more about the background to all this before I – what is the cliché? – "Take the secret to the grave."'

'The English; barking mad. Deranged people who prefer tea to Vodka and football to sex.'

'Rugby man myself,' Haversham replied evenly, raising one eyebrow.

'Do not try to make me like you, Mr Prosecutor,' Pavel warned.

'Wouldn't dream of it; anyway, how does one get into your line of work?'

'*One*,' he paused to emphasise Haversham's pomposity, 'cares.'

'Is that why you saved my life?'

'Are you thanking me? Really, there is no need, *one* does *one's* best.'

'Seriously. I want to try to understand.'

'You have, can have, no comprehension. If you did, you could not be part of a government that knowingly gives its own children leukaemia.'

Haversham nodded. 'You mean all this nonsense about the "Circle of Poison"?'

Pavel looked angry. 'Fact not non-sense'

Haversham shook his head.

'A defence smoke screen, that is all.'

'Do you deny it exists?'

'On the evidence I have seen and heard; yes. I have read the dead man's reports, nothing wrong with the samples.'

Pavel stubbed out his cigarette on the windowsill. 'Where do you think Jenny Fox received her samples from?'

The lawyer pondered the question for a moment. 'I see,' he replied. 'You were her digger.'

'Amongst other things.'

'An unimpeachable source,' Haversham muttered.

'Mr Prosecutor, I travelled the third world and your own country for those samples. They were untainted, unlike Easterman's.'

'You have to say that.'

'It can be the only explanation,' Pavel replied calmly, logic restored, but the insistent pain from his stomach was beginning to cloud his mind.

'You all right?' Haversham asked him, surprised at his own concern. Pavel winced and gritted his teeth.

'Just the legacy of my own government's caring policies.'

Haversham hazarded a guess: 'Chernobyl?'

Pavel's eyes flicked towards him.

'You were there?'

'Only at the end, during the clean-up.' Pavel laughed bitterly. 'At least that was how the Kremlin played the deadly farce out.'

He returned his attention to the world outside.

'They called them the Liquidators. Six hundred thousand souls bussed in as "volunteers".' He shook his head in bitter disbelief. 'In my country there are no "volunteers", only a choice between the worst of two evils; but Chernobyl was the worst fate. Most are dead. Those who are not would rather be. I was glad when my mother and father passed on.'

Haversham did not speak, did not move. Pavel continued his story.

'She was a nurse, he was a doctor, but they were genuine volunteers. Stupidly, they loved their country and its suffering people. I was with my unit on leave in a Black Sea resort when the rumours started. We all said it couldn't be true; no government would do that to its own people, but of course Stalin had done worse. My parents could not be contacted. The whole area was being kept under martial law. I deserted. Made my way there.'

He pursed his lips before continuing.

'It was worse, much worse than I could ever have imagined. Hospitals like charnel houses. Abandoned schools, a wasted landscape. Desolate and hopeless. I found them in their one-room apartment; dying.'

He shook his head to dispel the vision.

'And that, Mr Prosecutor, Geoffrey Haversham, is how *one* gets into this line of work.'

The lawyer was deeply moved. Pavel's grief was real, his story unquestionably so, and in that moment he suffered a dark insight.

'You helped them to die?'

Pavel did not respond.

'And now, you too are dying.'

Pavel studied the rooftops, watching for the first marksmen to arrive.

'Then I am a dead man,' Haversham whispered. Outside, a screeching choir of police sirens shattered the air.

1.02 p.m., The Jury Room

Bob was slick, Alex had to give him that much. Denzel's question had been answered smoothly in a mellifluous voice that silently accused the asker of ingratitude. Bob's lined face wore a 'more in sorrow than in anger' patina: Uncle Bob, martyr; Denzel, ungrateful child.

'He was just extremely lucky. I don't think he will be that lucky again.' Alex could discern the threat implicit in the comment. Denzel tensed. Bob pressed his advantage.

'No, not likely at all.'

'I owe you, man,' Denzel responded. 'I know that. If there's ever anything . . .'

'There isn't. There will not be, not now, but answer me one question, truthfully.'

'I'll try.'

'Who changed your mind about the verdict?'

'It isn't who, Bob,' Denzel replied, but was unable to prevent his eyes flicking over to Alex, 'but what.'

'Go on,' Bob urged.

'Just something that doesn't add up,' Denzel shrugged, then wrapped his arms around his muscular trunk.

'That something was enough to change your vote. Indulge an old man, explain; perhaps I'll be able to clear it up for you.'

231

'You mean change his mind,' Alex added. Bob tapped his pipe on the table.

'It's his turn on the clock, Alex. You'll get yours soon enough.' Bob's tone was dismissive, but seemed to find some sympathy with the others. Alex mentally buttoned his lip. Denzel continued.

'It's just, like, I don't get it, you know, how the shoot-out worked.' He gestured towards the Prof. 'Like Eric was saying yesterday about that cause and effect and stuff, got me thinking on last night and more today. Like, there are no witnesses, man, no one to tell us what happened, just a lot of scientists with slide rules working the thing out after the dust has settled and four people were, like, smoke, you know?'

He shrugged once more, seemingly embarrassed by the attention. Pearl nodded encouragement, Grace beamed a film-star smile in his direction, Bob lit his pipe and the Prof looked crestfallen that his scientific approach had propagated another not guilty vote, Danno and Pitbull just looked half-puzzled, half-bored. Mouse kept her eyes riveted to the table-top whilst Kaftan doodled idly on a scrap of paper; Kalsi listened carefully as he began to expand his thoughts.

'Well, it was like Jenny the Fox's barrister said in his speech, "How did she get her head wound?" 'Cos for one I'd surely like to know that thing.'

Alex shook his head in admiration. It was neat and a point that he had overlooked in his battle of wills with Bob. The evidence had come to light in the second week of the trial when the young, overworked doctor from the Accident and Emergency Unit of the hospital where Jenny Fox was taken under armed guard gave his nervous account of her examination.

Court Two, The Old Bailey, Day Nine of the Trial

The fresh-faced medic had stuttered slightly as he took the oath. Like so many others, he felt intimidated by the law and all its antiquated trappings. He grasped his examination notes like a talisman. The Attorney General, a consummate professional, noted the intern's discomfort and, after establishing his qualifications, smoothed his way into the evidence.

In the court, the professionals appeared nonchalant and dispassionate, the peering public gallery completely the reverse.

'Was she conscious when you examined her?'

'Yes, though obviously still in shock.'

The AG sternly raised one eyebrow. 'And what did your examination reveal?'

The witness glanced down at his notes. 'She complained of a pain to the,' he raised his right hand to the base of his own skull, 'right occipital: this part here.' He smiled shyly towards the jury. 'I examined the area: there was a contusion – bruising in laymen's terms – which could be seen through the hair, but the skin had not been broken.'

'And that would be enough to render her unconscious?'

'Yes, I suppose so; well, that's what she told me, and what the police said. Let me put it another way; whilst I'm no expert, it's certainly credible.'

'But was she *compos mentis*?' the AG asked.

'Was she in control of her faculties? Yes, I would say so,' the doctor answered, finding fresh confidence with each reply.

'Did you ask her what had occurred?'

'I did.' He found a portion of his notes that dealt with their conversation. 'She said she had been struck from behind whilst leaving a research centre.'

The AG paused for a moment. It had the desired effect: even Alex concentrated more fully.

'Was that all she said? Think carefully.'

The medic's new-found confidence deserted him, run to ground by the gravitas of the questioner's voice. He checked his notes more carefully, his lips moving slightly as he mentally rehearsed his reply.

'No. She said he was dead, murdered, and it was all her fault.'

The public gallery began to mutter, but an usher stationed nearby hushed them to obedient silence. The AG sank slowly, satisfied, to his seat. Jenny Fox's QC stood abruptly, then leant languidly with his elbows resting on a wooden lectern.

'But she never said that *she* had killed him did she, doctor?'

The medic began to glance down once more to his notes.

'No. Use your memory.'

233

He furrowed his brow.

'No, she didn't,' he stammered.

'And if she had, you would have made a note of it?'

'Yes, I suppose so.'

'Don't suppose anything,' he continued angrily. 'You would have noted it.'

'Yes, I su— Yes, definitely.'

'But you are sure she made the statement you recorded?'

'Yes, word for word; it's not every day someone comes to the A. and E. under armed escort. I wasn't going to get it wrong, at least I hope I didn't.'

He was still nervous, but his professionalism was being brought into question in a national trial; he steeled himself.

'But now you are not sure?'

'It's there; she said it.'

'And this is in the context of somebody, and I use your own words, "still suffering from shock"? Did you think that was fair?'

The judge growled, then spoke menacingly.

'Fairness is a question for me to decide, Mr Milton, and what the jury make of Dr Fox's words is a question for them.'

Milton nodded without verbal apology. It was clear to Alex that this was a damage limitation exercise by the defence. The prosecution would claim that Jenny Fox's words of remorse, recorded meticulously in the hospital, were the words of a killer, caught bloody-handed, and could not be interpreted otherwise. Then the barrister moved his cross-examination on to the subject of Jenny Fox's head injury.

'This contusion, this bruising, was consistent with a blow from a blunt object, was it not?'

The doctor looked to be on firmer ground as he answered. 'Definitely: as I said, there was no break in the skin.'

'And it is inconsistent with a ricochet from a bullet?'

The doctor faltered once more, one minute on concrete, the next on quicksand. 'I'm not really qual—'

'You are a doctor, please answer,' Milton demanded.

'Highly unlikely,' the witness replied.

'My lord,' Milton continued. 'The defence will call upon expert evidence, all of which has been properly disclosed to the prosecution, to prove that it is not merely highly unlikely, but impossible.'

'Then please be good enough to wait until your expert gives that opinion,' the judge answered testily. Milton smiled benignly.

'Nearly finished, doctor.' Alex thought the witness might faint with relief, then Milton asked him, 'She was attacked from behind?'

'It's very likely.'

'And I don't suppose that with three dead men and no other suspects you can tell us who the fourth man might be who attacked her?'

It wasn't a question, it was a rehearsal for a jury speech. The AG sprang to his feet; the judge barked a warning to Milton that any further misbehaviour would find him in contempt of court, but the point had been made and had lodged somewhere in the recesses of Denzel's brain.

Denzel shook his head as he continued to enhance his reasons for disquiet. The other ten listened intently. On the wall the air-conditioning kicked back into action and Pearl began to click away at her knitting once more.

'The way I see it,' Denzel said, 'is this: we got four people outside the building where the hit went down; Jenny the Fox, her two oppos, you know, the dead guys? And the security man who gets wasted. I mean, who smashed her on the head, man? That barrister man was right, there was another person there, must have been.'

Alex scanned around the table, all of them were nodding in agreement, even the Prof. Bob took a blow on his pipe, billowing more smoke into the now fuggy air.

'Not necessarily,' Bob said. 'What if the security guard hit her first, before the killing started, her two friends start shooting, he shoots back; that's what the ballistics expert said.'

'That wasn't what Jenny said in her evidence,' Alex stated firmly.

'And why should we believe her, Alex?' Bob replied.

Alex hastily recalled the Scenes of Crime evidence, from the team who had painstakingly recorded every item at the research centre. 'Because it doesn't fit with the measurements. I know measurements, it's my job. Look, the bodies of the Cresta brothers were fifteen yards away from the body of the security guard. They all died from injuries caused by entry wounds to the front, that means they were facing forward when they died.'

'Don't you mean facing each other, Alex?' Bob asked.

'No, I mean facing their killers, and that, Robert, is a very different matter.' Alex paused to allow what he was contending to sink in, then renewed his assault on the prosecution's case.

'The Attorney General said in his closing speech that it must have been the guard who knocked her unconscious, but that has got to be wrong. Think about it, he hits her from behind, why? He's armed, he's got them at a disadvantage, just has to say "stick'em up". But instead he hits her, runs fifteen yards, turns, and gets himself killed. It defies logic and common sense.' Alex nodded to the Prof, who belatedly blinked his eyes in recognition.

'People do all kinds of strange things in the heat of the moment, Alex,' Bob countered. 'You can't be sure it didn't happen that way.'

'I can't be sure that it did, and that's the test. If we aren't sure, where does it leave the rest of the case against her?'

The others shook their heads, apart from Bob who eyed Alex warily.

'You're bang on,' he said to a faintly embarrassed Denzel. 'Who hit Jenny Fox from behind? And why was she left alive?'

'Luck,' Bob replied. 'Her good fortune, or bad, depending on the outcome of our verdicts.'

'No, not luck, Bob, they needed a whipping girl, and they certainly achieved that, didn't they? I'm ready for another vote,' Alex concluded. 'Anyone care to join me?'

1.23 p.m., Wilberforce Street, Islington

Ray Prince pulled up outside the home of Mrs Joanne Dempster, feeling slightly dirty. It was the second house visit he'd made that day to a widow and for the first time in his career he began to wonder if anyone really cared. As he approached the front door he decided that they didn't. As long as it all happened somewhere else and not on their own doorstep, people really didn't care whether murder and terrorism were rife. It was a sort of complacency; people were more concerned with paying the mortgage every month and hoping there was enough left over to get by. Getting by, that was it; the thought was reinforced in his mind when he reached for the doorbell just as the neighbour came rushing out of her own door, head down, no time to even look, let alone care what a police car was doing parked outside the Dempsters' house.

Within seconds of ringing the doorbell Prince was face to face with Joanne Dempster. She was thirty-seven years old but looked younger, with her small frame, plain face, brown shoulder-length hair cut in a smooth bob. As Prince introduced himself, he could sense the wilfulness in her sharp little eyes.

'I wondered how long it would take you,' she said pushing the door wide open.

'You were expecting us?'

'Yes.'

'How come?'

'Just a matter of time, Adrian said,' she answered, her northern accent still stubbornly refusing to relinquish its grip on those flat vowels. She turned her back and headed down the hallway to the kitchen, which was fenced off from the living room by a childproof gate. Prince followed her and peered over to where a small boy played happily with brightly coloured toys.

'Alexander,' she explained nodding towards the toddler.

'Your only one?'

'No, Hannah is at school, she's eight now.'

'Been hard, I expect,' Prince said gazing at the child.

'At times,' she conceded.

'Why didn't you come forward earlier, Mrs Dempster?'

'I couldn't.'

'But that's what your late husband would have wanted, surely?'

'Ha,' she snorted, 'and so there it is again. He just can't leave us alone, even beyond the bloody grave he can't leave us.'

'I'm not with you.'

237

'He was always the same Adrian, for ever telling us that things would be all right, just listen to Daddy, he would say; well, look where that got us, the bloody coward. I wasn't going to give him the satisfaction of dying for something he believed in.' She rounded on Prince bitterly.

'But . . .'

'No buts about it, superintendent, think about it from the point of view of those who have to live with his mistakes; it's easy for him.'

'I can't pretend to know what it's like to lose someone so close, Mrs Dempster, but I do know one thing: whatever it was that your husband put in motion he did the right thing and for that you must be proud.'

'Pride! Is that what you'll call it when they come to repossess the house? When I have to tell Hannah that she won't be able to go to school with her friends any more? That there is no money to buy food and Christmas presents and God knows what else. That's nothing to do with pride, superintendent. That's what I call stupidity.'

'Where is the tape, Mrs Dempster?'

She opened up the gate to the living room and silently walked over to her young son, who gurgled excitedly as she bent down to retrieve the red and yellow children's tape recorder more used to playing nursery rhymes than the confessions of a whistle blower. The young lad watched his mother as she pressed the eject button and pulled out an unmarked cassette. She took one last look at it and handed it over to Prince who watched the scene unfolding with sadness.

'Here, take it, and don't bring it back. I've got to start again now and so have the children.'

'I understand.'

'He hasn't let anyone near it till now,' she said, indicating the youngster, 'listens to his daddy's voice every night before he goes to sleep, but he's got to move on now. Take it away, please.'

'Thank you, Mrs Dempster.'

'I won't be here if you come back. It's over now.'

'I understand, but there's bound to be an inquiry.'

'Can't you point them away from us? We've suffered enough because of this thing.'

'This thing, Mrs Dempster, as you put it, is beyond my control, but I shall do my best.'

Prince marched back to the car with the tape safely in his pocket. The Prime Minister had been right so far. The mail registration book at the laboratory had revealed that Easterman had indeed posted something to the house of Adrian Dempster the night of his death. Prince could only hope that the information the tape contained would be sufficient to end this mania. As the spools hissed into action and the car headed back to Westminster, he wasn't disappointed. The voice of Adrian Dempster came through on the speakers with all the answers they needed.

'I didn't really know which way to turn when I had to face myself. Silly, isn't it, really? After all these years not knowing anything, all of a sudden I hit the jackpot. I don't expect you to truly understand what it's like and nor do I expect that you would want to. But let me tell you, it's like nothing else on this earth.

'I'm sending this to you, doctor, because I know you're a man of your word. I have always respected you and even sometimes admitted my envy of you over the years. When I approached you about Biotron I should have told you the whole truth. That way I suppose there would have been a chance to survive this, but not now. By the time you're listening to this, I'll be gone. What I'm about to tell you now is the truth and only you can properly know what to do with it. I guess in a way it's a coward's journey, no doubt that's what my wife will say when it comes to pass. I would have taken the responsibility myself, but in the end I just can't face it.

'Two months ago when my father died a great many things happened to me. It made me look at the whole thing right from the beginning. You see, I was a clever boy at school. I did well at exams, sailed through them in fact. My parents were working people, salt of the earth I suppose you could call them. They never wanted anything else from me but to get an education and have a better life than they did. Ha, some ambition! It's so ironic, isn't it, that the life those poor people saw as being so much better than their own is no better at all. I know, because I have lived it.

'Joanne, well, she was different from the other girls at school, she knew what she wanted and I obviously figured in her plans to escape.

Not that I minded, in fact I'd been reminded so often that some day I wouldn't have time for the likes of my own friends from the estate, I began to believe it. That was the first mistake. Never forget where you've come from.

'*Anyway, on to university and I worked my way through it so easily. Deferring my gratification, said Joanne, and I believed her. That was the second mistake. Never trust in the future. When I joined the service, everything seemed so right, nice easy job, nice easy pension eventually, you know the sort of thing. I could have been a research chemist but the money wouldn't have been so good to begin with and Joanne wanted a house for our first baby. A house, for God's sake, that was all it took for me to cross the line.*

'*Within two years of working at the inspectorate I was in deep. But it didn't seem to matter. Everyone was doing it. First of all the senior guys laugh at you because you can't see past the principles. That's what keeps you poor, they say. A principled pauper. Then before I knew it I was laughing too, laughing with the others at our own cleverness, not caring about anything but the money. And the money paid for everything: it paid for the schools, the house, the cars, the holidays, the meals, the mistress, everything, and it kept Joanne happy. What more could I ask for? The first batch of samples wasn't that difficult. I collected them from the Biotron plant as normal, only this time I didn't even have to get my lab coat dirty. Instead I got to have lunch with one of the directors in the box at Ascot whilst they were brought to my car. Nothing could have been easier, could it? And beside the samples was a bundle of notes. I remember them so clearly, amazed at their freshness, how crisp and new they smelled.*

'*After that, everything I sent to you from Biotron was provided by them, no spot checks from me, no paperwork compiled by me, nothing. Anything could have been in those bottles as far as I was concerned. Then things changed. The more money I got, the less important it seemed to visit home like I used to; the phone calls became less frequent and for a short time I really had forgotten all about my past. As long as our Adrian is doing all right, then we need no more from him, my parents would tell my younger brother who worked in the factory beside my dad. He must have suffered something rotten because of me. They couldn't afford the money to send us both to college and so his life was over before it began. Thirteen hours a day inhaling paint at the local factory. It's no life at all, is it? But you see, it didn't matter to me because I was all right.*

'They told me my father was dying on a Saturday afternoon. Strange really, because we always watched the football on a Saturday afternoon when I was a kid, but now he was dying. They hadn't wanted to tell me before, knowing how busy I was. Of course, I went to see him straight away. He loved me with a passion, my father did. And suddenly I found I couldn't look him in the eye. Even as he lay there dying, I couldn't look him in the eye. All the lies and deceit came rushing into that space between us. What kind of a son was I really? He died not knowing that I was a liar and greed-driven con man. How can I ever look my own son in the eye with the same sort of honesty that my father cherished till his death? Because, after all, he was who he was and he was happy with it. Never been abroad in his life, never owned a fast car, never wanted to own his council house, never wanted anything but for me to make him proud. I let him down and that is something I cannot live with. He died not knowing what I was really like.

'The thing that made me approach you was the bereavement card from Chemitech. They owned the paint factory, which killed my father, drying up his lungs in a slow, painful death. All those years he worked for them and they still managed to get his name wrong on the card. It's not William, I thought, it's Bill, it's always been Bill.

'Not much, you may think, to cause all this trouble but when I realised that Biotron and Chemitech and the paint factory were all just part of one giant money machine to these people, I could stand it no longer. So that's why I am giving you the responsibility of telling the world what goes on. It's all corrupt, Dr Easterman, the whole stinking pile of it.

'Check the freight depot at Ashford and you'll find what you need. And one last favour, could you send this tape to my own son when you have got what you want? He has to know that I did it for him.'

2.05 p.m., The Jury Room

T he air-conditioning now spewed hot air into the room excessively, transforming it into a sweat box. Despite complaints to the chief usher, the unruly machinery refused to co-operate and was to be switched off. But nothing could have reduced the emotional heat contained in the room. Cold drinks of squash had been provided and were gulped down in contemplative silence, a variety of sandwiches consumed purely for energy. They were all sapped, sucked dry by the vitriolic discussions and the absence of an end to their dilemma.

Since the last vote had been taken, Bob had suggested a break, a chance to calm down and think clearly about their task. His suggestion was greeted with limp relief. From a low-backed padded seat against the outward wall, Alex surveyed the scene: Bob was chatting in a low voice to the Mouse at the table. The Mouse was listening without replying, except to shake her head from time to time; Bob continued smilingly to grind away, his tie unloosened at the neck.

At the table's other end, Pitbull and Danno, sweating foreheads, shirt buttons undone, scowled their way through their meagre lunch, the former gesturing to where Princess Grace and Denzel talked in low voices. The Prof and Kaftan sat in isolated silence, one seat apart, but a world away from any understanding. Pearl, still clicking,

243

clucked encouragingly to Kalsi, who appeared more animated than at any time over the past four weeks and Alex knew why: when they resumed discussion it would be her turn next, at ten o'clock on the jury dial.

The recent vote had changed the status quo, not hugely but enough to keep Alex's own hope alive and kicking. When Bob had trawled through the ballot papers, he had shaken his head whilst announcing, 'Six not guilty, four guilty, one not sure.' Alex wanted to argue that a 'not sure' meant 'not guilty', but something held him back. He reasoned that the writer of that confused statement could not be Bob, Pitbull or Danno. It was unlikely to be the Prof; therefore Kalsi was the only other possibility.

He was tempted, during the much-needed break, to persuade her of the declaration's reality, but he had enjoyed few conversations with the distant young woman during their jury service and knew that she might react badly to any intrusion. Besides, she was getting there under her own taciturn steam.

The air-conditioning whirred, gulped, then died. Bob took it as his cue to call the meeting back to order. Reluctantly, the eleven resumed their seats at the table as Bob outlined their position.

'As I see it, we're stuck until the judge releases us from our duty. At the moment, we're no nearer reaching a verdict than we were yesterday lunchtime.'

'Further away,' Pitbull muttered sullenly.

'We were 9–3 guilty then.' Danno's almond eyes switched to Alex for signs of argument.

Alex smiled hungrily, showing his teeth. Danno dropped his attention to the crowded table-top.

'I agree with you, son,' Bob replied wistfully, 'but folk are entitled to their opinion, however misguided.'

Alex tutted, Bob ignored him. Kalsi took up the debate.

'I'm a little tired of you men acting like spoilt boys.' She stared reproachfully at Pitbull, Alex and Bob.

'Speak, sister,' Kaftan said gleefully. Kalsi's flat stare caused her to straighten her smile. 'Well speak anyway,' she whispered. Kalsi nodded.

'The majority of this jury has been too wrapped up in petty personality battles to consider the case objectively.'

'Then that is my fault,' Bob offered, almost sadly. Here we go, Alex thought. 'I'm the foreman, clerk of works, should have kept better control.'

Another tack, Alex noted: power through humility. But Kalsi remained stern-faced and replied, 'Yes.' She paused, allowing the verbal slap to sting. Bob resurrected his role as ageing martyr, allowing his face to colour.

'But no matter, we are where we are, it is how we proceed that is vital.'

The quiet woman's voice carried an air of grave knowledge, even the aggressive Pitbull was hushed by her tones.

'Justice must be done.'

'We are doing our best,' the Prof said, stung by the implied criticism.

'Then we must do better,' she continued. 'This verdict will stay with us for ever: we must know that what we do is right and for the right reasons.'

'Which are?' Bob asked politely.

'That the verdict is just. I swore on the Koran to reach that state of mind, as yet I'm unsure: that was my view in the last ballot.'

Alex had been right, she was wavering. He began to speak. 'But doesn't that m—?'

She silenced him with a basilisk stare. 'As yet it means nothing, it will only have meaning when I feel in my soul that it does.'

'Bleeding Sunday school again,' Pitbull whispered to Danno. Kalsi nodded.

'I am not attempting to convert anyone, just to justify my viewpoint.'

Bob spoke. 'With respect, Kalsi, and I mean that, shouldn't we be getting to the point?'

'I am,' she replied, 'and as I have been patient during your questions, I ask the same from you.'

Bob scowled, but bit back any ill-tempered response. Kalsi gazed away and spoke.

'Another time, in another life.'

Kaftan's attention focused hopefully, but Kalsi shook her head.

'Before my conversion to Islam, I worked for a major shoe-shop chain as a buyer. As part of my job I knew intimately every style of shoe, every mule, stiletto, loafer, brogue and court shoe.'

Alex furrowed his brow; where was this taking them?

'But it also taught me to know the size of a shoe, just by looking down at a person's feet.'

'Bullshit,' Pitbull whispered. Pearl glared harshly at him. 'Well it is,' he said, defensively. Kalsi stared straight ahead.

'You,' she said to Pitbull, 'are a size 9, but your left foot is slightly larger than your right, so you buy 10s and wear an inner-sole on the right one.' She paused. 'You also have fallen arches.'

Pitbull's mouth gaped open. Kalsi continued.

'I can furnish the rest of you with the same details, if you like.' They shook their heads. 'As I was saying, it's just one of those things you pick up.'

'Where does that take you, Kalsi?' Alex asked.

'Back to the trial, where else? It was part of the prosecution's case. The Attorney General was proving that the clothing had been worn by the killer.'

Alex's heart leapt, just a little: she had said 'worn by the killer' not 'worn by Jenny Fox'.

'In the exhibit bag was a pair of black boots, do you remember?'

Alex did, and the video of the killing flashed across his memory. The woman had kneeled down on the victim's back; the camera caught it all. He wanted to see the video again, though its content sickened him; there had to be something he had missed, a clue, but he would wait his turn. Kalsi spoke again.

'It's just nagged at me since the exhibits were passed around.'

Alex had been feeling rough that day.

Court Two, The Old Bailey, Day Twelve

He was hungover. A savage night's celebratory drinking at a private club had left him with severe post-alcoholic distress. His head reverberated with the soundtrack of 'Zulu' pounding ferociously, whilst his stomach performed acidic acrobatics. It was not the ideal time to hear about blood spotting and staining.

Alex swallowed hard and reached for another glass of tepid water from the carafe provided as the Attorney General sank slowly to his seat on the front row of counsel's benches. In front of him lay several items of black clothing, still sealed in their plastic bags. Because of the blood on them the lawyers were unwilling to expose themselves to possible infection.

He had proved the provenance of the clothing earlier. It had been stripped from the person of Dr Jenny Fox at the police station, all in accordance with the Police and Criminal Evidence Act. In the witness box, a forensic scientist had just completed his evidence in chief for the prosecution. An expert on bloodstaining, he had examined all the items recovered from Jenny Fox and concluded that the splattering of blood was consistent with direct proximity to the murder. Jenny Fox's barrister took up the reins.

'Now, the seminal work on this topic is Professor John Glaister's *Medical Jurisprudence and Toxicology*, is it not?'

The scientist nodded then added, 'Very reliable source book.'

'He describes six patterns into which he groups bloodstains?'

'Generally, yes.'

The QC casually selected a copy of the book from his lectern, flicking to the page where a yellow post-it sticker featured prominently. He began to read.

'There are, firstly, drops, as the name suggests, caused by blood dripping directly from above.'

'Correct, and the shape of the drop will change according to the height from which it has fallen: it's called "starring".'

The scientist was enjoying the exchange.

'But none in this case?'

'No,' the witness replied. 'The victim's head, or what was left of it, was on the floor.'

The QC nodded, then moved on. 'Secondly, there are "splashes": this is where droplets have travelled through the air and hit a wall or surface at an angle?'

'Quite right,' the witness agreed. 'It is rather like an elongated exclamation mark; the "blob" indicating the direction of travel. It's useful where a body may have been moved after death in order to determine where the *actual* assault occurred.'

'But we know that in this case, do we not?'

'We do.'

247

'Next, Professor Glaister classifies "spurts"; now what are they?'

'Basic biology really, because the blood is pumped around by the heart under great pressure. If a major vein or artery is severed, there will be a forceful outflow of blood.'

'As was the case with the deceased?'

'It was.'

'And this spurting will stain the attacker? Will travel up the walls, sometimes even to the ceiling?'

Alex couldn't see where this was going – all it had served so far was to remind everyone of the hideous violence of Easterman's death – but the witness nonchalantly agreed with the last question.

'Quite. The clothing I examined, taken from the defendant, was stained with blood.'

'Thank you,' the QC remarked. 'That takes me nicely to the other classifications. "Pools" of blood, as the name suggests, mark the spot where a heavily bleeding victim will have lain dead for some time; "trails" occur if a bloody corpse is moved from the scene of the killing to another location by dragging?'

Alex glanced sideways: the Mouse looked ready to lose her breakfast, the Prof was noting the classifications assiduously, whilst Pitbull and Danno were nudging each other in macabre fascination.

'But, having explained five of the six, could you define "smearing", the last group, for me?' the QC asked politely.

'Certainly. Blood smears can be left either by a wounded victim or by his assailant stained with fresh blood whilst gripping or brushing against the sides of furniture, doors and walls.'

'True, true,' the silk answered. 'But isn't it also caused by the smearing of existing fresh stains?'

'It can be.' The witness was beginning to look less confident of his ground; his eyes narrowed as he waited for the next question.

'You mentioned earlier that the clothing you examined was stained with blood?'

'I did.'

'Look at your original report.'

Hesitantly, the witness did so.

'There,' the barrister continued, 'you say that the blood was "smeared heavily", not "dropped", not "splashed", not "spurted", not "pooled" nor "trailed", but "smeared heavily".'

248

'Yes, but . . .'

'Each is very different, is it not?'

'Yes, I'm trying to explain.'

Milton smiled. 'I haven't asked you a direct question yet.'

'We are all painfully aware of that fact, Mr Milton,' the judge drawled lazily. 'Do move this along.'

Milton nodded at the rebuke.

'Before beginning your initial examination, were you told how the murder occurred and where the clothing was recovered from?'

'I was.'

'That meant you knew that the defendant was unconscious on the arrival of the police?'

'I did.'

Alex could now see where the wily lawyer was going.

'You know the expertise of the Scenes of Crime Officers? You know that they would interfere as little as possible with any bloodstaining patterns whilst removing clothing?'

'Some interference is inevitable,' the witness replied guardedly.

'But not to the point of, and I use your own scientific expression, "heavy smearing"?'

'I would hope not, but we do not know what the defendant was doing prior to their arrival.'

Milton switched his attention briefly to the jury: his look said, 'Pay attention, boys and girls'. He spoke once more.

'Let me put another explanation to you.'

The uncomfortable scientist flicked his eyes to his questioner.

'If an unconscious person were to be dressed in clothing, already heavily bloodstained, would that not account for "heavy smearing": the smearing of existing fresh stains?'

The witness looked bewildered as the Court awaited his response. Reluctantly he replied. 'Possibly, but . . .'

'Thank you very much,' Milton interrupted. 'No further questions, my lord.'

'I have one,' the Attorney General said, rising swiftly to his feet. 'You were about to qualify your answer to my learned friend?'

The witness grinned smugly. 'I was: all I was going to say was that in thirty years of forensic science, I have never heard of such a ridiculous scenario.'

Alex wondered just how ridiculous it really was.

In the jury room, Kalsi expanded her disquiet.

'I looked at those shoes, I looked at Jenny Fox's feet and I am sure they did not belong to her; they were just too big.'

'Hardly scientific, though, is it?' the Prof remarked.

Kalsi shrugged.

'What about the OJ Simpson trial?' Pitbull asked. 'Those gloves he dropped, I mean, his lawyer made him try them on.' He adopted a bad American accent. 'If de gloves don fit, you acquit.' He smiled straight into Denzel's face, who let it pass.

Danno took up the baton. 'Yeah, why didn't she try them on?'

'Let's ask her to now,' Alex suggested, looking around the jury members' faces. They all nodded their approval, apart from Bob.

'Can't,' he whispered, 'the evidence is closed. Once the jury retires, no fresh evidence can be heard.'

'You seem to know a lot about it,' Alex said warily. Bob smiled coldly.

'Just one of those things you pick up on life's travels.'

'Really. Any other snippets of specialised legal knowledge you'd like to share with us?'

'Not at the moment, Alex, but if there is you'll be the first to know. Anyway, contact Edna the usher, write a note for the judge: he'll confirm what I've said.'

Twenty minutes later they were back in their room once more; Bob was right. The judge backed Bob's expert trial experience to the hilt; they had to decide the case on what they had heard and nothing else. Bob appeared too concerned to be smug, but Kalsi was unmoved by the judge's ruling.

'I know what I know. They are not her shoes. That means they belong to another person, the real killer. My vote is not guilty.'

Alex suppressed a smile, Pitbull was too deflated to argue, the Prof shook his head, but Danno appeared confused.

'What is it?' Alex asked him. Danno's face began to flush, his peripheral vision intercepting Pitbull's incredulous glare.

'I'm worried,' he stammered. 'I mean, I'm not sure about things any more.'

'Stupid Chink,' his ex-friend, Pitbull, spat. Pearl ceased her knitting.

'Apologise!' she demanded.

'Yeah, man,' Denzel agreed, 'you're very uncool.'

'I don't like racism,' the Prof muttered to himself. 'Nasty business.'

But Alex would not allow a side issue, no matter how distasteful, to swerve the debate away.

'Why are you unhappy?' he asked.

Danno shrugged. 'All you educated people apart from Bob, Eric and . . .' he nodded to Pitbull, 'think there's something wrong. I mean, am I missing something? It all seemed so easy, so open and shut, but now I'm not so sure.'

'Like I said,' Pitbull whispered menacingly, 'stupid Chink.'

Danno swivelled quickly. 'I'm as English as you, fascist bastard.'

Pitbull grinned. 'Later, coolie: give you a take-away you won't forget.'

Alex saw how Danno's fists were clenched; he couldn't lose the moment.

'So you're not sure?' he asked the red-faced young man.

'No, I am sure, sure now.' He pointed a finger straight into Pitbull's face. 'He's made my mind up for me: not guilty.'

Bob banged his hand down hard on the table.

'You can't do that!' he shouted.

'It's his vote, Bob, why not?' Alex demanded.

'Because he's voting out of petty dislike, not on the evidence.'

'That's my vote,' Danno reiterated quietly.

'That makes us 8–3 not guilty,' Alex said, but Bob wasn't going to let it pass so easily. He turned on Danno.

'What about the things you said yesterday, about the fingerprints? You were sure then.'

Alex didn't give him time to answer.

'Is that why you left the *Reader's Digest* book in his home, Bob?' Alex pressed. 'A little bit of subtle jury-knobbling?'

Bob's face went from pink to puce immediately.

'How dare you, Parrish? You accuse me of dishonesty: like to tell them how you got the contract for the leisure centre?'

Alex smiled, he smiled big.

'And tell me, Bob: how come you know so much about me, about all of us?'

2.51 p.m., The Jury Room

ob's colour continued to rise with the temperature in the room. He had categorically denied having any special knowledge of the jury members, but some of them wore deeply puzzled expressions. It was Pearl who demanded the resumption of calm. Alex and Bob continued to stare malevolently at each other.

'Now I've had just about enough of this,' Pearl said quietly through gritted teeth. 'Alex?' He nodded. 'Do you have a question or are you going to continue this schoolboy staring match until one of you blinks?'

'I have a question all right,' Alex replied, smiling ferally at Bob, then turning towards Pearl, 'and I've waited a very long time to ask it.'

'Well fucking ask it, then,' Pitbull demanded.

'Language,' Pearl reminded him, but Pitbull's own colour was rising sharply and the air was choked with the promise of violence. Alex reached for his bundle of jury documents and extracted a plan of the research centre. He spread it wide on the table.

'I want you all to see the videos again,' he said.

'Please, Alex,' the Mouse muttered, 'I don't think I can.'

'Me neither,' Pitbull snorted. 'Seen enough to know she wasted him.'

'Why?' asked the Prof. 'Don't we all know its hideous content by heart?'

There were murmurs of agreement from around the table. Alex turned to the Prof.

'Last night at the hotel, you said that if I could prove her innocence scientifically you would change your vote.'

The Prof looked embarrassed but did not dare to look Bob or the fearsome Pitbull in the eye.

'I said "might" not "would", and to be frank I only said that to get you off my back.' He shuddered involuntarily. 'This is all really too, too, much.'

'But you are a man of your word.' It wasn't a question and every jury member knew it. It was social blackmail but Alex refused to back down.

'Yes, of course,' the Prof mumbled. Alex looked from one face to the next, moving around the dial, trying to force his utter sincerity down their throats until he came to Bob.

'My question is, can I see the videos once more? That's all, no tricks. You made the rules, now play by them.'

Alex noticed that Bob's breathing was faster than usual: this was all getting to him. Good, Alex thought. Bob drummed his fingers on the table-top. It was his turn to move his eyes from head to head but Alex's earlier accusation had thrown suspicion upon him and most refused eye contact. Bob shrugged.

'If you want to put these people through that ordeal then who am I to stop you?'

Who indeed? Alex pondered.

Ten minutes later the video equipment was assembled in their room by Edna the usher and a security guard. It was placed on the table and their chairs were arranged in a horseshoe around it. Edna offered to operate the remote control. Alex thanked her for her kindness and plucked the slim, black, plastic object from her hand.

'Any nearer a verdict?' she asked whilst standing at the door.

'Yes,' Alex replied, 'and getting closer all the time.'

He waited until she had closed it before beginning.

'Now, Bob, you asked me how I got the contract for the leisure centre and the answer is because I'm a bloody good

254

architect. I know how buildings work, what makes them tick: as a watchmaker that should please you. But like anything else sometimes the truth is so obvious it can be overlooked, and for that I apologise.'

He flicked the play button. The monitor clicked into life and the fuzzed lines turned to a picture.

'This is the entry. All buildings have entrances and exits.'

They all watched the three eco-terrorists storm the front of the building. A number of other sequential clips monitored their violent progress through the centre. Mouse looked away during the beatings. The Prof shook his head. 'But where, oh where, is this leading us?'

'Patience,' Alex whispered. The video moved on to show the brutal execution of Charles Easterman.

'I never wanted to see that again, Alex,' the Mouse whispered accusingly, 'I've had nightmares about it.'

'We all have,' Kaftan muttered dreamily. Alex turned to face the Mouse.

'I'm sorry, truly sorry. If there was any other way . . .'

'Get on with it,' Bob ordered. It was at the point where the killers were walking away from the corpse and out of video shot. The tape returned to its fuzzy bars.

'Where did they go?' Alex asked.

'What do you mean?' the Prof asked, his scientific curiosity in the first stages of arousal.

'They had to go somewhere; everything goes somewhere,' Alex replied.

'Outside,' Bob said flatly, 'to murder the security guard.'

'Not from here they didn't,' Alex said, then turned to the plans of the building he had extracted earlier. 'This is the floor where it all happened.' He traced his finger over the spot where the prosecution had circled Easterman's corpse. 'The video clearly showed them moving in this direction.' They all watched intently as Alex followed the route with his right index finger. 'There are three doors on this corridor. Two lead up to the next floor, the other down to an underground car park. They couldn't have escaped outside by this route.' He raised his head to stare at the Prof. 'Exits and entrances: only so many.'

'They could have doubled back from the upper floor down a different exit,' Bob pushed.

'No, Bob,' Alex answered, 'no, they couldn't.'

'Why not?' the Prof asked whilst furiously tracing the route with his own finger.

'Because,' Alex raised the remote in front of him, 'it would have all been captured on video.'

The Prof nodded vigorously.

'You mean there would have been evidence of two sets of people leaving the building?'

'Exactly,' Alex replied with a smile. 'They probably changed their clothing in the downstairs car park. They must have known that Jenny Fox was due to arrive. They knock her out, kill her friends, dress her up in the black ski-suit.'

He turned to Kalsi.

'They couldn't get the shoes to fit, you were right, and the blood on the ski-suit was smeared, remember, heavily smeared, probably when they put it on her. They press her fingers on the murder weapon. The clothes already have the powder burns. The ski-mask picks up her hair samples; bingo, one patsy. They needed her alive to carry the can.'

The Prof shifted uneasily. 'But I can't be sure she didn't do it.'

Alex reached forward and placed both his hands on the Prof's shoulders, staring deeply into his glass-framed eyes.

'Eric,' he whispered, 'you can't be sure that she did.'

Alex began to nod his head; after a second or two the Prof began to nod his too.

'Just hold on one fucking minute,' Bob shouted, his voice vicious beyond all recognition.

'Robert!' Pearl said, disgusted.

He raised one finger and pointed it directly into her blushing face. 'Shut the fuck up.'

'Out of order, Bob,' Pitbull said nervously. 'Well out of order.'

The Mouse began to whimper miserably. Denzel, Grace and the others were stunned by the outburst.

'Come on, Bob,' Alex spat, 'tell us who you really are.'

Bob smiled, a smile that sent a cool shiver sprinting down Alex's back.

'I'll do better than that,' their foreman replied bitterly, 'I'll tell you who *you* really are.'

3.05 p.m., Outside the Bolthole

The street was cordoned off and all civilians evacuated from the potential bomb blast area. Brian 'Taker' Chance was quietly pleased with the way his men had dealt with this part of the operation, now it was down to him. It had taken solid police work and a touch of much needed luck to find the flat. A suspicious member of the public had telephoned to report a sighting of a man carrying what looked like a corpse, from a van to a car in an underground car park. The informant had written the registration of the vehicle down on her receipt from Sainsbury's. This was later circulated in the Greater London area. The car, a Saab, was found abandoned with its ignition barrel snapped at the back of the premises. The kidnapper had had no choice. He would have had to carry an unconscious, possibly dying man, through the teeming streets of the capital to do otherwise. They had then checked the records of the flat rental agency to acquire the occupants' details and telephone numbers. All were genuine taxpayers and registered voters apart from the occupant of the single attic flat. A description of the man who had rented it tallied with that of Pavel, 'the Liquidator', Boniak. He was up there, Chance knew it. It was almost time to make contact. He received the all clear from the ground forces and radio confirmation that the teams of marksmen were in place. There was still no word from the jury – that was good. It gave him time to bargain, that's what his training was all about. He stood on the rooftop of an adjacent building, a mobile telephone in his hand. The sun shone brightly but he felt cold. If the kidnapper blew the package then he and his men would die. All had been given the choice to retire from the operation without shame or blame. Those who were married with children had been ordered to. There was no way out and this entire episode had to end, and end soon. He tapped out the flat's telephone number; the call was answered on the second ring.

Pavel was surprised they had taken so long to make contact, then reminded himself that they would have taken time to sweep the adjacent buildings clean of potential casualties and position their marksmen strategically. He could see five or six of them peeking over the parapets, baseball caps back to front, like a gang of murderous 'rappers', each looking for 'the' shot if the occasion arose. Pavel had closed the curtains, strapped Haversham to the front door, his arms pinioned by his sides. As he took the call, he immediately switched it to conference mode on his laptop.

'Speak!'

'Let me talk to the Attorney General.'

'Speak, Mr Prosecutor.'

'I'm all right.'

'Do you need any more insulin?'

'We have sufficient,' Pavel said. 'My demands?'

'Working on them.'

'Of course you are,' Pavel replied, his voice thick with Soviet irony. 'This is still a race against time, perhaps you had forgotten?'

'Please, can we talk in a civil manner?' Chance asked, his voice reasonable, measured, designed to placate.

'There is nothing to talk about. Either the Prime Minister has met my demands or he has not.'

'We are trying, really we are.'

'For your information, Mr Haversham is tied to the door; any assault will injure him badly. That also places him directly in the line of your sniper's fire. Until you have the information, please do not contact me again; my guest only has so many fingers.' He closed the connection. 'Never thought I would die with a member of the British Establishment; many strange things have happened in my life, but I did not expect this.'

'Why didn't you ask him about the girl?' Haversham asked over his shoulder.

'She is dead. That is what we all agreed.'

'Now what?'

'Well, I am afraid you must remain where you are. By now heat-

seeking probes will tell them where we are physically. They have
to know I am telling the truth.'

'And?'

'And, I hope that your brother is a very stubborn and inquisi-
tive man.'

He knew his brother possessed both of those attributes but if it
came down to a bitter choice between brotherly love and patriotic
duty, Geoffrey Haversham did not care to guess which Edward
would choose.

3.07 p.m., The Jury Room

The jury room seemed to be breathing as heavily as Bob as he held
them with his menace.

'You people have no idea what you are dealing with.' He glared
around the table. 'Not a clue, and yet you want to let Fox walk. But
you won't. You see I know. I know all about you, every single one.
There is no such thing as a blameless life. Secrets can only be hidden
not destroyed.' He smiled, but Alex could see the sweat on his brow,
marking the lie of his confidence.

'Where shall we start?' His eyes were flinty slits. 'Let's stay with
the programme, shall we? Yes, let's stay with the clock. At number
one we had the doughty Dave Conran,' he said referring to Stalin.
'Interesting man, even sold time-shares in the early days before
moving into the world of mobile phones. Nice scam. Took the
money without providing the service. Used a large number of
limited companies that he collapsed when the writs started flying,
set another up straight away. The Fraud Squad are very interested
in *his* activities.' He smiled icily. 'A little bit of consecutive prison
sentences issued on top of what his lordship dishes out for the
contempt of court.'

He turned to look at the Mouse. 'At number two we have the shy retiring Jayne Pitt.' The Mouse had her hand over her mouth in anticipated horror. 'But not so shy or retiring when shagging her brother-in-law. Been quite a while now, hasn't it? Still like the Holiday Inn? Remind me, which of the Ten Commandments is adultery?'

The Mouse began to cry, silently.

'Stop it now,' Kaftan whispered, placing an arm around the Mouse's shoulders.

'I will if you'll stop cultivating cannabis plants in your greenhouse,' Bob replied, warming to his task.

'It shouldn't be illegal,' she said defensively.

'No,' Bob agreed, 'but it is, particularly when you've got over two hundred of the leafy little devils sprouting up. A yield of about £10,000 by my reckoning. Still, you can always tell the judge that it's for personal use; might keep the sentence down to three years.'

Kaftan gulped. 'How do you . . .?'

Bob shook his head. 'Does it matter? And don't start any of that karma crap on me either.'

Kaftan and Mouse held each other like children in an air raid.

'Where was I?' Bob resumed, his cheeks puffing out with righteous zeal, as he looked through his glasses into the troubled eyes of the Prof.

'Eric, Eric, how could you?'

The Prof looked away. 'You're a bloody madman,' he said.

'Just well informed,' the foreman replied. 'You should feel at home with killers. When was it, five years ago?'

'She was in pain,' the Prof replied, his voice wavering with emotion, hands trembling on the table's top.

'Gave her a helping hand, didn't you? Still, a little bit of euthanasia never harmed anyone. Police were very suspicious, ladies and gentlemen, but not enough to press charges.' He wagged a finger at the Prof. 'Never, ever, keep a diary. Case is still open, of course: no statute of limitations on murder.'

'Me next,' Pitbull snarled, shoulders set for battle, fists clenched.

'But this is our England, isn't it?' Bob said. 'Green and pleasant, a land fit for heroes, white heroes. That's what your leaflets say, don't they? Send 'em back to Wogland, they're taking our jobs.'

He glanced over to Denzel and Princess Grace.

'And what they do to our women, well it's a disgrace. Shame is you have half a warehouse full of racist bile at your lock-up. Incitement to Racial Hatred is a serious offence.'

'They can be destroyed,' Pitbull replied. Bob smiled.

'Not before the police receive an anonymous tip-off, they can't, so shut up and listen.'

He switched his attention to Danno.

'You have a large family, all enjoying life in the West. Now that life could suddenly disappear for three of your cousins. The immigration rules are so complex these days, but your cousins must have known they needed visas to stay.' Bob nodded reasonably. 'I'm sure the Home Office will understand.'

Danno's mouth opened and closed like a fish.

'So many busybodies about,' Bob said, 'whispering to the authorities: they'd have to investigate, be a shame.'

Pearl sat with her arms folded, face set.

'And what lying poison do you have for me, Robert?'

'I hate to do this to you, I really do,' the foreman replied, awash with insincerity. 'Could destroy the very foundation of your life. Sure you want to take the risk?'

There wasn't a moment's hesitation before Pearl said, 'I've got nothing to hide.'

'I know,' he said, 'you're a fine woman: led a hard-working, law-abiding life.'

Pearl's face lightened momentarily.

'More than I can say about your old man,' Bob said.

'What?'

'Docker's strike; your old man was union convenor. They didn't want to strike, they even voted that way, but he wanted it, rigged the vote. How many of those poor bastards did he put on the dole queue?'

Pearl slammed her hand down on the table. 'That is a filthy lie.'

'Have to let the press decide, won't we?' Bob answered sweetly. 'You'll excuse me whilst I move on.'

'Bastard, lying bastard,' she shouted, then appeared shocked by her own language and began to shake. Alex watched in morbid fascination. Bob was becoming more animated as he continued his exposé of them all. He noticed a vein throbbing in Bob's temple as he turned his attention to Princess Grace.

'The icy Helena,' he began. 'How many affairs this year: is it twelve or thirteen? Still, that's not the worst of it, is it?'

'I have no idea what you are talking about, you appalling little man.'

'You tell him,' Denzel said supportively. Bob hosed him down with his eyes.

'I'll come to you in a moment.' Then returned his full basilisk stare to Grace. 'You see, ladies and gentleman, poor little Helena has a problem: a husband that she doesn't love. But he is so rich and he wants a baby so badly, but Helena, you see, she doesn't, that would tie her to him for ever.' He nodded sympathetically. 'You really should have told him before you got rid of it: it was his too.'

Alex saw the tears well in her eyes, then watched them track down her beautiful face. Denzel reached an arm around her, she shook it off with a shrug.

'She doesn't want you now,' Bob said. 'Besides, you have more pressing matters to attend to.'

Bob was breathing even faster now, as if he were in a sprint to trash them all, and his body couldn't keep up with the relentless speed of his mind.

'That little brother of yours should keep away from drugs. Wouldn't surprise me in the least if he was picked up again for possession.'

Denzel shrugged. 'He's a big boy, he knows the risks.'

'Yes,' Bob replied, 'but your mother, Edith, with her bad heart and all; how long is it since her last attack? Three, four months?'

'You don't look so well yourself,' Alex spat. Bob reached into his pocket and removed the bottle of pills Alex had seen him take, regularly, during the trial. He placed it on the table and reached for a cup of water. Alex snatched the bottle and read the label.

'Digitalis, what's that for?'

'Angina,' the Prof replied. 'Had it myself, before the by-pass.'

Bob made a lunge for the bottle; Alex easily held him off.

'Your turn, Bob. The stakes are high: your life for the truth.'

Bob reached for the telephone to the ushers' room. Pitbull clamped a hand over it.

'Do as Alex said.'

Bob's brow was now wringing with sweat. He looked from one impossibly hard face to the next, each as unforgiving as a death camp commandant.

'You . . . you can't.'

Alex rattled the bottle of pills in Bob's scarlet face.

'With these I can do exactly what I want.'

'Do we have a majority, Alex?' the Mouse asked. Alex turned to Pitbull.

'Well?'

'I want something on him first: he's got plenty on me.'

'Fair enough,' Alex said. 'Now Bob, you really look rather unwell, why don't you tell us all about it?'

3.10 p.m., The Jury Room

'This is murder,' Bob gasped. 'All of you are murderers, I'm just an old man, never done anyone any harm.'

He was clutching at his chest. Alex opened the bottle of pills and counted them out into his hand.

'Six,' he said, then took one and crunched it into pieces on the table-top.

'Five.' Alex repeated the exercise once more.

'Four. Running out of life-savers, Bob.'

Bob turned to each of the other jury members but all their faces remained as unforgiving as stone.

'All right,' their ex-foreman said. 'A pill first.'

'No deal, Bob. Start talking, but make it quick,' Alex replied, balancing one of the small round pills on his index finger.

'They got me on the jury, said to make sure she was convicted,' he gasped.

'Try again,' Alex said, grinding another lifeline to dust.

'I got myself on, they paid me.'

Alex removed one more.

'For Christ's sake,' Bob spat, then paused to regain his breath. 'What I'm telling you will never be evidence, it was gained by torture, non-admissible. It was part of the operation. We'd been monitoring Fox and Easterman for months. He'd started acting

265

strangely, had to be watched even closer. We'd had the team trained up and waiting nearby. Two men, one woman, identical heights, weights, builds. When Easterman called her to arrange the meeting he signed his own death warrant. We had Fox followed and knew exactly what time they would arrive. In the meantime the plan went ahead. Our people executed Easterman, then slipped out of video camera surveillance, stripped down, then waited for Fox.'

Alex watched the harsh faces of the jury melt into something approaching shell-shock.

Bob was reddening even more, straining to get the words out. 'The hit on Easterman had to be spectacular, the Cresta brothers had to die, Fox live and be tried.'

'What was the point, Bob? If that's your real name,' Alex asked.

'Work it out, Alex,' Bob answered, exasperated and fading fast.

'The Circle of Poison,' Alex said.

'The Fox girl was right. She had to be stopped, locked up, the organisation discredited.'

'Very neat.'

'Thank you,' Bob responded bitterly. 'Now the pills.'

'No,' Alex shouted.

'You can't,' the Mouse whispered. 'You promised.'

'That's right, man,' Denzel added. 'Gave the man your word.'

'Alex, dear,' Pearl said. 'Unlike this piece of human filth' – she nodded to Bob, her face eaten by contempt – 'none of us are killers, and I don't intend to start now, whatever the temptation.'

Danno, the Prof, Princess Grace, Kalsi and Kaftan nodded, only Pitbull kept his head still. 'I want to hear what Alex has got to say,' he said. Alex stared hard at them all before speaking. Bob's breath was more rapid now. 'For mercy's sake,' he whispered.

'About as much mercy as you showed Easterman and the others. But it isn't about mercy, is it? It's about profits and law suits, leukaemia and filthy lucre? That's what we are up against. Look at his employer's resources, look at what they have done already. If we let him live, he'll complain to the usher about torture, we'll be discharged and then next time around they'll get it right, she'll go down for a murder we all now know she didn't commit. Do we really want that on our consciences?'

'We can give evidence about what he said, can't we?' Grace asked.

'Just look at what he has on all of us. Do you think for one moment his employers don't know the same? Then what? Mere blackmail would be a relief.'

'Let him die,' Pitbull muttered.

'We can't,' Mouse and Kaftan replied together.

'We have to,' the Prof whispered. Bob's eyes were beginning to bulge out of his head.

'There is an alternative,' Alex said, but just at that moment Bob collapsed on to the floor and lay still and unconscious. Alex dropped down quickly to take his pulse.

'Still alive.' He popped one of the digitalis pills into Bob's mouth.

'Right,' Alex said. 'That's what I was waiting for. Now, let's get poor Uncle Bob to the hospital and whilst that's happening I believe we have a verdict to return.'

'I don't understand, Alex,' the Mouse said.

'It's over once we find her not guilty, it's a done deal, and we are all out of here.'

'What about Uncle Bob?' Danno asked.

'Do you really care?' Alex asked him.

He shrugged.

'I thought not, but even if he survives, he won't trouble us again.'

'Why not?' Pearl asked him.

'He's got no evidence against us and we have no evidence against him; classic standoff. Besides, he's a mercenary. Let's get this verdict delivered and go home. I don't know about the rest of you but I want to hang this jury business on a peg and get out of here.'

3.14 p.m., The Bolthole

Haversham was stiff with inertia, his face pressed hard against the door. He could tell that Pavel's suffering was increasing rapidly. They had talked on and off, each brief conversation punctuated by the terrorist's spasms. If the time came when he passed out Haversham was ready to bellow the message across the rooftops.

'Pavel?' he whispered.

'Not dead yet, Geoffrey, I'd try the same in your position. But do not shout to them too loud; you might wake up the dead.'

Somehow it seemed to Haversham that it would take more than some form of cancer to finish off his kidnapper. The telephone rang suddenly and cut across his train of thought. Wearily Pavel pushed himself to answer it.

'You have news?'

'The best news, it is over. Jenny Fox was acquitted by the jury three minutes ago.'

Haversham's hope, long abandoned, welled up.

'I shall verify,' Pavel said. Haversham could hear Pavel typing into his computer keyboard. Then he exhaled deeply and brought round his pager for Haversham to see. There on the running ribbon of the readout the verdict was confirmed.

'Then it's over, Pavel.'

'I like your jury system,' he replied. 'So unguessable.'

Pavel returned to the table and spoke into the conference mouthpiece.

'I verify, Jenny Fox is innocent, but then again she always was.'

Chance smiled. 'Now we need to ascertain the details of your surrender.'

'Surrender?' Pavel whispered. 'But the job is only half done. I await the Prime Minister with the answer to my question: Who really killed Charles Easterman? You have fifteen minutes.'

The Attorney General wanted to scream; instead he subdued his quaking voice to a small whisper, 'Why?'

'This chemical poison is bigger than your life or mine. Think of the children; their suffering.'

'They know they can't trust you now.'

'I know.'

'That means we will die.'

'In fifteen minutes to be precise. Still Jenny is free, that should please you, no?'

268

Haversham felt it begin in his stomach, cannon through his lungs and burst through his mouth; he was laughing.

'Pavel, you mad bastard, you sad, mad, strange, berserk bastard. Pleased? Pleased? I am over the fucking moon!'

Pavel smiled, then sniggered, then laughed himself.

'You asked me how does the world end, Geoffrey? Now I know, it ends in laughter, laughter at God's great joke: mankind.'

3.16 p.m., Cabinet Room, 10 Downing Street

Edward Haversham, looked around the ancient room. The faces stared back, forthright and grim, reflecting the expressions of the large portraits, which adorned the walls.

'You all know why I have called this emergency meeting?' Haversham said slowly, waiting for everyone to settle. The Chancellor of the Exchequer sat to his right scribbling notes with the assistance of one of his treasury advisers. Opposite him was the Secretary of State for Trade and Industry, shuffling sheets of paper. The Chief Whip and Lord Chancellor sat side by side and to the right of them was the Minister for the Environment accompanied by the Chief Medical Officer.

'Have you listened to the tape personally, Prime Minister?' asked the Chancellor.

'I have.'

'So there is no possibility that this is a hoax?'

'None whatsoever, I'm afraid.'

'What are we going to do?'

'That's the only thing on the agenda.'

'Do you want to give us your thoughts first, Prime Minister?'

'There is no option. We have to tell the truth.'

269

RANKIN DAVIS

'But looking at the overall situation, that may not be the solution which is most acceptable.'

'Especially in light of the fact that this administration is so young it could be disastrous,' the Minister for the Environment interjected. 'I mean, do we know one hundred per cent that this Dempster chap is telling the truth?'

'Was,' Haversham stated flatly.

'I'm sorry?'

'I said was, he's dead.'

'Looking at it from the treasury's point of view we have to conclude that, whatever we do, in the eyes of the public, we will be held responsible ultimately.'

'How can that possibly be so?' demanded the Chief Whip.

'Haven't you followed the situation here?'

'As well as anyone else.'

'Are you seriously suggesting the possibility that we can simply pretend this entire affair never happened?'

'Why not?'

'I don't believe you said that,' Haversham stated forcefully. 'My brother is being held hostage by someone who is prepared to risk his own life for the sake of something he believes in. I ask you now. Would you?'

'I don't think you want an answer to that question. Furthermore I find it grossly offensive that you should seek to question my commitment to any cause when clearly your judgement has been clouded from the outset by the relationship that exists between you and your brother.'

'I hear what you say,' Haversham said menacingly. 'But given that wholesomely honest view, Charles, do you think I would seek to force your loyalty were there not a higher responsibility placed on our shoulders?'

'What higher responsibility?'

'The one which dictates that government demands honesty.'

'Rhetoric.'

'No, not this time, Charles.'

'Look at it again, I implore you, Prime Minister.'

'I can't. The truth has to be told.'

'What is the truth though?'

'You're asking me? Don't you realise that we are faced here with the prospect of a collapse of confidence, which will put all other issues into the shade?'

'You're assuming a great deal, Prime Minister. Charles may have a point worth exploring,' said the Chancellor of the Exchequer.

'You think so?'

'I do.'

'And are you prepared to enlighten me as to why you too think we should go down the road of deceit?'

'I can try to put the alternative view. Yes.'

'I'm listening.'

'What we are really talking about is an issue which goes beyond our jurisdiction.'

'What? Like Chemitech, you mean? No boundaries, just profit?'

'If you don't want to listen, then I'm wasting my time, Prime Minister.'

'I'm sorry. Go on.'

'When the public discover that Dempster and the other Inspectors have been running this operation, it's laying the trail right to our door.'

'And should we be frightened of that? Is it not better that we admit to our failings in the hope that the people will applaud our honesty?'

'Not when the cost is so great, Edward.'

'So our predecessors have involved themselves in the worst piece of profiteering ever seen?'

'Yes, and we have picked up the baton, Chemitech are huge contributors to our funding.'

'I ask you though, at what cost?'

'At the cost of ensuring the greater good prevails. If you tell the truth, it comes all the way to us. We granted the export licences; we may as well have granted death certificates according to Easterman's findings and so the compensation claims will be never ending, not to mention the way we will be perceived by the rest of the world. It will finish us, Edward.'

'It might be the end of the old order but it could be the beginning of the new.'

271

Just then Donald Taylor burst through the door.
'Prime Minister, the conference is ready, you have two minutes.'

3.26 p.m., Outside the Bolthole

The only way the message could be delivered was by megaphone. Startled bystanders watched in amazement as a uniformed police officer put the contraption to his mouth and bellowed for all to hear.

'You inside the flat, turn on your television set. The Prime Minister will answer your question.'

3.28 p.m., The Bolthole

Pavel turned the tiny television set off and slumped down on the bed. Geoffrey Haversham expelled a huge draught of air and said, 'What now?'

'Now, I let you free.'

'They will kill you,' Haversham warned, surprised that he cared.

'I know. But then again I am a dead man already.'

'Let me negotiate,' Haversham offered.

'I have nothing left to bargain with.'

'You still have me.'

'No,' Pavel replied sharply. 'Your brother has earned your life, I will not break my word.'

Haversham could hear the terrorist shuffle towards him then felt his bonds being loosened. 'I must go with dignity,' Pavel muttered. 'No cancer ward, no drugs.'

'A blaze of glory?' Haversham spat.

'Why should you care? Look what I have done to you.'

Haversham stretched his aching limbs as Pavel began to unstrap the Semtex waistcoat. 'You saved my life.'

'I put your life in jeopardy. I only saved it to barter with your brother.'

'I don't believe you,' Haversham replied.

'You should,' Pavel said quietly and stared deep into his eyes. Haversham had to struggle to stop himself from flinching.

'Any loss of life is repugnant to me,' Haversham muttered.

'You are a good man, Geoffrey Haversham, Mr Prosecutor, but things are as they are. We may not choose to die, but we can choose the manner of our death.'

Pavel strapped himself into the waistcoat. 'Now shout to them and tell them you are coming out.'

'Please, Pavel, if you choose to die now, then so be it, but don't take anyone else with you.'

'Go now,' Pavel ordered.

Haversham felt confused, completely at a loss for how to react. He stuck out his hand. Pavel looked down at it and smiled wryly, took it, then pulled the Attorney General towards him in a fierce bear hug.

'I always thought my last living contact would be with a nice big woman, not a bony lawyer,' he whispered and laughed. 'Now, go!'

Haversham did as he was bid. As soon as he left the attic flat, uniformed arms grabbed him and spirited him away to safety.

An hour later, when Pavel failed to answer the telephone for the hundredth time, and the heat-seeking probes could only register a vague warmth, it was stormed. There was no loss of life. They found him dead; convulsed on the floor. He had drunk the nitro-glycerine from the explosive device. There was no note and, despite what must have been unimaginable pain, Pavel Boniak, the Liquidator, was smiling.

EPILOGUE

12 Noon, September 9th, St James's Park

Jenny Fox buried the ashes of Pavel Boniak at the foot of a mighty oak tree. The Attorney General, along with Frazer and a team of armed guards, watched from a discreet distance. Since the story had broken, the government had barely survived a vote of 'no-confidence', but Edward's frankness had helped them to weather the storm; more than could be said for the pesticide industry. He had already drafted the Indictment that would see many of the guilty ruined, and behind bars. Boniak had been hailed by eco-activists as a martyr to the cause, just as he had intended. But the real question, 'Who really killed Charles Easterman?' had yet to be answered. Haversham believed he knew the answer: 'We all did, and we did it through a selfish cocktail of fear, greed and indifference.'

But Alex Parrish and the other members of the jury knew the real answer and Uncle Bob was last seen on an emergency trolley on the way to hospital; he never made it, and was pronounced dead at 4.02 p.m. They had sworn never to see each other again or discuss what had happened inside the jury room. Contrary to that promise, Denzel and Princess Grace had continued their brief affair until the realisation that it was born of the moment killed it for good. Princess Grace divorced her husband for *his* adultery and the lawyers were becoming ever richer arguing over the settlement. Denzel's mother

275

recovered from her heart by-pass operation and even his brother's three-year prison sentence for possession of crack cocaine couldn't shake her away from regular, noisy visits. Pearl returned to her doting family armed with four weeks' worth of knitting and never once asked her husband whether he had rigged a Union ballot; she didn't have to. The Prof emigrated to Australia to join his son and grandchildren and no matter how long it took was determined to make them understand why he had done what he had done for their grandmother. Stalin was imprisoned for fraud and contempt of court; his lawyers are still seeking leave to appeal against the convictions. Pitbull moved his racist pamphlets to what he believed was a safer lock-up. Unfortunately it was raided on an anonymous tip-off and he is currently on remand, awaiting trial. Kaftan, appalled by how close Jenny Fox came to conviction, decided to up-sticks and cannabis plants and move to a more tolerant regime in Amsterdam. Kalsi continued to practise her faith and has no plans to return to selling shoes. Danno warned his cousins about their predicament and the three are awaiting a decision from the Home Office.

The Mouse ended the affair with her brother-in-law. The guidance she had received from the Almighty during the trial had reaffirmed her Christian faith. She and her husband are currently attending Relate. Nothing could save the relationship between Alex and his girlfriend Lucy; it just blew itself out. He buried himself instead in building the sports complex, using up his spare time in the fight to clear his brother's name.

Jenny Fox was appointed head of an independent research team, set up to combat carcinogenic foodstuffs and pesticides, by the Prime Minister Edward Haversham. Hers is a mighty task.

> '*In this broad earth of ours,*
> *Amid the measureless grossness and the slag,*
> *Enclosed and safe within its heart,*
> *Nestles the seed perfection.*'
> Walt Whitman, 'Song of the Universal'